GWEN BRIS

THE GUTENBERG MURDERS

GWEN Bristow was born in Marion, South Carolina in 1903, and Bruce Manning in Jersey City, New Jersey in 1902. In 1924, following Bristow's graduation from Judson College, her parents moved to New Orleans. In the late 1920s, Gwen Bristow and Bruce Manning, both Louisiana journalists at that point, met and married.

Their first joint novel, *The Invisible Host*, was a success, and enjoyed stage and film adaptations. Three further mysteries by the writing duo were to follow.

The couple moved to Hollywood in the early thirties, and there Bristow established herself as a prolific and bestselling writer of historical fiction, while Manning became a respected screenwriter, producer and director.

They continued to live in California until their respective deaths: Manning's in 1965, Bristow's in 1980.

FOR

BETTY

INTRODUCTION

OVER several years in the early 1930s the spousal writing team of Gwen Bristow (1903-1980) and Bruce Manning (1900-1965) published four crime novels: *The Invisible Host,* (which possibly inspired Agatha Christie's classic mystery *And Then There Were None*), *The Gutenberg Murders, Two and Two Make Twenty-Two* and *The Mardi Gras Murders*. The couple later went on to enjoy highly successful careers in entertainment, she writing historical fiction, including her bestselling Plantation Trilogy, he writing screenplays in Hollywood, including most of the scripts for the hugely popular films of youthful star Deanna Durbin. Before turning to writing crime fiction and these other rewarding pursuits, however, Bristow and Manning had experienced at first hand, during their time as Roaring Twenties newspaper reporters working the mean moonlight and magnolia streets of New Orleans, Louisiana, more than their share of real life crime, including a great deal of bloody murder. Bristow, a diminutive but daring brunette originally from South Carolina, particularly distinguished herself as what George W. Healy, Jr., a colleague of hers at the *New Orleans Times-Picayune*, the Bayou State's leading newspaper, termed "our star sob sister." Although "sob sister" was a somewhat condescending term for women journalists covering human interest stories (the most interesting of which invariably concerned murder), another of Bristow's colleague's recalled of her, with what he no doubt meant as the highest of praise: "She was the kind of woman reporter you'd send to do the type of story you'd send a man on. She was perfectly capable of doing it."

Bristow proved just how capable she was of doing nasty jobs in 1927, a banner year for bizarre and grisly killings in Louisiana, even by the old French colony's own impressive Baroque Gothic standard. First there came in July the murder of Morgan City utility company engineer James LeBoeuf. Murder in this case was only outed when the engineer's bloated body, which had been submerged with three hundred pounds of railroad irons in the depths of Lake Palourde, was exposed by receding water in the aftermath of the Great Mississippi River Flood. James's unfaithful wife Ada, the mother of the couple's four young children, was arrested and brought to trial for his shocking murder, along with an older, socially distinguished local doctor named Thomas Dreher, with whom Ada had been having an affair. The trial, which dragged on for two years, became an immediate sensation in the state and even made national newspaper headlines, with Ada LeBouef finally becoming the first white woman in the state's history to be judicially executed. The state hanged Dr. Dreher as well, on the same day as Ada.

Along with her colleague, drama critic Kenneth Thomas Knoblock (who later authored three crime novels himself, including one which drew directly on the infamous Moity murders; see below), Bristow handled coverage of the LeBoeuf-Dreher trial for the *Times-Picayune*. She "manfully" detailed every aspect of the affair for her readers, despite admitting in an anguished letter to her mother, written after the guilty verdicts had been handed down, that her job exacted an enormous emotional toll on her. The two year LeBoeuf-Dreher trial was "the most horrible experience I ever had," she confided. "When I rushed into the Western Union office behind the courtroom to flash my story, my hand was shaking so I could hardly write. I slept only three hours that night. . . ."

Bristow proved considerably more hard-boiled when, about four months after the James LeBoeuf murder, she and her colleague George Healy found themselves on the scene of a ghastly double trunk slaying in the French Quarter. Early on the morning of October 27, black "scrub woman" Nettie Compass, who lived in the back of the small stucco French creole style two and a half story building at 715 Ursulines Street with her husband Rocky and daughter Beatrice, trudged upstairs to clean at the second-story apartment of housepainter Henry Moity and his wife Theresa, a couple who lived unharmoniously in cramped and dingy quarters with their three small children and Theresa's sister Leonide, who recently had left her own husband, Henry's brother Joseph, and two children. Discovering a pool of blood seeping out from under the door to the Moity's apartment and down the stairs, Nettie promptly fled for her life, screaming for help in classic crime novel fashion.

Nettie's cries attracted two insurance salesmen who ran a business next door. After a brief inspection of the premises one of the men,

Frank Silva, doubtlessly did what any other true blue American would have done. He alerted the press, which soon arrived on the scene in the form of the *Times-Picayune*'s intrepid George Healy. Silva, Healy and several local neighbors effected entry into the Moity apartment, where they found more blood on the floor and a large, partially open trunk in the couple's bedroom. Upon lifting the lid of the trunk, Healy discovered a dismembered woman's body, its severed limbs and head piled over the torso. Healy then doubtlessly did what any other true blue American reporter would have done. He alerted his city desk, asking for a lady reporter to be sent to the scene as soon as possible to help chronicle this blockbuster story. He also suggested that the city desk might want to get in touch with the police and the parish coroner.

Star sob sister Gwen Bristow arrived on the scene at the same time as the coroner, George F. Rowling, but she was in no way intimidated or inhibited by this man's official presence, bounding into the apartment at his side and immediately sighting several repellent objects on the bed in the Moitys' bedroom. "Look," she ghoulishly announced as she held these loathsome items up for the others in the room to descry, "ladyfingers." Four human fingers they were, severed from a woman's hand. Placing the "ladyfingers" back on the bed, Bristow then charged into the second bedroom, where Leonine had slept, and thereupon discovered a second trunk with another woman's body. The disjointed bodies being identified as those of the Moity wives, New Orleans Police Superintendent Thomas Healy, a "ruddy, pot-bellied Irishman" (who was no relation to George, though the two men had an amicable relationship), sent out an all-station bulletin calling for the arrest of the dead women's husbands.

Joseph Moity soon turned himself in the authorities, opining all the while that his brother Henry, driven to madness by Theresa's wanton ways with other men and resenting Leonide's influence over her sister, had committed the murder and fled; this indeed proved to be the case. There followed another bulletin from Superintendent Healey to the seven ships which had sailed from New Orleans on the day of the murders, warning their crews to keep a lookout for a desperate man with "dark, bushy hair," "very dark brown eyes" and a tattoo mark on his arm, depicting a flower with a woman's face and a nude female body.

The telltale tattoo did the trick and Henry, who had been working under an assumed name as a deck hand on a fishing lugger on Bayou Lafourche, soon was identified and turned over to the police. Once confronted with the ghastly killings, Henry attempted to pin the blame on a big, red-haired, psychotic Norwegian sailor he had dreamed up, but soon he broke down and confessed to the awful crimes. He admitted that after hearing rumors his unhappy wife was planning to run off with Joseph Caruso, the Moitys' landlord and the owner of a store on the ground floor of the building, he became possessed with thoughts of killing her and her meddlesome sister. Catching sight of Nettie Compass on the evening before the murders, he had whispered to the cleaner not to be frightened if she and her family heard the Moity children crying in the early morning hours. A few hours later, Henry after a heavy bout of drinking stabbed Theresa and Leonide to death, then expertly disjointed their bodies and deposited the pieces in the trunks. (His former employment as a butcher proved most helpful in this regard.) After cleansing himself of his bloody work in the bathroom he gathered the children and deposited them at a relative's and made his futile attempt at escape.

At the conclusion of his trial the next year Henry was sentenced to life imprisonment for the murders. Deemed a model prisoner by authorities, he was eventually placed under minimal supervision and as a result casually strolled to freedom by catching a cab in 1944. Although he was recaptured two years later, Henry received a pardon from Louisiana's governor in 1948, on the ground that he had committed the murders during a fit of temporary insanity (i.e., that bout of heavy drinking). It is interesting, and perhaps instructive, to compare the difference in the punishments which the state meted out to Ada LeBeouf for peripheral involvement in the murder of her husband and to Henry Moity for the bestial slaying and dismemberment of his wife and her sister. Henry went on eight years later to shoot his then girlfriend in the state of California. For this attempted murder (his bullet had pierced the woman's lung, but she managed to survive), he was sentenced to a term in prison at Folsom State Prison, where he passed away the next year.

George Healy and Gwen Bristow covered the Moity murder trial from start to finish, Healy writing the straight news report and Bristow the imaginative "color" (i.e., the sob sister stuff). However, near the end of the trial the two reporters, having gotten rather bored with the whole sordid mess, secretly switched bylines. George ruefully admitted that his color was not up to Bristow's impeccable standard and that it "was my last attempt to write like a woman." While he did not divulge how successfully Bristow had written "like a man" on this occasion, certainly she proved able to put her experiences covering murder trials to good use when she wrote four crime novels in collaboration with another male, her husband Bruce Manning, a fellow New Orleans newspaper reporter with black hair, dancing eyes and an infectious grin, whom she met and married while covering the LeBoeuf-Dreher trial.

* * * * * * *

Critics of Bristow and Manning's most successful crime novel, *The Invisible Host*, have carped over the wickedly baroque novel's artificial setting and general lack of realism, criticisms which to me seem entirely beside the point. The Golden Age of detective fiction for a time gloried in its very artificiality. However, the trio of Bristow and Manning crime novels which followed *The Invisible Host* are, if less outrageously inspired than *Host*, also more credible as well as quite enjoyable in their own right, demonstrating that the crime writing couple had not exhausted their murderous imaginations with a single book.

Although not published consecutively, *The Gutenberg Murders* (1931) and *The Mardi Gras Murders* (1932)—both of which novels, like *The Invisible Host*, are set in New Orleans—comprise a two book series and share a number of characters, both major and minor. The major series characters in the novel, all of whom are memorably presented, are Dan Farrell, district attorney of Orleans Parish ("not society but . . . nice people"), ace crime reporter Wade of the *Morning Creole* (decidedly homely but the possessor of a "sardonic grin that conveyed a perpetual assumption of the superiority behind the grin and the stupidity in front of it"), Captain Dennis Murphy of the New Orleans Homicide Squad ("broad, ruddy and Irish") and the *Creole*'s star photographer Wiggins (a "very small, very brown young man with a screwed-up face, hopping like a firecracker"). These colorful characters, along with assorted police and press men (sadly no sob sisters ever put in appearances) link and enliven the two novels, providing as well an air of big city verisimilitude to a genre that was then still dominated by the country house setting, both in the United Kingdom and the United States.

Although its milieu is more realistic than that of *The Invisible Host*, *The Gutenberg Murders* nevertheless offers readers an ingenious, highly classical puzzle, with D.A. Farrell, the police and the press all working together to discover the malefactor behind a rash of gruesome, fiery slayings of individuals associated with the Sheldon Memorial Library, which had already been reeling from the scandalous theft of its recent prized acquisition of nine leaves from the Gutenberg Bible. (Farrell improbably deputizes Wade, although in real life Bristow herself would seem to have had rather a cozy relationship with the police in the Big Easy.)

For murderous inspiration Bristow and Manning unexpectedly drew on the ancient Greek playwright Euripides. (Indeed the novel might have been called *The Euripides Murders*.) Another source of inspiration very likely came to the authors from England's recent Blazing Car Murder, a notorious killing which took place shortly after the passing of Guy Fawkes Night in the early morning of November 6, 1930. After a slain body was discovered in a burning automobile, another man, Alfred Rouse, was arrested and brought to trial for the crime on January 26 1931, and convicted and sentenced to death five days later. Upon the failure of his appeal, Rouse was executed on March 10. Bristow and Manning published *The Gutenberg Murders* four months later in July, likely after having been composed the novel during the winter of 1930-31, so assuredly would have been familiar with the case.

The second and final entry in what might be termed the Wade and Wiggins mystery series, *The Mardi Gras Murders*, was published in November 1932, about sixteen months after *The Gutenberg Murders* and eight months after the non-series *Two and Two Make Twenty-Two*. Farrell, Murphy, Wade and Wiggins all reappear, with Murphy's and Wiggins' roles enlarged from the first novel relative to Farrell's and Wade's. Indeed, Wiggins, whose first name we now learn is Tony, plays the leading role in solving the crime, as Wade had done in *Gutenberg*. The story concerns another rash of bizarre murders in New Orleans, this one taking place over Collop Monday, Shrove Tuesday and Ash Wednesday and plaguing members of the secretive and sinister Mardi Gras parade society Dis, dedicated to the Greek god of Inferno. Once again Bristow and Manning served up an intricately plotted mystery with fiendish murders (including a "locked room" killing on a parade float) and plenteous local color, although it must be admitted that *Mardi Gras Murders*, completed after the publication of Dashiell Hammett's hugely popular novels *The Maltese Falcon* and *The Glass Key*, has a more hard-boiled consistency to it than *Gutenberg*.

In particular Police Captain Murphy, with his repeated bellicose threats of inflicting the "third degree" upon persons of interest in the case and his bigoted treatment of Cynthia Fontenay's black butler Jasper (an important witness in the case), likely will be viewed far less indulgently by modern readers than he is by Farrell, Wade and Wiggins. Yet should we really fault authors like Bristow and Manning for portraying things as they were in those days? (And of course many would question just how much things have changed today.) As New Orleans crime reporters themselves, Bristow and Manning knew of what they wrote, unlike most crime writers of the day (Dashiell Hammett certainly excepted), although they often shared the cynicism of their profession, a quality which they portray in their depictions of Wade and Wiggins, who often get so caught up in the story they are covering that they forget about the finer human feelings. Bristow and Manning refer to "the newspaperman's paradoxical quality of combining a genuine sympathy for people who got into trouble with a naïve eagerness to put their troubles in the paper," which is perhaps a bit too indulgent a way of characterizing it.

Wade and Wiggins are similarly indulgent in their view of Murphy's practice of "stowing away recalcitrant suspects" in the "dripping, rat-ridden, unlighted depths" of the Ninth Precinct station house under the authority of Ordinance 1436, on the assumption that a night or two spent there would loosen stiff tongues. "[E]ven the toughest of gangsters had been known to confess with teary appeals for mercy after two days in sparse fare among the rats," write Bristow and Manning, without any obvious sense of disapproval. As the pair of former reporters would well have known, in real life Henry Moity had made his confession at the Ninth Precinct station house a few years earlier in 1927 and at his trial his legal team argued that he had confessed essentially, as George Healy out it, "to get away from the rats" in that "disintegrating, ill-kept, rodent-infested dungeon."

Two and Two Make Twenty-Two, the crime novel which appeared between *Gutenberg* and *Mardi Gras*, is more of a throwback to the pleasing artificiality of *The Invisible Host*, at least in terms of its enclosed setting on an island off the Mississippi Gulf Coast, which is obviously drawn from the time which Bristow and Manning themselves spent in the area in 1930-31. As a powerful storm bears down on the high-toned pleasure resort of Paradise Island, the small number of hotel personnel and guests remaining there has to cope not only with a squall but drug running and a most determined murderer. Regular police being absent from the scene, the case is solved by a sprightly and engaging elderly genteel lady sleuth, Daisy Dillingham, one of a series of well-drawn women characters who appear in the Bristow-Manning detective novels. At one point Daisy pronounces: "Men always see the obvious. You'll run around putting two and two together and making your own chesty fours out of them. Sometimes two and two make-twenty-two." And the novel's jaw-dropping conclusion proves that she is right. Gwen Bristow and Bruce Manning may have only moonlighted in mystery for but a short while, but vintage mystery fans are fortunate that they did.

Curtis Evans

PART I
WEDNESDAY

CHAPTER ONE

DAN Farrell, district attorney of Orleans Parish, was not society but he was nice people. He was not brilliant, but he was both a good politician and a good prosecutor; he was honest, and endowed with a good deal of respect for the sort of learning which he regarded as a mental luxury, and this was one reason why he had called in Wade of *The Morning Creole* to consult him on what Farrell thought might prove the most salient features in the case of Quentin Ulman.

The case of Quentin Ulman puzzled Farrell because Quentin Ulman was an unusual man and he was suspected of an unusual crime; and when Farrell was puzzled he did one of two things: either he locked himself into the room off his main office and thought his way to a solution, or he called in his friend Wade and they sat and smoked and talked until they saw the way out of the tangle. The first process having failed, Farrell now sat looking across his desk at Wade, who stood leaning his many-angled person against the wall and squinting at the white midsummer glare of the windows behind the district attorney's head. Wade blinked, plunged his bony hands deep into his pockets and regarded Farrell with a grin.

"Sure, I know Quentin Ulman. His racket is wine, women and books. He's assistant librarian over at the Sheldon place. What's he been up to?"

The district attorney permitted himself the relaxation of a somber smile.

"Well, they tell me that this morning somebody looted the safe of the Sheldon Memorial Library and made off with those famous nine leaves from the Gutenberg Bible."

Wade jerked to attention. "What!"

"Exactly. And here's where Ulman comes in. Somebody, apparently Ulman, has been robbing the library for the past six months, and taking some very valuable treasures."

"'Apparently Ulman'—whose guess is that?"

"Mine. I've just had quite a conference with the head librarian—old Dr. Prentiss."

His eyes on Farrell with an intentness at odd variance with his lazy slouch, Wade came across the office and let himself down into a chair.

"This looks like a pretty story, Dan. That Bible's been the cause of a lot of dirt around the Sheldon Library."

Farrell swung his chair sharply around. "But this is private dirt," he said with provocative slowness. "Prentiss doesn't want Ulman or anybody else arrested; he wants the Bible fragment back, then he wants the rest of the rare books that have been taken. He doesn't definitely accuse anybody, Wade, but in talking to him about the losses I got the idea that he believes Ulman is the most likely suspect."

"I see," said Wade. "Do you know what that Bible fragment is worth?"

"Prentiss says about forty thousand dollars."

Wade thoughtfully scratched the back of his ear before replying. "It's a pip of a story, but it has some peculiar angles."

Farrell frowned. "Angles?"

"A lot of them." Wade leaned forward. "That Bible fragment is a big prize for anybody who knows the value of stuff like that. And I can think of several people besides Ulman who might have been glad to lift it from the Sheldon Library for one reason or another."

"What do you mean?" Farrell leaned his chin on his hand as if somewhat befuddled by this hint of a new complexity.

"Well," said Wade sharply, "here's something that might interest you. Prentiss is a smart man, and he's got just one obsession and that's rare old books. He's famous all over the country for his knowledge of them. He lives for that." Wade had dropped his usual air of bored cynicism; he was catching a picture of the librarian and projecting it for Farrell with rare eagerness.

"Prentiss," he went on, "is very jealous of his position as an authority. When he brought this Gutenberg Bible fragment here to New Orleans last April, Alfredo Gonzales said Prentiss had been fooled—the thing was a fake. Now Gonzales had a perfect right to voice an opinion: he's head trustee of the library and he knows as much about books as Prentiss does—but that Bible fight was the climax of twenty years' squabbling between those two."

Wade's broad mouth crinkled confidingly at one corner. "Gonzales seems to resent Prentiss' having been made head of the Sheldon Library, and ever since it was founded he has been hitting Prentiss in the one spot where Prentiss can't stand to be hit, his judgment of books. And now it looks as if Prentiss has got a chance for a sly comeback."

"How's that?"

"Do you know Mrs. Alfredo Gonzales?" Wade puckered his forehead unbelievingly, as if he had said "Do you know Cleopatra?"

Farrell hesitatingly shook his head as though ashamed to admit his lack of experience. "No—I assumed there was such a person, but nobody ever mentioned her to me."

"Well, I've never met her," said Wade, "but I've heard about her. She and Quentin Ulman are thus and so. Everybody in their crowd knows it. It seems she's very charming and not very discreet, or something, and she's gotten herself mixed up with this big book and binding man—"

"You don't think she stole the Bible, do you?" Farrell asked. Farrell was a decisive realist with little aptitude for imaginative theories, and his tone conveyed his incredulity.

"No, but somebody did, and it's Prentiss' chance to take a stab at Gonzales. The Bible disappears—Ulman is in the grease. It's a front-page story; the tabby-cats get it, and everybody whispers that Ulman sold the damn thing to buy pearls for Mrs. Gonzales, and of course Gonzales is stung where it hurts a Cuban gentleman worst. Don't you see?"

"Hm," said the district attorney thoughtfully. "Sounds interesting." He took a cigar out of his breast pocket and studied it as though expecting to find the solution written on the paper band.

"It *is* interesting. By the way," Wade broke off suddenly, "how much of this can I put in the paper?"

"Nothing about Ulman. You can break the story of the theft of the Bible in the morning paper, but don't mention that Ulman is suspected. I don't want anything at all in this evening's papers—I figure to keep it quiet until after the library is closed. We're starting an investigation this afternoon."

wonder. From what I know of Gonzales he's very much the Spanish nobleman—he'd probably do anything before he'd divorce his wife and advertise that he couldn't keep her where she belonged—but the frame-up might not work either—"

"Why not?"

Wade shrugged. "Ulman might go, and Mrs. Gonzales go with him. At any rate, Farrell, I'll take it easy. And don't you get mixed up in this battle between those two bookworms, but at the same time don't overlook the Gonzales' domestic rows. Somebody may be trying to railroad Ulman."

He paused an instant, warily balancing the connotations of what he had just said. "You know," he went on, "the publisher of my paper was a good friend of old Mike Sheldon—the man who founded the library. I'll talk to him about this mixup if you like. All we've got to be careful about is not to let anybody make us look like monkeys. I'll wait to see what the investigation turns up before we print anything about Ulman, although I don't see how you can keep him out very long. This Bible burglary is a big story. But Ulman—if the tabbies are right, and in a case like this they often are—Ulman might have a lot of Mrs. Gonzales' gold to fight with, if he needed it."

Farrell nodded soberly. "So be careful what you print, Wade. Don't force the Ulman feature until it becomes official. Remember—Prentiss doesn't suggest Ulman stole the Bible. Ulman's guilt is my theory."

Wade smiled with mock gravity. "But I hope you're right. It seems a shame not to tie him into it. Think of the papers we'd sell. Handsome blond Viking accused of theft—fighting for honor against cruel district attorney—beautiful woman in the background—love, library and intrigue for the lady readers of *The Creole*—"

"Seriously, Wade," Farrell interrupted, "I don't want to involve Ulman till I have some definite reason for doing so. His professional reputation might be ruined if he got mixed up in a thing like this, even if later events exonerated him. We are going after the thief who took the Gutenberg Bible with all we've got, and whether it's Ulman or Prentiss or Gonzales or the ghost of old Mike Sheldon, he isn't going to be spared. But for the present let's consider Ulman carefully as a suspect but keep him out of the picture till—"

The telephone rang.

"—till we know more about it," finished Farrell. "Excuse me a minute. Hello? Yes? What? *What?*"

He slammed the receiver into place and reeled around to face Wade.

"All off," he said briefly.

"What?"

"We can't keep Quentin Ulman out of the picture now. He has been found murdered."

CHAPTER TWO

ALGIERS is a disgruntled suburb of New Orleans that sprawls along the west bank of the Mississippi River and is reached from the city by the Canal Street ferry. Farther up the river, opposite the ferry station at Napoleon Avenue, is Harvey, another sulky little suburb, and between Algiers and Harvey is a dirt road that winds lonesomely through the shadowy chaos of live oaks and moss and red lilies that grow in the marsh on either side.

The little road is bright with traffic at night, when the people of Algiers and Harvey finish their day's work and go to ride, but in the daytime passing autos are few, and for this reason Dr. Prentiss and the Sheldon Library had selected a spot on this road as the site of the bindery where repairs might be made on those of his literary treasures that had been mishandled in the course of years. The bindery was a compact little building isolated among the moss-hung oaks.

When questioned by the police on the day of the Bible's disappearance Dr. Prentiss said that he had sent Quentin Ulman to the bindery about noon, to have him out of the library when the district attorney's men came to check the list of lost books, and this information, coupled with the blackened cigarette case bearing Quentin Ulman's name, left little doubt as to the identity of the charred and smoking skeleton that was found on the dirt road shortly after two o'clock by a laborer walking from Harvey to Algiers. The call from the Algiers precinct station reporting the laborer's grim discovery began the Bible Murder Case when it sent Wade and Farrell rushing up the river road.

After giving his office a quick telephone call Wade had scrambled into a police car with Farrell, and with a motorcycle escort clearing the way before them they crossed by the Canal Street ferry and reached the scene of the crime while police from the Algiers station were forming a cordon to keep onlookers away from the thing that lay there, covered by an old army blanket. An officer hurried up to the car as it came to a stop.

"We've been waiting for you, Mr. Farrell. Glad you're here."

Farrell sent a glance toward the blackened area around the edges of the blanket and beckoned to Wade.

"Let's get inside the lines. Is Murphy here yet?"

"Yes, sir, he's over to the bindery," another officer answered. "We sent for him when we saw your car coming."

"Hello, boss." Captain Murphy of the Homicide Squad came plowing through the crowd. "We're standing around till the coroner comes. Torch murder. Dirty job, sir." Captain Murphy made a wide gesture that included the beating sunshine, the officers hurrying about, the mob beyond the police line and the blanket with its hidden awfulness, all in one sweep of distaste. The captain was broad, ruddy and Irish; he had been on the force twenty years, and a single experience of his brisk authority was enough to convey that his elevation to head of the Homicide Squad represented to him the attainment of a pinnacle at which lesser men were supposed only to gasp from a distance. He turned his blue eyes on Wade, who stood surveying the scene with the look of a veteran appalled in spite of himself.

"You here already, Wade? Well, you beat the others. No reporters but you so far. Sure, Mr. Farrell, there ain't a doubt but that it's Ulman. Here's the cigarette case."

He produced the blackened case, rubbed off on one side to show the engraved name.

"Found it on what was left of the poor fellow. So I ran right up to the bindery—it's not but twenty yards or so, beyond those trees. It was unlocked. There's a phone there, so we rang the library. Got that old duck Prentiss. Took quite some explaining to get over what had happened, but finally we got out of him that he'd sent Ulman to the bindery about twelve o'clock and hadn't heard from him since."

"Did he say Ulman had a cigarette case like this?" Wade put in.

"Said he'd never noticed. But Ulman was at the bindery, and he ain't there now, and here's somebody who was carrying a case with Ulman's name on it. We figured it must be him."

"Who found the body?" Farrell asked.

"Laboring man. He's here. At least I told them not to let him get out of sight." Murphy sent a threatening look around and jerked his thumb to where a laborer in overalls stood between two policemen, fidgeting in scared importance.

"There he is. Lives in Harvey and was walking to his job in Algiers. Saw the remains smouldering in the road about two-fifteen or two-thirty."

Farrell nodded briskly. "That places the time of the murder between noon and two-thirty. Probably Ulman was killed somewhere else and the body brought here. They usually use the torch to make identification harder. Any signs of a struggle in the bindery, Murphy?"

"Not a thing, sir, as far as I can see. Of course we've got men there to keep people out and we're keeping traffic off the road, waiting for the Bertillon man. I've a couple of fellows from headquarters going all over the ground."

"Fine. Murphy, go back to the bindery and call Dr. Prentiss again. Get the names of all persons who saw Ulman leave the library today and also the names of those who know the combination of the safe where Prentiss kept the Gutenberg Bible leaves."

"The what, Mr. Farrell?"

"The Bible. Just say Bible to Prentiss and he'll understand. I'll explain later. Tell him I want all who were there to come to the library at seven o'clock tonight for questioning. Have headquarters notify them to appear. I'll wait for the coroner."

"Sure, Mr. Farrell." Murphy thrust his shiny-backed notebook into his pocket. Wade turned suddenly.

"Mind if I go with him, Farrell?"

"No. Keep your eyes open. You might be useful." Farrell gave him a cheerless smile and Wade started trudging through the dust with the captain. "Say, Murphy," he inquired, "if that laborer has a job in Algiers, what was he doing wandering around here?"

"Said he had a sick baby and his boss let him have time off to go home. Said he walked to Harvey and there wasn't anything on the road, so he went home and found the baby was better and started back. Then he runs into this thing smoking in front of him, gives a yell and beats it down the road to Algiers. Tumbles into the first house he comes to, where there's a lady and her five children who'll never be the same again, grabs the phone and calls the Algiers station."

"Does his story stand up?"

"Seems to. I've got a man checking it. Here's the bindery."

The officer on duty opened the door and they went in. The bindery was a cool, well-equipped little workshop, with supplies in cabinets against the wall. Wade took an appraising look around.

"No sign of a struggle here," he summarized.

"Not a bit," Murphy agreed, going over to the telephone stand. "Not even a paper on the floor."

Wade gave a cursory glance at the sewing-frame and the cutting and standing presses, none of which appeared to have been in use when Ulman left, then he crossed to the work-table. He looked curiously at the glass case on the wall above the table, where a long knife used for cutting leather lay among other tools, but the case was locked and appeared not to have been disturbed. On the table were two undecorated leather covers, and by them lay several brass stamps with wooden handles, engraved with letters and decorative designs. Apparently Ulman had been about to prepare these covers for the stamping of their titles. Wade noticed an unlighted gasoline burner.

"Where's the gasoline for the lamp?" he asked Murphy.

"Didn't see any. But we found an empty gasoline can by the body."

"Any chance for fingerprints?"

"Not much. It had a wire handle. The rest was all gritty from being spun in the road. It's wrapped up and in my car." Murphy picked up the telephone. "I'll call Prentiss. You look the place over, but be careful of anything that might have prints on it."

Wade stuck his hands safely in his pockets and wandered about. The bindery was, as Murphy had said, in perfect order. Ulman had evidently left it unsuspecting. Wade went into the entrance-hall in front of the workroom and looked thoughtfully out of the window at the flagged pathway leading from the door to the road, fifteen feet or so in front of the bindery. The bushes growing close to the walk were not broken or trampled, and the stones gave no hope of footprints.

On the rack just inside the door hung a white linen suit, as if placed there by Ulman when he changed into the overalls he wore while working. Wade began methodically to empty the pockets of the suit.

He found a couple of bills addressed to Quentin Ulman at the Sheldon Library; a couple of handkerchiefs, a stray match, one or two coins and a monogrammed wrist watch, evidently placed there for safekeeping while Ulman worked. Rummaging further he discovered a wallet, apparently unmolested, for it contained forty dollars in bills. Besides the money there were several cards, a gold university seal and a book of postage stamps, and in an outside pocket a rolled copy of the current issue of the magazine called *American Architecture*. While Wade was thoughtfully laying them in a line on a handkerchief, Murphy reappeared.

Murphy saw the handkerchief and smiled approval at Wade's care against smudging whatever fingerprints there might be. "What'd you find?" he inquired.

"Robbery wasn't the motive," said Wade, nodding toward the table, "unless the robber was looking for something besides money and jewelry. Here's Ulman's wallet untouched, and here's his watch—worth seventy or eighty dollars at least. Get the library?"

"Yeah." Murphy's shrug implied that he would have been just as happy if he hadn't. "Old Prentiss is no treat to talk to. Wants to know if we found a Bible. Any loose Bibles, Wade?"

"Not even a tract. But I'll tell you about the Bible." He summarized his interview with Farrell, and Murphy heaved a portentous sigh.

"That does put a quirk in it. So maybe that's what the firebug was after." He soberly busied himself wrapping the contents of Ulman's pockets and stowing the smaller articles in a large Manila envelope. Then patting the envelope as if to say "Stay there and be good to us," he looked up at Wade. "You'd better be asking Mr. Farrell before you print these names," he offered, "but just for your own information I don't mind telling you who was at the library today."

He scowled at his notebook. "There was Dr. Prentiss, of course, and his secretary—a fellow named Luke Dancy—and a girl named Marie Castillo—"

When Murphy said a girl, he said a "gurl." His gutturals were rich as charlotte russe. The look in his eyes, the cock of his head, all added, "We'll watch this girl. When there's murder we always watch 'em."

"Marie Castillo?" Wade repeated. "Spanish?"

"Cuban. Professor Alfredo Gonzales' cousin. Anyway, she's a medical student who works in the library during the summer. Then there was Mrs. Alfredo Gonzales." And to "Mrs. Alfredo Gonzales" Murphy added another look that said, "And we watch 'em single and married, we do."

"What was she doing there?"

"How should I know? Readin' books, she'll say. Ain't that what people do in libraries?"

Wade grinned. He had always liked Murphy.

"Well, according to Prentiss that was all the people that was there and saw Ulman before he went out, but there was a fellow named Terry Sheldon in just after Ulman left." Murphy turned his book lopsided so as to read a note that traveled up the margin of the page. "This here Sheldon is a sculptor. He's a nephew of old Mike Sheldon that started the library that started all this trouble. Those are all, but Prentiss says that the professor, Alfredo Gonzales, can open the safe, so I'm having him invited for tonight too."

For a moment Wade grimly wondered about Murphy's list, and how those men and women would like being questioned in a murder case. He wondered if any of them mourned Ulman. He remembered that once when he had been sent to interview Ulman their talk had turned on rare books on criminology, and suddenly he wondered what Quentin Ulman would be thinking now if he could know that the extinction of his glittering vitality was only another abstract crime.

Turning the coat inside out he saw a hitherto over-looked inside breast pocket, in which he found an envelope of heavy bevel-edged stationery addressed in an angular feminine hand. "From a lady friend," he commented dryly. "Do we read it?"

"Sure. What'd we come for? Let's see it."

Wade obediently drew out the single sheet inside.

"QUENTIN—

If you are taking Marie to the Chinese ball Thursday night I'll see you there. And for heaven's sake get your phone fixed. I don't like to write, even to you.

WINIFRED."

There was no date and no address, and Murphy grunted unhappily, but Wade's eyes had already narrowed at the green-embossed initials in the corner.

"The Chinese ball, Murphy," he explained, "is to be given at the Vincennes Club tomorrow night. And this W.G. stands for Winifred Gonzales."

Mentally he had scored a victory for the tabbies who talk.

"Winifred Gonzales?" Murphy repeated.

"Mrs. Alfredo."

Murphy gave a profound nod. "So that's how things were?"

"So it seems. You'd better take this. I suppose I'll have to see Farrell about it. Shall we get back to him?"

"We'd better. Then I kind of thought I'd take a trot up the road. There's a filling-station around the bend on the other side of where the body was found. Folks there might've noticed something."

They went out of the bindery, down the walk and back to where Quentin Ulman's body was lying. The coroner had just arrived and behind had come a bevy of reporters and the police ambulance. The area around the body had been roped off, and unofficial observers were being held outside, where the ambulance was clanging its way among the police and newspaper cars; inside the area reporters were scuttling, policemen were giving and taking orders, photographers were clicking their cameras, and standing together near the edge of the blanket under which lay the thing nobody had looked at since the first policeman covered it, were Farrell and the coroner. Wade and Murphy elbowed through the crowd beyond the ropes and approached Farrell.

"—and now you can do whatever you think you should here, doctor," Farrell was saying, "but I'd like to have the body moved as soon as possible."

The coroner turned to the assistant at his elbow. "All right, Sam," he said casually. "Unwrap it."

Wade took a step backward and looked at the hideous black skeleton that had been Quentin Ulman, and though he had seen death often in his ten years of newspaper work, he felt sick. The coroner's detached air steadied him.

"A man, I'd say, and a rather big man," the coroner was saying as he pulled out a tape measure. "The size and conformity of the bones give that much. Well over six feet."

Farrell looked questioningly at Wade. "Was that about Ulman's size?"

Wade nodded, and the coroner went on. "Of course it's impossible to tell now how he was killed. Have you found a bullet?"

"Not a sign, doctor," said Murphy. "I've had men looking."

The coroner bent over for a closer inspection. "The skull's cracked, but I'd say that was from the fire. Doesn't look as if it was done by a blow. I can be more certain, of course, after looking at the brain tissues. Suppose we take it in. I'll give you a full report tonight, Mr. Farrell."

Murphy had Wade by the elbow. "Say, do you want to stay and stare at these ruins any more? Then let's get going, will you?"

Relieved to be dragged away, Wade acquiesced and started with Murphy toward the filling-station around the bend. The station was out of sight, for the oaks on either side of the road were draped with moss that swung in heavy festoons to the ground, shutting off any view across the curve. As they walked along Murphy rubbed his ear and sighed.

"Damn it," he said. "Hear that radio?"

Wade did, because it was hard to hear anything else. They came in sight of the filling-station, which stood alongside of a trim little building with an open counter in front, where pop and hot-dogs were offered to passers-by. Over the pop-stand blared a loudspeaker, by means of which the world was being exhorted to drink to dear old Maine, and precluding the possibility that any calls for help could have been heard by either the hot-dog boy or the filling-station attendant, both of whom were now leaning on the counter listening bulgy-eyed to accounts of the murder from a cluster of customers.

Eagerly and with many words they informed Captain Murphy that they had heard nothing, nothing at all, for if they had, did he think they'd have stayed peacefully by their jobs while a man was getting burnt up around the bend? Sure, they remembered the man with the sick baby. He'd passed about noon, when the filling-station man had been over at the pop-stand having lunch. They remembered him because he had stopped to buy some sandwiches to take home to his old lady, saying she was too busy with the baby to fix anything.

They also remembered his passing on his way back.

"Yeah. Now this is what I want to know," said Murphy, spreading his elbows on the counter. "How many cars passed here between the time that fellow stopped here on his way to Harvey and the time he passed on his way back to Algiers?"

The hot-dog boy scowled. Wade, placidly consuming a bottle of pop, looked over the straws toward the captain.

"Think the murderer got away by automobile, Murphy?"

"Might have. Now, boy, how many cars passed here?"

The hot-dog boy shook his head lugubriously.

"Don't remember none."

Murphy turned sharply to the man from the filling-station, who was lustily enjoying the excitement.

"How about you?"

"Didn't notice any. But there might have been some."

"Haven't you been here all the time?" Wade asked.

"Sure, but not out front. Too hot. After I'd had lunch me and Willie here went inside the station and kind of sat around talking awhile. If anybody'd stopped for gas or anything, they'd have blowed their horn and we'd have known they were here."

"But it's possible," Wade persisted, "that a car, or several cars, might have passed while you were inside and you wouldn't have noticed?"

"That's right." The man nodded importantly. "We might not have heard, see, because the radio was going all the time."

"I got you," Murphy retorted crossly. "Just sitting around inside instead of looking out for trade. Now if you'd kept your eyes on the road where they belonged you might have seen a murderer go by just fresh from having set a man on fire." Murphy gave him a look that simply removed him from the landscape, and turned to Wade with an expression indicating that he took no great joy in people who didn't look out for trade.

When he had asked one or two other unproductive questions they made their way back to the center of their investigation. The body of Quentin Ulman was gone and the crowd had thinned. Farrell was waiting for Wade.

"I told the photographer from your paper that you'd drive back to town with me," he said. "Get in. I think we're through here for the present and I want to talk to you. Coming along, captain?"

Murphy shook his head. "I'll be over after a bit. Thought I might give the whole layout another look." He turned back toward the bindery, and Wade got into the police car with Farrell. The corporal at the wheel turned it toward the ferry.

For a moment neither Wade nor Farrell spoke, then Farrell began with abrupt energy.

"This looks like a tricky case, Wade."

"You're mighty right it does." Wade was studying his bony knuckles with unwarranted attention.

"How'd you like to work with my office till it's over?" Wade started and sat up. "What?"

"I've been thinking," said Farrell. "The publisher of *The Creole* is the man behind the present city administration, and he'll want this thing cleaned up as much as I do. Besides, he was a friend of old Mike Sheldon's. I believe he'd release you for awhile if I asked him. There are several reasons why I want you."

Wade nodded, puzzled.

Farrell went on. "There's a lot about this business that will bother the police, and there's a lot about the people involved that will handicap Murphy. I need a man now who knows how to handle the sort of people who rarely come into contact with the police. You know how. What do you say?"

Wade slowly shook his head. "And not cover the story for *The Creole*?"

"Sure, if you want to, but with me acting as censor. They'd have to give the routine to another reporter; you'll be pretty busy. You could do a daily story, though, based on my regular press statements. You won't have any advantage over the rest of the reporters. But if you'd like the job, I'd like to have you."

Wade leaned back and ruminatively lit a cigarette. "Farrell," he said earnestly, "you can't understand this, I'm afraid. A big story like this, an exciting story, a baffling story, is what keeps men in the newspaper business. No reporter wants to work from regular press statements. He wants to do it all himself and scoop the town. If you knew the days and months we put in on tripe, waiting for big stories to break, you'd know better why I've got to turn you down."

He stopped, half ashamed of himself. Farrell had been his friend for years, and Farrell couldn't be expected to understand. But Farrell had laid his hand on Wade's knee, and was looking at him with a face that suddenly made Wade think of a corporal bullying his soldiers into battle.

"You big silly ape," said Farrell. "Don't you know this is bigger than a big story? Don't you know that if Mr. Wade of *The Creole* ropes in the murderer of Quentin Ulman it will be the biggest story any newspaper man has made in years?"

He paused, and their eyes met.

"You'll have the full authority of my office behind you," Farrell went on. "You can't print the details of the investigation, except what I'm willing to give out. But if you bring in the murderer of Quentin Ulman—"

Wade's lean cheeks suddenly creased with a grin of great understanding.

"Lord, Farrell!"

"Then I'll call your publisher as soon as we get back to town." Farrell chuckled. "Now, Inspector Wade, what do you think of this murder?"

Wade meditatively blew out a cloud of smoke and grinned impishly.

"I think—" he looked at Farrell out of the corner of his eye—"Mr. District Attorney, I think it's just a case of where somebody stole an old, old Bible, and forgot to read the page whereon it is written

"Thou Shalt Not Kill."

CHAPTER THREE

THE burnished day had settled into twilight when Wade stopped his car in front of the gray stone castle that housed the Sheldon Library, where he had come to begin his work as special investigator for the district attorney. He had read the reports of the police and the coroner with growing bafflement, and had come to the library convinced that only those who knew Quentin Ulman's gayly complicated life could tell him what he wanted to know. Waving at the policemen on guard at the main door, he went around the mob of miscellaneous people who stared curiously up at the towers, made his way to a private entrance concealed between two pilasters at the side of the building, and went through a dim little hall into the main exposition room.

Just inside the door he stood still a moment, wondering at the paradox that had made this shadowy grandeur the background for a murder. Though the curtains were drawn, he could see the outline of the ramparts of books that lined the walls. On the north side of the room were windowed cases shielding precious manuscripts, and between them stood a square Flemish cabinet guarding the richest of the time-hallowed volumes that filled the life of Dr. Prentiss. At either side of the exposition room were heavy uncarved doors, one leading to the private office and one to the reading-room, and near the latter door a stone staircase curved to Dr. Prentiss' living-quarters on the upper floor. The very austerity of the library made it beautiful, and as Wade stood smiling thoughtfully in front of the door he half forgot that he had come here not to admire but to discover why a charred skeleton had been found across the river that afternoon. The shadows were thickening in the room, and he had stood at the door a full minute before he noticed a girl standing by one of the windows.

She had evidently not heard him come in, for she was half turned away from the door, drawing one of the heavy silk tassels of the curtain-cord over and over through her fingers. Her head was bent, and he had a glimpse of black hair and an impertinent profile. He took a step forward; she started and gave an abrupt push at a button, turning on the light above the staircase.

He saw that she was very dark, with heavy black eyebrows and a straight mouth; her dress of bright orange linen made an incongruous splash of color in the gray room. "You are Mr. Wade," she said inquiringly, "from the district attorney?"

"Why yes." Wade went to her and stood leaning on the rail of the staircase. "Were you expecting me?"

"Mr. Farrell phoned and said you might come over before the others."

Recalling what his reception as a reporter would have been in these circumstances, Wade marveled at the ease provided by his transition of office. The girl was silently looking out beyond the tapestry curtains, and he had a chance to study her expressionless profile. But it profited him little, for she was betraying no more emotion than if he had come to ask for a look at the library catalogue. After a pause she turned to him, so frankly that his appraising scrutiny seemed something like peeping through a keyhole.

"Is there anything you want me to tell you now, Mr. Wade, or do investigations wait for a signal with all the contestants present and on guard?" There was an odd little flicker at the corner of her lips.

Wade smiled back at her, mentally slipping her into his catalogue of personalities as "dark and blazing, hard as nails, maybe dangerous." Aloud he said, "You must be Miss Castillo—Marie."

Her manner changed sharply. She frowned. "How do you know that?"

"Captain Murphy said that a medical student named Marie Castillo worked here as assistant during the summer." He smiled reassuringly. "You fit the description. And I think I've seen you here once or twice, though you wouldn't remember me."

"I'm Marie Castillo—but why should Captain Murphy be inquiring about me—?" She stopped. Suddenly her hands twisted together in front of her. "It's all so dreadful—I suppose I'm frightened."

He tried to analyze her fear. She was very young, with a flashing aliveness that warned even as it appealed to him. "Won't you sit down somewhere," he suggested, "and talk to me? I'm really quite harmless, but if I can get a few preliminary facts straight for Mr. Ferris he won't have to spend so long questioning you tonight." He spoke as gently as he could, for he had guessed that her aloofness was covering nerves still trembling from the tragedy of the afternoon. She smiled as if with sudden penitence.

"All right. We can sit down over here. I'd really rather you didn't worry Dr. Prentiss any more than you can help—he's dreadfully distrait." She led the way to the desk at the front of the room and they sat down. Marie turned on the lamp. "You'll pardon me if I'm awfully rude, won't you?—but I'm pretty jumpy. I—I knew him rather well, you see."

"I understand. You were here when he left this morning, weren't you?"

She nodded. "I work here. Naturally I saw him this morning."

There was a curious self-defensiveness in her manner again, as though she were trying to justify her presence and at the same time have the interview done as soon as she could. He wondered what she was really thinking. A cousin of Alfredo Gonzales, employed at the library alongside of Quentin Ulman—Marie might have plenty to tell if she chose to tell it. He managed to speak casually.

"If you were here all the morning, then you can tell me what happened."

"Nothing happened," said Marie.

"Nothing?" Wade lifted his eyebrows. "But he was murdered."

"Not in the library," she flung back.

He swung one of his long legs over the other. She sat stiffly, her cream-colored hands laced in her lap.

"You're going to make this interview interminable, you know, if you won't talk," said Wade. "Naturally I'm not exactly a pleasant visitor, and I understand that you'd like to get rid of me as soon as possible—but the district attorney will be here in about half an hour and he'll ask you—"

"I'm sorry," she said sincerely. "You can't know how nervous I am. Ask anything you like." But she smiled with a demureness that added quite plainly, "And try and make me answer."

"That's splendid," said Wade. "You knew Mr. Ulman well, I think you said?"

Her black eyes fixed themselves on him as though to emphasize her answer. "We worked together, Mr. Wade."

"I think you knew him better than that," he returned quietly. "You had intended going with him to the Vincennes Club tomorrow night, hadn't you?"

For several seconds Marie did not answer. She simply looked at him. In spite of himself he regretted having put that question so soon.

"I don't know who told you that," she said at length. "But if Quentin Ulman had lived until tomorrow night, I should not have gone with him. Not there or anywhere else. That's all I'm going to say about it." Wade knew it wasn't all she was going to say, but because he found himself sorry for her he temporarily laid aside the subject of Marie's relations with Ulman and switched his questions. "You were here when Dr. Prentiss left this morning for the district attorney's office? Suppose you tell me about that."

Marie relaxed. "I came in about nine o'clock," she answered without hesitation. "Mr. Ulman was already here, and so was Mr. Dancy—he's Dr. Prentiss' secretary. Dr. Prentiss came down and went into his office, and it was not long after that he said he was going downtown. He didn't say where, but of course I know now it was to the district attorney's office. That was about ten o'clock, I think. He was gone till about eleven-thirty or maybe a little later. Then he came back and sent Mr. Ulman to the bindery."

"Mr. Ulman seemed to be his normal self?"

"Why, yes—I suppose so." But he saw that her hands had doubled up on her knees. He looked at them and his eyes traveled slowly up to the quivering muscles of her throat.

"What time was it," he asked very distinctly, "that Mrs. Alfredo Gonzales came in?"

Her eyes suddenly shifted and looked past him. "Mr. Ulman telephoned her as soon as Dr. Prentiss was gone."

"May I smoke?" asked Wade.

Marie looked back at him with swift momentary relief. "Ordinarily you couldn't," she answered with a faint smile, "but tonight I suppose the rules are suspended. Give me one, won't you?"

When he had lit her cigarette he sat down again and asked,

"Does Mrs. Gonzales often drop in?"

"Frequently," said Marie.

"And how long was she here this morning?"

"Till Dr. Prentiss came back."

"So you and Mr. Dancy and Mr. Ulman and Mrs. Gonzales were together in this room all the morning?"

"No. Mr. Ulman and Mrs. Gonzales were in the reading-room. They went into the reading-room shortly after she came and were there till Dr. Prentiss asked me to get Mr. Ulman for him. That was when he told Mr. Ulman to go to the bindery."

"When you went into the reading-room," said Wade, "what were he and Mrs. Gonzales doing?"

Again, for an instant, she simply looked at him, and he knew she was going to lie.

"They were looking at an eighteenth-century prayer-book," she said.

Wade wanted to smile, and checked himself. "When did Mrs. Gonzales leave the library?" he asked.

Marie looked at her cigarette.

"They went out together."

Wade leaned forward. "They went out together—to the bindery?"

Marie stood up abruptly. "I don't know where they went, Mr. Wade." She took a step away from him. "I don't know where they went. Winifred—Mrs. Gonzales—had her car, and she told him she'd drive him to the ferry. They drove away together. Nobody saw him again." She pushed her hair off her forehead with a quick desperate gesture. "Why did you make me tell you that? I didn't—"

"Marie!" A man's voice called through the great room. "Marie, Alfredo just called to say he'll take you home when this business tonight is over—oh, pardon me." A slim young man with a rumple of light hair was coming toward them. He had stopped questioningly.

"Mr. Wade, from the district attorney's office," said Marie hastily. "Terry Sheldon, Mr. Wade."

Terry sauntered forward, his hands in his pockets. "So they sent you out for the dirt, did they? Well, there's plenty."

"Terry!" Marie's voice was sharp and pleading at once.

"Well, there is. Quentin Ulman is dead, Mr. Wade, and so you're here. What can we do for you?" He swung himself to the edge of the desk and dangled his legs. Wade was still standing, looking appraisingly from Terry to Marie. Marie was twisting her belt, gazing at Terry Sheldon with a sort of harsh terror.

"You can do a good deal, I think, Mr. Sheldon," Wade said quietly. "First, you can tell me what you mean by the dirt. Then, you can tell me how you happen to know it."

"Second question comes first," retorted Terry easily. "Did you get that my name was Sheldon? That's how I happen to know it. I'm the last of the Sheldons. Old Mike who founded this blasted library was my uncle. Naturally I hang around a bit and so get a look at what's going on. Such bits of excitement as a lost Gutenberg Bible fragment, for instance."

"Did you know it was gone this morning?" Wade put in.

"I did not. I learned it about noon. I learned it while our friend Ulman was on his way to his execution. Prentiss got Dancy to give me a ring and ask me to come by on important business, and as soon as he had gotten Ulman and Dancy out of the way he shut himself up in the office with Marie and me and told us Ulman had been raiding the place. Said he thought we ought to know—being related to old Mike and all that sort of thing."

"You are related to the Sheldons?" Wade asked Marie.

She was still standing by him, her eyes fixed on Terry as though in frightened appeal to him not to say too much. She started at Wade's question.

"Indirectly," she answered. "Mrs. Michael Sheldon was my aunt. She was a Cuban—my mother's sister."

"Old Mike married her in his sugar-raising days when he was making his fortune," Terry amended. "Now what else did you want to know, Mr. Wade?"

"I told you," Wade returned inexorably.

"O Lord, don't you know? Ulman is dead, and before he died he stole the fake Gutenberg—"

"You agree with Mr. Gonzales that it is a fake?"

Terry shrugged. "I'd rather trust Alfredo than Prentiss. I've tried to keep out of their altercations because I don't know enough to tell an incunabulum from a novel—I'm a sculptor—"

"Yes, I know. I've seen your work. What time did you get here this afternoon?"

"I don't know—noon, maybe. Everybody was gone but Marie and Prentiss."

"What time did you leave?"

"Don't know. About one."

"Then where did you go?"

"I went riding around in my own little automobile," said Terry impudently. "No, Wade, I have no alibi for the so-called tragedy. I hadn't seen Ulman in weeks. Prentiss told Marie and me that somebody from the district attorney's office was coming up about four to check up on the missing books, and asked us to be back then. We met on the steps and when we walked in Prentiss told us about the murder, and if you'll pardon me, I believe that's all I've got to say." He slid off the desk.

"Just a minute." Wade stopped him. "Where were you this afternoon, Miss Castillo?"

"At home," said Marie. She was still looking at Terry. "I live in the French Quarter—on Royal Street."

"Seems to me," Terry commented, "we've all talked enough."

"There's one thing more I'd like to ask both of you now," said Wade slowly. "Has either of you an idea of who might have had a motive for killing Quentin Ulman?"

Marie caught her underlip between her teeth and did not answer. Terry gave a cynical grin.

"Why, for the life of me, Mr. Wade, I can't think of more than six people who would have liked to kill Ulman, and to be perfectly fair to the other five I don't mind saying just privately that I shouldn't have minded doing the job myself."

"You're a beast, Terry!"

Marie whirled about and left them, slamming the office door behind her. Terry looked up at Wade and tilted an eyebrow.

"So was the late lamented," he observed, "and she knows it. You might go easy on her, though. Now am I excused from making any more mud pies?"

Wade shook his head. "I think, Sheldon, you might elaborate on that interesting statement you made just now."

Terry stood quite still. His eyes narrowed. "Why bother, Mr. Wade?" he queried slowly. "This little business is just another murder to you, but it means hell has cracked loose in the Sheldon clan and before it's over there'll be blood and tears, and God knows whether it will ever be over at all."

He stood looking at Wade with a sort of lazy defiance. Wade regarded him coolly.

"You were bluffing Marie, weren't you?"

"No I wasn't. I don't give a damn about the public interest in this imbroglio. Ulman's dead and what of it? My personal regret is only that he wasn't struck decently by a taxicab instead of ripping up all this fuss."

"Still bluffing?"

"You think so. What do you want to know?"

"When you left the library at one o'clock," asked Wade, "did Marie leave with you?"

"Yes."

"You drove her home?"

"No. I left her at the main entrance."

"And you rode around till four o'clock?"

"Yes."

"That wasn't very polite, was it?"

"Oh, don't be so cross-examinish. Neither of us was in any state of mind to be polite."

"Why was that?"

"I'd been giving her my opinions after we came out of Prentiss' office."

"You didn't accuse her of taking the Gutenberg Bible, did you?"

"Hell no." Terry kicked at a knot in the floor. "I told her how she was letting that big Swede make a fool out of her."

"You mean Ulman?"

"Of course."

"Listen to me, Sheldon. If you make me drag this out of you sylla-ble by syllable you aren't going to do a thing but stretch tonight's meeting till morning. You and Marie quarreled at the library entrance because you told her you thought Ulman wasn't sincere in his admir-ation of her eyes and nose and ankles?"

"He didn't admire her eyes and nose and ankles any more than he admired mine. I told her so."

"You told her," said Wade slowly, "that Ulman was going to the Chinese ball tomorrow night not because he wanted to be with Marie but because he wanted to see Mrs. Gonzales there?"

"Yes," snapped Terry. "And you can go to hell."

"Did you tell her—"

The side door opened. Wade stopped, and Alfredo Gonzales came into the library.

Terry said, "Hello, Alfredo," and Wade, who had interviewed the professor once or twice, stepped forward with a word of greeting. Gonzales gravely inclined his head and came toward them.

"You told Marie I would take her home?" he asked Terry. He spoke with the exquisite precision with which some rare foreigners master the English language.

"Yes. She's in the office. D'you want to talk to Wade? He's doing some preliminary digging for the district attorney."

"If Mr. Wade wishes."

"Thanks." Wade indicated a chair. Gonzales crossed to the desk with quiet acquiescence, and Wade stood marveling at his self-possession. For Professor Gonzales looked less like a savant than like one of the adventuring grandees who in more ample times had gone subduing alien tribes; tall and sunburnt, he walked not only with an outdoor grace but with the calm assurance of authority. His face was proud, his lips thin and more than a little arrogant; he had black eyes under heavy brows, cold and threatening by turns. Alfredo Gonzales could be both gracious and cruel, but it was easy to understand that he would never be otherwise than elegant, and that he had never been meek in his life.

Terry stood leaning negligently against the back of a chair. Wade sat down.

"I'll be grateful if you can spare me a few minutes, Mr. Gonzales—or is it correct to say Dr. Gonzales?"

The professor smiled. "I prefer Mr.," he said. "The other is correct, of course, but I dislike the particular form of egotism that insists upon recognition of a scholastic degree. The name, Mr. Wade, is Alfredo Miguel Gonzales y Castillo—*Mr.* Gonzales."

"Mr. Gonzales, then," Wade agreed smiling. "I'm clearing up a few points before Mr. Farrell arrives. Did you know Mr. Ulman well?"

Gonzales made an ambiguous gesture. "I knew him fairly well. I was acquainted with his work, of course—he was a very promising young man."

He spoke without the faintest emotion, as though discussing the tennis game of an absent acquaintance.

Wade frowned thoughtfully. "Then you were satisfied with the way he performed his duties at the library?"

"I believe," returned Gonzales, "that Dr. Prentiss considered him a most able assistant."

"Couldn't you have had him removed if you had not thought so too?"

"Certainly not," Gonzales responded simply. "My position as head trustee of the library permits me to supervise no one but Dr. Prentiss, and that supervision extends merely to his use of the Sheldon funds. If, in my opinion, Dr. Prentiss buys books the inclusion of which in the library is not justified, it is my duty to say so."

"And in your opinion," Wade added, "the lost Gutenberg fragment is one such purchase?"

Gonzales stood up. "I believe I made myself clear on that subject when the fragment was brought to New Orleans last April. My official statement will of course be issued at the time of Dr. Prentiss' regular report to the trustees the last of July. Until then, I prefer to say no more. Shall I wait in the office for Mr. Farrell?" Wade glanced at Terry, who was still hovering belligerently in the background, then back at Gonzales.

"Another question, Mr. Gonzales. Have you any idea who might be responsible for Ulman's death?"

"Pardon me, Mr. Wade, but if I had I should hardly venture to express it."

"But you have a suspicion?"

"It is impossible not to look for suspects," Gonzales returned smiling, "but you must excuse me from voicing an opinion."

"Rats, Alfredo!" Terry cut in shortly. "If opinions could have killed Ulman he'd have been dead months ago."

"My dear Terry." Gonzales spoke like a professor rebuking a schoolboy. "To speak of the dead—"

"Oh, sacred dead be damned. I'm tired of all this palaver. I think I'll tell Prentiss you want him, Wade." He banged his way into the office, and Gonzales turned apologetically back to Wade.

"You must pardon Terry. He is young and impetuous—and very jealous of the reputation of the library that bears his name. Is there anything more I can tell you?"

Wade was standing, leaning one elbow on the back of his chair and wondering what lay under the suave exterior of his companion. "I've been talking to Terry for quite a while," he said. "Terry was perfectly frank in saying that he did not admire Ulman, and from one or two things he said I gathered that he had no great opinion of Dr. Prentiss. Am I right?"

"Dr. Prentiss is a reticent man," Gonzales answered, "wrapped up in his library work—hardly the sort to appeal to a lusty young sculptor like Terry." He was speaking slowly and with evident carefulness. "Terry is an artist, and an unusually good one for so young a man, but he cannot endure working in solitude for more than a day or two at a time, and he finds it hard to understand how any man could pursue his work year after year in cloistered seclusion, with few intimate friends and no social life to speak of. Dr. Prentiss is quiet, reserved, and, I believe, quite happy in his mode of living. But what you want of Dr. Prentiss, you must ask him."

"And I shall be glad to give you any assistance in my power, Mr. Wade."

They started as they heard the voice from the office door. Dr. Prentiss stood an instant in the doorway, then came toward them, the scholar of pictures and legends, tall and slender, with a droop to his shoulders that suggested much bending over a desk and long delicate hands that seemed made for caressing the crumbly pages of old books. His white hair waved back from a high, commanding forehead, and his gray eyes were at once piercing and contemplative; an odd mixture of shyness and arrogance, he looked like a man with a passion for supremacy but at the same time one who had the born aristocrat's dislike of indiscriminate contacts. Suddenly keyed to a rare pitch of critical sensitiveness, Wade glanced from Prentiss to Gonzales, remembering their antagonism, but they hardly looked at each other. Gonzales stepped aside with punctilious formality and went into the office, but Wade was somehow conscious of a disturbing cross-current of bitterness in that instant's meeting. He looked keenly at Prentiss as he turned toward him. Prentiss was still standing by one of his high square-cut chairs.

"You will be brief, Mr. Wade?" he asked. "It has been—a difficult day." He passed his slender blue-veined hand over his hair and sighed.

"As brief as I can," Wade promised. "All I want now is some information on this missing Bible fragment. You've had it about three months, I believe?"

"Yes. I bought it in April. It was discovered in a walled-up cell of the monastery of St. Emmeran in Bavaria. I went to Europe as soon as I heard of its being found, and bought it after convincing myself of its authenticity. The purchase was widely heralded in intellectual circles."

"Yes, I remember. Nine leaves, isn't it?"

"Nine leaves, in almost perfect condition. One of the greatest literary treasures procurable at any price. This morning," he added wearily, "it was gone."

"Will you tell me," Wade went on, "why you are sure Mr. Ulman robbed you, instead of someone else?"

Prentiss gave a faint smile. "That is a natural question from one who is unacquainted with the library," he returned. "The others who know the safe combination, Mr. Wade, are beyond suspicion. Mr. Gonzales, the head trustee, comes to the library so rarely that his visits may be called events. His presence here is virtually unknown except on the occasions of my semi-annual reports to the executors of Michael Sheldon's will. Terry Sheldon is an artist, not a bibliophile. He visits the library often to do research, but he is totally unacquainted with the value of books, and would have no idea of where to dispose of a Gutenberg Bible fragment at anything like its true value. Marie Castillo—I have known her all her life. It is unthinkable."

"Dancy, your secretary—" Wade prompted.

"I have never told him the combination of my safe. Besides, you overlook the fact that I have during the past few months missed other valuable books from the locked cases. Several of those thefts took place on occasions when every one of the others I have mentioned was out of town."

"Including Dancy?"

"Including Dancy."

As if the mention of his name had called for his appearance, a trim and rather young man in a very correct sack suit strolled languidly out of the shadows by the side door. Wade recognized him at once as one of the group that hung about the French Quarter on the fringe of the writers' colony and referred to themselves as the intellectual minority. Dancy vouchsafed a nod at Wade and then at Prentiss, and stood negligently by the desk, so at ease that Wade was faintly amused at his pose. He had catalogued Dancy in a minute—one of the regular American-Anglomaniac school, with clothes patterned after what he thought young men in Mayfair were wearing and manners that he had carefully adopted after a week in London or a course of English novels. The handkerchief up his sleeve was a touch, along with his striped club tie and his thick brogues and the cuffless trousers. Wade listened for him to speak, betting with himself that his phrases too would be London-borrowed.

"They're all here," Dancy announced, and his accent was not disappointing. "District attorney, carload of policemen, pressmen no end. All coming in." The side door opened to admit Farrell and his followers, and as Dr. Prentiss with a word to Wade went to greet the district attorney the gay Mr. Dancy placed himself on the arm of a chair. "Are you," he inquired, "one of the pressmen?"

"I'm Wade of *The Creole*, temporarily of the district attorney's office."

"Righto. I'm Luke Dancy. I'm secretary to Dr. Prentiss. And while he brings in the rest of you chaps it might be jolly for you to know that the whole show has been held up because the swanky Mrs. Gonzales has been acting ducky, with one foot on the running-board of the district attorney's car. Even the bluff old inspector who is with him was all muddled."

Wade grinned politely, not sure yet whether Dancy was as much of an ass as he sounded. "You see," Dancy went on in a lower voice, as the group came nearer and Dr. Prentiss explained the geography of the library to Farrell, "the dear old doc is too tush-tushy, all shut up in his ivory tower, to know much about the world, the flesh and the various devils. But I thought that might amuse you, eh what?"

Wade considered the loquacious Mr. Dancy with relish. "If you had come in earlier," he observed, "you and I might have had a very interesting time."

"Quite." Dancy slid off the chair-arm and stood looking from Wade to the group of police officers and back again, with his slightly supercilious smile. "I don't know who turned our up and coming young bibliophile into a cinder, Mr. Wade, but—" he raised his voice and took a step toward the door—"Mr. Wade, may I present Mrs. Alfredo Gonzales?"

CHAPTER FOUR

MRS. Gonzales might have been thirty and she might have been forty; she was one of those women whose charm is too rich for youth and whose faces are too young for middle age. She slipped her hand into Wade's and lifted to him a pair of tantalizing amber eyes.

"Mr. Wade? Oh, yes, Mr. Farrell told me about you a minute ago. A reporter turned detective, aren't you?"

"That's about right." Wade was cordial, but he felt a sudden need for vigilance, as though he and not Mrs. Gonzales were about to undergo official scrutiny. She was looking at him with exasperating candor, like a woman who has just told a secret across a tea-table; he was conscious of Dancy's half-amused, half-pitying observation and the murmur of voices from Farrell and his group of policemen. "Won't you sit down?" he added. "I think we can wait here a few minutes before Mr. Farrell is ready."

"Thank you." She took the chair he drew forward and glanced at his cigarette-stub on the floor. "I suppose I may smoke? Ordinarily Prentiss would as soon turn the garden-hose on his books as run the risk of a spark, but tonight should be different." Before he could reach for his matches she had flipped a little flame from a lighter and was inhaling mischievously. Her eyes met his again with balanced provocation; Wade drew a chair for himself near her and studied her in silence for a moment. She was dressed simply and in exquisite taste—a suit of honey-colored crêpe with gloves and shoes and hat a shade darker. The brim of her hat shaded her face effectively, and he guessed that she had worn it for that reason, but as she dropped her lighter back into her bag and looked up again her self-possession was perfect.

"You probably know all about these things, don't you?" She had an odd, cool little voice, and her words were like the clink of ice in a glass. "Tell me—will it be very terrible? Do they bring in a mannikin and poke pencils in where the ribs would be? Or do we all have to go down to the morgue when this is over? And is anything we say used against us? And do you put it all in the papers?"

Wade regarded her bright naïveté with a practised eye and owned that she did it well. "This little bit of procedure," he said smiling, "is like *Through the Looking-Glass*. Do you remember what the Red Queen said to Alice? 'It takes all the running you can do to stay in the same place.' Or, I should say, it is less frightening than a half-hour with the dentist, but it's much like that. The same monotonous boring."

"It sounds perfectly dreadful. Look—here come the victims." She waved at Marie, who had come out of the office with Terry. "Hello, darling."

"Good evening, Winifred." Marie's voice was toneless, almost curt. She carelessly took the arm of the chair Wade offered her. Terry perched himself on the desk.

"The cop who dragged us out says Farrell wants us to stay out here while he turns the office into an inquisition and puts us on the rack one by one. Charming, isn't it?"

He was blandly addressing the room at large. Winifred blew a smoke ring into the air. "Will this take very many hours, Mr. Wade?" she asked.

He shook his head. "I don't think so. Mr. Farrell will do his best to keep it short."

"I hope he does. I'd intended going to bed ever so early tonight, for I've lots of things to do tomorrow—that Chinese ball at the Vincennes Club tomorrow night, you know, and my costume not half ready." She cocked an ambiguous eyebrow at Marie. "Are you going there?"

Marie jerked up her head. "Of course not. Try not to be a fool, Winifred."

"I do, angel, but I don't seem to have much luck."

Winifred stepped on the end of her cigarette and lit another. Wade glanced from her to Marie and back again; the flat self-assurance of Marie, and Winifred's whimsical determination to make everybody as uncomfortable as possible, both amused and puzzled him. Then he heard his name in a quizzical whisper.

"Gargoyle to see you, Wade."

Dancy, who had been standing in the background as though the whole tableau was affording him excellent diversion, indicated the gargoyle—a very small, very brown young man with a screwed-up face, hopping like a firecracker—Wiggins, the star photographer from *The Creole*. He beckoned frantically, and Wade, somewhat relieved to eject himself from the glittering confusion of Winifred Gonzales, walked toward the door. Wiggins grimaced at Prentiss and the district attorney, who were engaged in low-toned conversation, and dragged Wade out to the steps.

"Say, will Farrell stand for pictures in there? That monkey at the door won't let anybody in with a camera and he's keeping all the reporters out. You sure got an inside track. Who's the dame?"

"That's Mrs. Gonzales—pipe down."

"The missus, eh? Whoops! Would I go wrong for that? See if you can get her out here for a picture."

"Don't rush me." Wade thrust both hands into his pockets and looked sternly down at his mosquito-like assistant. "If you keep on with this racket Farrell will have somebody hog-tie you and I won't blame him. We've got two hours to get pictures. Farrell says it's okay if the people will stand for it. O'Malley's covering this story—I'm not—so you stay with him."

"Rats," said Wiggins. "Don't try to high-hat me. I didn't murder that sap. I just shot the little that was left of him. I've mugged 'em all, big boy, from presidents to leap-year babies, and I didn't have a thing to do with any of 'em."

Wade strolled down the steps and out to the curb, where the newspapermen stood in a little group with Captain Murphy. The reporters glared as Wade approached.

"Hello, *Mister* Wade," said McFee of the *Star*. "And how do you get into the holy of holies?"

"He knows where Farrell buries his dead or something," contributed Kennedy of the *Telegram*.

"Say," put in Churchill of the *Clarion*, "what does Farrell think this is—the Rockefeller wedding?"

"Humph," said Kennedy. "The trade is sure going to hell. You get one good story in this town every three months and then Farrell decides he's going to make rules like the Court of St. James. Do we have to wear knee-breeches to get into his party?"

Wade grinned appreciatively. "Don't be griped. Class tells."

"And tells damn little," grunted Churchill. "When my city editor finds out that his reporter wasn't in on this there'll be plenty of fever for Farrell."

"Horse feathers," said Wade languidly. "Now listen. Farrell isn't going to give anybody a special deal. I'm not covering this story. I can't write a thing I find out in there. You know Farrell better than to think he'd give anybody a washout. From the way this story looks now I'd say there'll be plenty for all and that the guy that did this killing isn't going to be easy to put a rope around."

"Who did it?" asked McFee suddenly, turning to Captain Murphy.

The captain, who had stood listening, smiled broadly across his blooming Irish face. "Well, it might have been the Archangel Michael. The dead man stole himself a Bible, you know."

"Maybe," said Churchill.

Wiggins was hopping. "There's a broad some place in this story. When a guy gets fried, sachet da femme."

"Mr. Wiggins of the Sûreté," grinned Kennedy, making a bow.

"Listen, smart guy. I'll tell you something. You can talk about books and you can talk about Bibles, but when a guy thirty years old gets knocked off, some place in the picture there's a—"

An officer came out of the library. "Mr. Wade and Captain Murphy."

Wade grabbed Wiggins' elbow and made some remark about O'Malley, but Wiggins had not paused in his speech.

"—there's just one thing you can be sure of behind a big murder—"

Wade shoved him away. "Go find O'Malley, half-portion!"

Wiggins, undisturbed, leaned back and waved a forefinger. "—and it's always the same—a *woman*!"

Wade good-naturedly dragged him off and went inside. Murphy had preceded him, and was sitting ungracefully alongside of the sheriff, at one end of the half-circle that faced the district attorney. Farrell stood behind the main library desk, speaking in the professionally-modulated voice of the courtroom.

"—and I realize, of course, that with the exception of Mr. Wade and the officers present, you folks are far removed from the world of violence. Our purpose in holding this conference is to ascertain as far as possible facts about the life, habits and associates of Mr. Quentin Ulman which may serve to throw light on the motive behind his murder."

Wade lowered himself into a seat near Farrell and examined the group. Dr. Prentiss was watching the district attorney, his fine-cut face drawn with anxiety. Next him sat Winifred, lightly drawing at her cigarette, but she was looking not at Farrell but at Wade. On the other side of her was Alfredo Gonzales, giving the district attorney the same polite, nondescript sort of attention he would have bestowed on a not very interesting lecturer at the university; to the end of Farrell's talk he did not once glance at his wife. Marie sat very still, a line between her dramatic eyebrows, stiff determination in her tight mouth; once or twice she looked questioningly at Terry, who was gazing moodily at the wall beyond Farrell. Between Terry and the sheriff was Dancy, faintly interested as though at a not very exciting second act. Wade cast an appraising look at Farrell, who, having explained his reasons for swearing in Mr. Wade of *The Creole* as a special investigator, was finishing up the preliminaries.

"I do not mean to detain you long, and I do not want to embarrass you. If I ask for information of a personal nature it is because my duty as the holder of this office is to bring before the bar of our court whoever the evidence indicates is guilty of this crime, and before charging any person with murder I must have evidence sufficient to justify the charge. Tonight, with your help, I shall begin to look for the facts behind Mr. Ulman's death.

"Now I shall ask each of you to step into Dr. Prentiss' private office for a short discussion of points I have already outlined. Mr. Wade, will you come with me?"

Wade followed him. Farrell opened the office door and placed himself at Dr. Prentiss' desk. Wade took a chair by him and looked admiringly around, for crossing the threshold from the main library into the sanctum of the Sheldon custodian was like stepping from the rigor of the Middle Ages into the richness of the Florentine Renaissance. Against the paneled walls stood Italian book-cases holding the doctor's private collection, and the cabinets that contained his files looked as if they had been intended to hold diplomatic documents in the days of the quattrocento courts. Farrell and Wade set in two broad-backed chairs facing the door across a great carved desk copied from one on which Lorenzo the Magnificent had detailed his commissions to Leonardo. "Quite a sybarite, this Prentiss," Wade observed.

Farrell smiled soberly. "What do you think of these people, Wade?"

"I haven't struck oil yet, but I'm keeping up my spirits. They all look like people who've made a compromise with life and don't like it. Except possibly Marie."

"I had a word or two with Prentiss. He seems to be more concerned about the removal of his main chance to get back his Bible than by the fact of Ulman's murder."

"Wiggins offers an opinion," Wade volunteered, "that there's a woman in the woodpile somewhere."

"It's a primary theory," Farrell assented, "but this particular job seems a little bit too gruesome for the average woman."

Wade produced a cigarette and desecrated the temple by scratching a match on the floor. "Farrell, old dear, judging by the looks of those six varieties of the Great Stone Face I'd say that you'd better keep that sentiment on ice till something resembling the average woman shows up."

Farrell chuckled. "Well, we'll start the fireworks. Ask any questions you want, Wade. Seems to me you're in a newspaperman's paradise."

"Paradise lost," Wade retorted dryly. "Worse not to know things than to know things you can't print. Who's first?"

"Prentiss. He can give the best general background, and that's what we need before we see the others."

As Farrell opened the door Wade had a flash of the room beyond— Terry leaning over the back of Gonzales' chair in close conversation, Mrs. Gonzales chatting brightly toward Marie and Prentiss, neither of whom seemed entertained, and Dancy sitting off to one side, watching with sardonic detachment. Murphy was engaged in an inaudible oration to the sheriff.

"Dr. Prentiss," said the district attorney.

Prentiss rose, compliant but questioning, as though in spite of his inevitable eagerness to see the case done with he could not quite understand its intrusion of his privacy. He entered the office, took his seat and waited, like an aristocrat trying not to show his indignation at the processes of democratic law. Being a visitor in his own office seemed not to his liking.

Farrell was an expert questioner, and he went rapidly through the details of Prentiss' charge against Ulman earlier in the day. Prentiss answered readily, but a bit nervously; Wade, from his place by Farrell, gravely looked on. In spite of the deceptive impression of Prentiss' white hair, Wade decided that he could not be more than five or six years older than Gonzales, whom he had judged as being somewhere in the middle forties; and in spite of the scholarly lift of the doctor's brow and the quiet evenness of his voice there was something indefinitely disturbing about him—he was undoubtedly, Wade reflected, noting the harsh lines at the corners of Prentiss' mouth, a man who might shudder before circumstances, but never acquiesce, a man who would fight his way with appalling and ruthless determination.

"Just when did you say you discovered the loss of this Bible fragment?" Wade asked suddenly.

It was his first question. Prentiss answered without hesitation.

"This morning—a few minutes after nine."

"I believe Mr. Dancy, Mr. Ulman and Miss Marie Castillo were in the library then?"

"Yes. I had just come downstairs. I spoke to them in the main room, and went on into the office."

"What time was the library closed last night?"

"It was about five o'clock. Two students of the university summer school were working here, or it would have been closed earlier. I like to give my assistants as little as possible to do during the hot weather."

"Who closed it?" Wade asked.

"I locked it. Mr. Ulman and Mr. Dancy were here until closing time. Miss Castillo had been gone about half an hour."

"All three of them had keys to the building, I suppose?"

"Yes, but not a key to this office. Mr. Ulman was the only one who had that. However, the porter who cleans the library every morning has a key. He usually dusts the office sometime between seven and eight, so that the door was open this morning at least from eight o'clock on."

Wade nodded slowly and glanced at Farrell, who took up the interrogation.

"Had you seen the Gutenberg Bible fragment in the safe last night, Dr. Prentiss?"

"Yes—that is, I last opened the safe shortly before closing time to put back some papers, and the Bible leaves were there."

"Those leaves are immensely valuable, aren't they?"

"Certainly," said Dr. Prentiss with a faint smile, as though pitying the man who could ask such a question. "The Gutenberg Bible was the first book printed in Europe, Mr. Farrell, about 1450, and this together with the fact that most of the copies have disappeared in the course of centuries, makes even one genuine Gutenberg leaf of enormous value to collectors. My fragment consisted of nine consecutive leaves, in nearly perfect condition."

"I seem to remember," Wade remarked irrelevantly, "that your fragment included the Ten Commandments, didn't it?"

"It did. Why do you ask?"

"I was—just thinking." Wade stared at the ceiling.

"Dr. Prentiss, who lives in the rooms above the library besides yourself?" asked Farrell.

"My housekeeper, Mrs. Selwyn, and her husband, who acts as caretaker."

"I talked to the night watchman," Farrell said to Wade. "He's a young chap going to school and he seems trustworthy. He's absolutely certain nobody entered the library last night." He turned back to Prentiss. "I think you told me that you discussed the theft with Marie Castillo and Terry Sheldon after Mr. Ulman left for the bindery. After they had gone, what did you do?"

"I had lunch upstairs."

"Then after lunch," Wade put in, "what did you do?"

"I talked to my housekeeper a few minutes, then returned to my office."

"What time was this?"

"I don't recall precisely—some time after one o'clock."

"When did you get news of Mr. Ulman's death?" Wade persisted.

"About three."

"And how did you occupy yourself from one o'clock till three?"

Dr. Prentiss, who had answered the previous questions with expressionless courtesy, suddenly grasped the arms of his chair and leaned forward, his face drawn with harshly-controlled anger.

"Mr. Wade, are you suggesting that I crossed the river and killed Mr. Ulman?"

For an instant Wade studied the doctor's face, thrown into clear relief by the lamp on the table. Then he answered.

"My dear Dr. Prentiss, we're merely trying to clear up a horrid puzzle. The tabulation of your actions is only part of a plan to discover where everybody was between noon, or shortly before, when Mr. Ulman left the library, until shortly after two o'clock when his body was found. If we go far enough we'll eventually find somebody who can't tell us where he was for that length of time. Now Marie Castillo told me a few minutes ago that it was about one when she and Terry left here; it therefore must have been considerably thereafter when you finished lunch and returned to your office. Were you in your office from lunch-time until you got the call from the police about three?"

"Yes," said Prentiss, apologetically.

"Was anybody else with you?" Farrell asked.

"I don't think so—yes, Mrs. Selwyn came down a few minutes after lunch." He paused as though to adjust his memory. "I had been too disturbed over the discovery of the Bible theft to eat much, and she brought me a cup of coffee, and stayed quite a while straightening some papers that the wind had blown about and talking about household affairs."

"Dr. Prentiss," said Farrell suddenly, "with the facts as they stand—pointing to the probability that the Bible fragment was taken from the safe sometime this morning, will you tell us why you sent Quentin Ulman, the man you suspected, from the library to the bindery before the investigation by our detectives, giving him a chance to take the fragment with him and hide it or dispose of it?"

"Certainly. Have you ever seen a Gutenberg Bible, Mr. Farrell?"

Farrell shook his head.

"If you had, you would be better able to appreciate why I sent him away. It is absolutely unthinkable that he could have had the leaves concealed on his person—my thought was that he had probably hidden them in what he considered some secure place in the library. The size of the leaves would make it impossible to conceal them anywhere about an ordinary linen suit without their being sadly folded and wrinkled, and nobody with Mr. Ulman's knowledge of the value of those leaves would have put them where this would happen. The only way to carry them safely would be in a large flat case or package, and Mr. Ulman carried nothing of the sort out of the library with him."

"Then you think he may have hidden the fragment while you were talking to my assistant this morning?"

"No. If he took them this morning and hid them he did so before I came down. He was in the front room with Marie and Mr. Dancy till Mrs. Gonzales arrived, and she was with him until I returned from downtown and sent him to the bindery. So if he hid the fragment before I came down he had no opportunity of taking it from its hiding-place unobserved. I decided to send him to the bindery when I learned that Mrs. Gonzales had been with him all the morning—so that we could discover his hiding-place before he returned. I specifically told him he need not return during the afternoon, so that if he did I should have had every reason to ask him what he wanted. Frankly, I thought sending him away was very good strategy."

"It may have been," said Wade non-committally. He took out a cigarette. "Of course, there's a possibility that Mrs. Gonzales took the Bible leaves out of the library with her."

Prentiss started. "Mr. Wade, that is not to be thought of."

"My dear doctor." Wade's cool scrutiny was almost insolent. "Our talk is absolutely confidential. We're merely exchanging ideas, you know. No record is being made of what we say, so you may as well agree that not even your loyalty to the library could keep you from seeing that the relationship between Ulman and Mrs. Gonzales was hardly what might be called casual."

"I decline to discuss that, Mr. Wade." Prentiss spoke crisply.

Wade tilted an incredulous eyebrow. But before he could answer Farrell had interposed.

"Dr. Prentiss, if the Gutenberg fragment was not destroyed on the person of Quentin Ulman, you have a better chance of recovering it than you could possibly have had if Ulman were alive. The mark of murder is on that book. Even collectors are not so thick-skinned that the charge of accessory in a murder will not strike through."

Dr. Prentiss' polite attention had suddenly become avid interest. "You think you can recover the fragment?"

"The point of my remarks," said Farrell sternly, "is that I don't think we can do a damn thing unless you take us into your confidence. We'll have our men help you search here, if you like—but this case is murder first, robbery after."

The librarian considered. Wade shot a glance of congratulation at the district attorney.

"What is it you want me to tell you?"

Wade leaned over the desk. "What do you know about your assistant and Mrs. Gonzales?"

"Nothing," said Prentiss firmly.

"Dr. Prentiss," insisted Wade, "have you never once heard any mention of a love affair?"

"It is not my habit to listen to gossip of that sort, Mr. Wade. Mrs. Gonzales frequently visited the library. It was natural that Mr. Ulman should show her the books she wanted to see. That was why he was here."

"You have never heard any suggestion that she might not have come here entirely for the purpose of looking at old books?"

"Mr. Wade," said Dr. Prentiss with the slightest tinge of reproof, "there are some people who enjoy repeating talk of that kind. It is not my habit to listen to it, and I cannot believe that your listening to it will help you discover the murderer of Mr. Ulman. I have discussed the subject only once, and then against my wish."

"With whom?" asked Farrell insistently.

"Terry Sheldon. Terry is very fond of Professor Gonzales, and also of Marie, and he came to me once, several months ago, to insist that I discharge Mr. Ulman from the library. I replied to him that I had no reason to believe what he said about the relationship of Mr. Ulman and Mrs. Gonzales, and that Marie was quite capable of attending to her own affairs."

Wade sat up. "Marie? Why Marie?"

"Why, it was understood, I believe, that she and Mr. Ulman had intentions—"

"Whe-ew!" Wade gave a low whistle. "Did Marie tell you that?"

"Oh, no."

"Who did?"

"Terry mentioned it. It was generally understood, however—Mr. Ulman was very attentive to Marie." Wade lay back, considering. Farrell took up the inquiry.

"Would you say that Mrs. Gonzales and Marie were good friends?"

"Good friends? I don't know. They moved in the same social circle, and Marie is a frequent visitor at the Gonzales home—she is extremely fond of her cousin."

"I suppose that Mr. Ulman moved in the same social circle?"

"I believe so."

"If you were Marie's father," said Wade, "would you have objected to Ulman's actions as a suitor?"

"I can't say." Prentiss smiled leniently. "Marie is an independent young person, Mr. Wade, and while I am very fond of her I am sure she would resent anything that might be interpreted as an attempt on my part to meddle with her affairs. She seems quite able to take care of herself."

"So she does." Wade studied his shoes, and Farrell asked another question or two. But he looked up when he heard Farrell ask slowly and with penetrating distinctness,

"Dr. Prentiss, why do you think Quentin Ulman was murdered?"

Prentiss was standing. He looked at Farrell intently.

"Mr. Farrell, I am a bookish man, and I have led a retired and rather circumscribed life. I do not know why men kill each other. Mr. Ulman may have been killed by his accomplice in the theft of the Gutenberg Bible, if he had one, or because of complications in his personal life of which I am unaware. If you will permit me, I should prefer to go no further."

"Thank you. That's all."

But when Prentiss had gone out Wade sat a moment grinning cryptically at the district attorney. Then he said,

"I hope we didn't shock the venerable doctor with our tattle about the goings on among the booklovers."

"Booklovers—!" Farrell's shrug was conclusive.

Wade chuckled. "Well, he puts us right back with Wiggins. Ulman in love with Winifred—Ulman engaged to Marie—"

"Shall we have in the women, then?"

"Danny, my boy, don't be like that." Wade patted the district attorney's head patronizingly. "Looking for women is all right, but you'll find them sooner if you talk to their husbands. Call in Alfredo Miguel Gonzales y Castillo and for God's sake brush the ashes off your coat before His Elegance arrives."

CHAPTER FIVE

FARRELL went to the door. "Professor Gonzales," he said.

The professor stood instantly. Wade had a momentary glimpse of Prentiss as he laid a gentle, reassuring hand on Marie Castillo's shoulder, then the professor crossed the threshold of the inner room and the door closed. Gonzales gave an inaudible greeting to Wade and Farrell as he took his seat, and looked at them guardedly. Farrell made a brisk beginning.

"We shan't waste time on formalities, Mr. Gonzales. We want to detain you as little as possible."

Gonzales smiled courteously. "You are very kind. I shall be happy to tell you whatever is in my power. Mr. Quentin Ulman was a distinguished colleague of mine, and if I can do anything to bring to judgment the author of his horrible death I am at your service."

"Thank you," said Farrell, moving his chair an inch closer. "First about this Gutenberg Bible, Mr. Gonzales. Your doubt of its authenticity was based, I suppose, on a careful examination?"

"I do not say that. A good book is like the face of a friend. It would not be necessary to make a detailed scrutiny of an impostor. After a few moments' study of the fragment I felt that it was not what it was said to be. The newspapers, with apologies to Mr. Wade, sensationalized a report that had not been prepared for the layman. With the exception of the article which was signed by yourself, Mr. Wade, none of the reports seemed written by men who understood what I had in mind. I only stated that the fragment did not appear genuine, and that I should welcome a chance to make a complete study of it."

"Did Dr. Prentiss," asked Farrell, "decline to let you make the examination necessary for a definite opinion?"

"Oh, no. I did not put the request. I planned to make a very definite examination at the time of Dr. Prentiss' report to the executors the last of July. As you may already know, it has been my policy under the trusteeship to discuss the affairs of the library with Dr. Prentiss twice a year, and twice a year only."

"Just what is your relationship to the library?" asked Farrell. "And will you explain also the relationship of the others outside?"

"Certainly. By the terms of the will of the late Michael Sheldon I am head trustee of the library, and co-executor of the will with the Exchange Bank. Dr. Prentiss is required to make a semi-annual report to the executors, showing all his activities in connection with the library over a period of six months. Terry Sheldon is a nephew of Michael Sheldon, and Marie Castillo is a niece of the late Mrs. Michael Sheldon, who was before her marriage Miss Juanita Gonzales of Havana. Mr. Dancy is Dr. Prentiss' secretary. Mrs. Gonzales has no connection with the library."

"I see," said Farrell, and paused. Wade guessed that the pause was an invitation to him.

"You knew Mr. Ulman pretty well, didn't you?" he asked.

"Very well." Gonzales spoke without self-consciousness. "He was a friend of both myself and Mrs. Gonzales."

Wade caught himself in an incredulous frown and hastily smoothed out his face. "He was a frequent visitor at your home, then?"

"Fairly frequent."

"You talked about books a great deal, I suppose?"

Gonzales smiled. It was like the set smile with which one faces a photographer. "Hardly. Very few people spend their evenings chatting in these days. For myself, as I nearly always spend my free afternoons at golf or tennis, I am more inclined to read in the evenings, or to play chess with my friends, but Mrs. Gonzales takes more pleasure in social amusements. She is younger than I—she was only sixteen when we were married—and as Mr. Ulman was frequently the escort of my cousin Marie at parties, Mrs. Gonzales found it convenient to go with them when my own presence was not necessary."

His ambiguous politeness nearly betrayed Wade again; he halted himself in a shrug and made as if to adjust his tie. "Marie Castillo is a near relative of yours, is she not?"

"No, the relationship is very distant. She is my third cousin. However, as she is the only member of my family in New Orleans and as she is a very attractive girl besides, both my wife and I take a great deal of pleasure in her company."

Wade hesitated; he felt himself floundering, and he was not accustomed to flounder. But Farrell plunged into the breach.

"It was generally assumed, was it not, that Ulman was to be a member of your family by marriage with Marie?"

"I believe so, Mr. Farrell, though there had been no definite announcement—I suppose it was delayed because Marie is still a student."

"Then Mr. Ulman did not discuss his regard for Marie with you?"

"No, but his devotion was quite obvious." Gonzales was benign, as though he were conveying how well he understood the manifestations of young love. It looked like a deadlock. Wade reminded himself that it was time to get something said.

"Mr. Gonzales," he plunged in, "you know people and their frailties, I suppose, as well as either Mr. Farrell or myself. What I'm going to tell you may be embarrassing both for you and for us."

"Please feel free to go on, Mr. Wade." Gonzales' face was as expressionless as a cameo.

"Thanks. It's not easy. A great many people seem to have thought it unusual that Mr. Ulman should be so devoted to your wife as well as to your cousin."

Gonzales looked sternly at Wade and then at Farrell, then his eyes rested on Wade again.

"Gentlemen, the men of the house of Gonzales do not question their wives. They trust them—" his ominous pause was discounted by his next suave phrase—"or they do not live with them."

He faced them across the circle of light, a man of a race that both Wade and Farrell suddenly knew was not theirs, a man who would close the door of his house when he left it and permit no stranger to see inside. Abruptly Wade thought of Winifred, almost blatantly Anglo-Saxon when contrasted with her dark, proud husband. He felt himself half abashed.

"Yes, I understand that—I merely mentioned the gossip because I wondered whether or not you could offer any idea as to how it might be traced back to an enemy of Quentin Ulman."

"Mr. Wade," Gonzales answered quietly, as if the question implied that he might have given the gossips unwarranted attention, "I have not the remotest idea."

"Then do you think," Farrell suggested, "that the murder motive was the Gutenberg Bible?"

"I have no ideas on the subject, Mr. Farrell. It is hard to conceive of a man who is at once bibliophile and thug. Possibly Mr. Ulman was killed by an assassin in pay of someone else, someone who knew the whereabouts of the Bible leaves and wanted Mr. Ulman out of the way. But that is only a guess."

"When did you first learn of Mr. Ulman's death?" Wade inquired.

"When I bought an evening paper as I left the university campus this afternoon."

"You teach in the summer school?"

"Not always. This year I lecture once a week."

"When did you last see Mr. Ulman?" Farrell asked. "Two days ago, I believe. I met him on the street, but had no conversation with him. We merely greeted each other and went on."

"Will you tell us," went on Farrell, "what you did today, before you learned of Ulman's death?"

"I left home about ten. My class met at ten-thirty. After the class I spent a few minutes talking to one of the students, and at noon I met two of my colleagues for lunch at a restaurant near the campus.

We sat at table for about an hour. I went from the restaurant to the university library, where I stayed long enough to take out a book, then I went into my office and prepared my lecture for next week. I left the campus about four."

"Quite right," said Farrell smiling. "That has been checked, in case it interests you, professor."

"I am very glad. Otherwise it might be annoying." He looked squarely at Wade.

"Just one more question," said Farrell, "and we shan't keep you any longer. We're trying to find out as much as possible about Mr. Ulman himself—what kind of a chess game did he play?"

"He was never my opponent at chess."

"Did he go in for athletics?"

"Sometimes, I believe."

"Ever play tennis or golf with you?"

"No."

"That's all, Mr. Gonzales. Thank you."

The professor rose, bowed from the waist, and went out. Farrell looked questioningly at Wade. "What do you make of the battling bookmen?"

"Precious little, yet. But it's a cinch they were both on this side of the river during the crucial two hours."

"Yes. Murphy says he saw one of the profs who lunched with Gonzales, and a couple of students who saw him in the library afterwards, and another who spoke to him as he came out of his office on his way home. Also, Murphy saw the old lady who manages things for Prentiss. She said she brought him down some coffee ten minutes or so after lunch, and stayed there quite a while, arguing that he ought to eat more green vegetables or something."

Wade picked up his hat from the desk and looked reflectively at the brim. "Gonzales is making a valiant effort to keep his domestic life clear, but this pretense of friendship with Ulman is pretty bald."

Farrell nodded. "A little bit pathetic," he agreed moodily. "But it looks as if he couldn't have killed Ulman, no matter how much he might have liked to. Alibis are usually tricky things, but we've got to remember that whoever did this business went over the river and then came back. Whoever it is ought to have nearly an hour unaccounted for."

Wade squinted at the lamp. "Gonzales might have sneaked out of his office and back again unobserved. But that hardly seems likely. He's one of the best-known professors on the campus."

"Suppose we try one of Wiggins' femmes."

"Get the Castillo youngster in. But one thing you'd better remember. She's hard—every nerve dipped in shellac."

Farrell gave him an understanding nod and went to the door. "Miss Castillo," he called, "will you come in?"

Marie entered. She stood an instant just inside the room, surveying the two men who faced her, then, slowly, she advanced toward them and sat down. Farrell went back to his place behind the desk. With deliberate coolness Marie crossed her legs and lit a cigarette, looking at him with a gaze bright and sharp as a surgeon's knife.

Her bright orange dress was like a sullen flame. Her ink-black hair glistened green under the light. This girl's resistance would die a hard death, Wade told himself, if it died at all.

But Farrell had cross-examined a great many defiant witnesses in his career, and he knew that beginning with professional inconsequentialities calculated to put his answerer at ease.

"Miss Castillo, you told Mr. Wade this afternoon how and when you last saw Mr. Ulman. You don't want to amend that account, do you?"

Marie considered for a moment. "No. I know of nothing to change." She spoke flatly. Wade thought he had never seen a girl with so absolutely blank a face.

"Very well," Farrell said. "You have worked in this library since the beginning of the summer, I believe?"

"Yes."

"What are your hours here?"

"I come at nine and work as long as I am needed. Sometimes the library is open till five. Sometimes if no visitors are here, Dr. Prentiss closes it earlier."

"You have worked for Dr. Prentiss before this summer?"

"For the past three summers."

"And you attend the university during the winter?"

"Yes." Her syllables were like the clicks of a ping-pong ball.

"Why do you work at the library, Miss Castillo?"

"To make a living."

"It pays part of your college expenses?"

"Yes."

"Very commendable, I'm sure." Farrell gave her a friendly smile, but Marie's face did not change.

"Not particularly. I don't do it from choice."

Farrell continued to be genial. "Most of us don't work from choice. How do you pay the rest of your university costs?"

"With my father's life insurance."

"I see. What are your duties here?"

"Clerk."

She lit another cigarette, stepped on the stub of the first, and lifted her eyes again to Farrell in a bleak uncompromising gaze. Wade wondered how long she would be able to hold out. He knew she wanted to talk and perhaps to cry. The strain was telling in her face, and as much as he wanted to be impersonal he could not enjoy seeing her being tortured. Farrell went on.

"You were born in Havana, I believe?"

"Yes."

"How long have you been in the United States?"

"Since I was three."

"Have you lived anywhere besides New Orleans?"

"No."

"Your father has been dead for some years?"

"Six."

Wade leaned forward, expecting her to break down after that question. Her "Six" was like the snick of a scalpel. But she sat rigid; since lighting her second cigarette she had not moved.

"How long have you been a student at the university?" Farrell asked.

"Seven years."

"You are studying medicine?"

"Yes."

"I suppose you intend to practise?"

"I am going to be a laboratory technician at a hospital. I am specializing in chemical research."

"And you graduate next year, do you not?"

"Yes."

Farrell was discouraged; he had vainly tried to relax her with unimportant questions, but Marie had not changed. Wade was sorry for her; he guessed the strain behind her terrific impassivity and wished that Farrell would put a question that would force her to some display of emotion. Evidently with the same idea, Farrell veered the line of his inquiry.

"Now this is a personal question, Miss Castillo, and I wouldn't ask it if it could be avoided, but were you planning to marry Quentin Ulman?"

"I was not!"

The answer flared from her. Wade was on his feet. This was what he had been waiting for.

"Well, we're glad to hear that," he said, "because during the short time we've been investigating Mr. Ulman's death it has been variously intimated to us that you and he were engaged."

She had closed her shell around herself again. Her answer was as carefully devoid of emotion as her earlier replies had been. "That is not true."

"Of course," said Wade easily, "Mr. Ulman paid you a great deal of attention."

Marie sat up. "I am not engaged to all the men I dance with, Mr. Wade," she snapped waspishly.

Wade smiled. This was better. "Of course not, but you must have danced a great many times with Mr. Ulman to give that impression to so many people."

She stiffened angrily. "As an amateur detective, you perhaps need to be reminded that the number of times I dance with anybody is none of your business."

He frowned thoughtfully, trying hard not to be exasperated at her defiance. He knew that it took all her nerve to stem the hysteria that must be sweeping through her. He knew too that in a few minutes all her reserve was going to smash against a question that would force out the fact she was trying so desperately to keep hidden. But Farrell had changed the subject with a business-like query.

"You are a cousin of Professor Alfredo Gonzales, are you not?"

She leaned back in her chair. "Yes, a third cousin," she said wearily.

"Can you tell us then," said Farrell, very slowly, "your impression of the relationships of Professor Gonzales, Mrs. Gonzales and Mr. Ulman?"

"That is something, Mr. Farrell, that I know nothing whatever about."

Wade interposed. "Oh, come, Miss Castillo," he said. "You were frequently in company with Mrs. Gonzales and Mr. Ulman at social affairs."

She looked at him with cold antagonism. "I have been at parties," she answered acidly, "where I saw a great many men and women, and I did not inquire whether the men beat their wives, or whether the women bullied their husbands, or whether they drank orange juice or rye whiskey for breakfast."

This, thought Wade, was much better. If he could only keep her talking.

"So we'll leave that for the moment," he said. "Let's get this established. When did you last see Mr. Ulman alive?"

"I told you. When he left the library."

"He had been in the reading-room, out of your sight, for most of the morning?"

"Yes."

"Mrs. Gonzales was with him there, wasn't she?"

"Yes."

"Did Mr. Ulman and Mrs. Gonzales leave the reading-room together?"

"No, Mr. Ulman left alone."

"Then that left you and Mrs. Gonzales there. What did you talk about?"

"The weather, I think."

"Yes, there's lots of it these days. But didn't you talk about anything else?"

"I suppose so. I really don't remember just what was said."

"Did you leave the reading-room together?"

"Yes."

"It was shortly after that, wasn't it, that Mr. Ulman left for the bindery?"

"Yes."

"Was Terry Sheldon there when he left?"

"No. He came in a few minutes later. Really, Mr. Wade, if you will stop to recall what I told you before Mr. Farrell came it might refresh your mind on all these facts."

"Yes, I remember: you and Terry had a conference with Dr. Prentiss in which he told you the Bible fragment had been stolen."

"Yes."

"Is that all you talked about?"

"If you want to know what happened at that conference, I think you might ask Dr. Prentiss."

"At any rate, Miss Castillo, this much is true, isn't it—that you did discuss Mr. Ulman and Mrs. Gonzales?"

Marie stood up. "Mr. Wade, I have no intention of staying here to answer that sort of question, no matter what is the official status you have recently acquired. I do not care to discuss Mrs. Alfredo Gonzales and her relationship with anybody. I have no interest in Mr. Ulman's personal affairs nor in those of Mrs. Gonzales. What Mr. Ulman did was entirely his own business."

Her words were fast and clipped. Her eyes flamed at him. Wade leaned back in his chair and looked up at her with a lazy smile. If he could only keep her angry!

"Have you ever thought of directing your talents to the stage instead of to the laboratory?" he asked.

Her only answer was a continued fiery stare.

Wade lit a cigarette. If she would only unbend, he thought. Maybe if he could make her mad enough it wouldn't be so hard for her. Farrell was annoyed, but Wade went on with a slow drawl. "I am very sorry to bother you with this unimportant little murder, Miss Castillo," he said, "but before you go I'd like to ask you just one more question, if you don't mind."

Marie still stood motionless. Wade decided to fire his telling shot. She had to take it some time.

"If you were not interested in Mr. Ulman, if what he did meant nothing at all in your peaceful life and if you did not give a whoop what happened to him," Wade said deliberately, "it can't possibly embarrass you to tell us why you got off the ferry-boat coming from the scene of his murder just twenty minutes after his smoking skeleton was found on the road between Algiers and Harvey this afternoon."

Marie's hands gripped the edge of the desk between them. Her lips parted.

"Mother of God," she whispered, and collapsed.

He was glad it was over. As Farrell sprang up Wade went to the door, opened it and went out, closing it behind him.

"Mrs. Gonzales," he said, "will you be good enough to come into the office? There will be no further investigation here tonight. Marie Castillo has fainted."

Winifred was already at the door of the office, where Marie lay limply in one of the big leather chairs, with Farrell chafing her hands. The others had followed, frightened and indignant; Alfredo Gonzales fairly thrust Farrell out of the way.

"I'll take her home. What in God's name have you been doing to her?"

Wade, in a corner of the room, hardly noticed them. He was holding a little wad of paper that had been dropped on the table in the confusion. He had snatched it up unobserved, and smoothing it out quickly he had read, "Marie—that was only adios. Quentin."

CHAPTER SIX

"BUT I did get one swell piece of art. Shot the bunch coming out of the library. All of 'em look kinda spooky in the flash. But I got the picture, see?"

Wade stopped in the doorway of the city room and glared good-naturedly down at Wiggins.

"Look here, chimpanzee. If you don't be quiet I'm going to drop you down the elevator shaft. I've got things to think about. Understand?"

"Sure. I got things to think about myself. Whadja do to that Marie person? She looked like a woman who'd just had a baby in a burning building."

Wade put his hands in his pockets and wrinkled his forehead thoughtfully. "What do you think of her, Wiggins?"

"Well, I said there was a woman in this case, but she ain't it. If she'd knocked off a guy she's the kind that would brag about it and expect a loving cup." Wiggins gave a ponderous shrug.

"Maybe," suggested Wade, "she knows who did it."

"Maybe. Now me personally, I think it was that high-hat young feller with the Bond Street look—Dancy—that's the kind that always thinks they can get away with anything. But don't you go pestering Marie. She's got a good camera face and she's a nice girl."

Wade patted his little photographer genially. "She is nice. What else do you think?"

"Well now, the professor's missus—she looks like a million dollars and she's nice too—but you get what I mean—she ain't *nice* nice. You trust me, smart boy. I know this racket. I know too much about it. Mighta been a petty officer in the navy now if I'd stuck—did I tell you about—"

"Yes, you did, and I've got a story to write. You go rush that picture."

Wiggins made a face and bobbed down the hall. Wade, his hands thrust into his pockets, ambled wearily into the city room. It was approaching the rush hour, when copy boys dash in and out, laden with smudgy sheets that will be the morning news, and reporters hunch furiously over their typewriters and write tensely, looking up at the clock and jerking half-finished stories out to be put into type, knowing that after the first pages of copy are gone all the bright remarks that should have been in the opening paragraph will rush to the surface stillborn. The great room rattled and quivered and seethed; it looked like the last epitome of confusion, as if every man there was enduring such a peak of strain as would leave him shaken for weeks to come, but it happened every evening and they were used to it, and they knew that all the noise and the tight nerves would be smoothed down to cool type for breakfast.

Wade kicked crumpled evening papers and sheets of discarded copy out of his way as he walked to the city desk. He tipped his hat back on his head and slid into the chair opposite Koppel, the city editor.

"O'Malley's doing the story from Farrell's regular press statement. Anything special you want me to write?"

Koppel considered. "Much fireworks?"

"Lord, yes; but that's graveyard. I can tell you what happened but it won't do to print." He recounted the details of his interviews. "I saw this girl getting off the boat when Farrell and I drove the car on, and I thought I recognized her. I'd seen her once or twice in the library without speaking to her. What's your idea now?"

Koppel pushed back his eyeshade and carefully refilled his pipe. "Hm. There's one large mass of landscape that nobody has touched yet, Wade."

"Yes, I know. The Sheldon will."

"Exactly. I've a vague recollection of that will—back in 1911, I think it was, and I wasn't here then, but it's been cropping up now and then when Prentiss and Gonzales have indulged in their favorite pastime of calling each other boobs. I've a notion, Wade, that this Bible Murder might have started twenty years ago with that will. A will can be a sinister document sometimes."

"Most of them are." Wade slipped down on the end of his spine and stretched out his legs. "It's a nasty proposition, you know— when people can't realize that the world will jog along very well after they're dead and insist that they've got to reach their clammy hands out of their graves to throttle folks who are still living. I'll take a look at the will."

"Do it tonight. I'll order the 1911 files brought down for you. Print it under a special head—murder of library assistant rouses interest in terms of will by which library was founded—maybe we ought to get this will into the light."

Wade nodded agreement and stood up.

"Well, here's luck," said Koppel. "It's a good thing this broke in the off season—great for circulation." Wade grinned and waved as he went off. For the next hour he gazed ruminatively through the twenty-year-old files of *The Morning Creole*. At last he brought another story to the desk. Koppel took it.

"The will story? How is it?"

"It'll do. Pretty good feature. But no wonder Gonzales and Prentiss hate each other, after that."

"What do you mean?"

Wade shrugged. "Well, here's Prentiss with the income of three-quarters of a million being paid to him every year, and Gonzales lost his chance at it because he married three months too early. But here's Gonzales with a legal right to censor everything Prentiss does at the library. And that's not all. Listen." Wade slithered himself between the chair and the desk. "Don't read the story yet—there's a lot of buttery phrases that don't do a thing but make the information easier for the public to swallow—but here's the idea.

"Mike Sheldon died in 1911, leaving his fortune to found the library. He'd spent a long time in Cuba, and he came back to New Orleans in 1907 with six million dollars, a beautiful Cuban wife and a beautiful half-Cuban daughter named Muriel. Alfredo Gonzales was some kind of distant cousin of Mrs. Sheldon, and both he and Prentiss had been studying medieval literature here. Muriel had been educated all over Europe, specializing in medieval literature too, so when her engagement to Prentiss was announced it all seemed quite suitable.

"But Prentiss unwisely betook himself to Europe, and while he was gone Alfredo won the heart of Muriel, so about the time Prentiss got back it was announced that Muriel was going to marry Gonzales. Then came the tragedy. Two weeks before the date of the wedding Muriel drank poison, for a reason that nobody knows.

"Mrs. Sheldon died in 1909 and Mike Sheldon two years later. Both of them had manifested great fondness for both of Muriel's suitors, and when Sheldon's will was opened it was found that he spoke of them in the most flattering terms and said that either of them would be an admirable guardian of his daughter's memory. The will established the Muriel Sheldon Memorial Library to perpetuate Muriel's memory and her love of classical research, saying that the library was to be a scholarly institution with emphasis on the collection of manuscripts, incunabula and rare editions.

"Now comes the hitch. Sheldon says the organizer of the library must live absolutely for the library, without family cares or other outside interests, so he specifies that the first custodian must agree to remain unmarried, and the income of three-quarters of a million dollars is to be paid to him annually. If either Prentiss or Gonzales should be unmarried at the time of the opening of the will, the unmarried one is to be custodian of the library with the other head trustee and co-executor of the will jointly with the Exchange Bank. If both were unmarried, the bank was to choose between them; if both were married, another custodian was to be appointed.

"Well, just three months before this Gonzales had married Winifred, so Prentiss got the library.

"Prentiss has absolute control of the purchase of books, the engaging of assistants and other expenditures, from his appointment until his death, or until his incompetence or his misuse of funds has been legally proved. But he has to make a semi-annual report to the executors, showing how he has been spending the money, and these semi-annual reports have for twenty years been the occasions for the famous Prentiss-Gonzales squabbles.

"But there's more yet. When Prentiss dies, the trustees are to appoint another custodian whose salary will be paid from the regular library funds. He doesn't have to be a bachelor, by the way. The three-quarters of a million that Prentiss has been using to buy his socks and ties will be given to Terry Sheldon, who'll have the income for life, and when he dies the principal will go to his children. But if Terry dies without children the principal goes to Marie Castillo.

"There's another possibility of a tangle, but we don't know what it is. The will was accompanied by a sealed codicil, which was to be opened only at the death of either Prentiss or Gonzales, or upon Prentiss' being judged incompetent to handle the library funds. The codicil is in custody of the bank."

Wade stopped. Koppel raised his head and stared profoundly at Wade, who was regarding him with a curious frown.

"Pretty hellish, isn't it?" said Wade.

"It's abominable. Enough to make all those people hate one another. No wonder Gonzales keeps pawing at Prentiss' reputation."

"Precisely. And what about Gonzales and his wife? He's been slaving away in a classroom these twenty years because he married her—and now look at her!"

"Lord!" said Koppel. "Can you imagine the pleasant domestic scene in the Gonzales household when this will was filed for probate?"

"No," said Wade shortly, "I can't." He looked down, then back at Koppel. "Particularly as I understand that the beautiful and frisky lady has plenty of money in her own right. You know that gorgeous big house of theirs with the palms in front? You don't imagine that's kept up on a professor's stipend, Koppel?"

Koppel twirled his pipe between his fingers. His twelve years at a city desk had taught him to regard most human problems with the casual tolerance that comes of being too well acquainted with them, but as he looked at Wade his face wrinkled thoughtfully. "Can you imagine," he suggested, "what Marie Castillo is planning to give Terry's first baby as a christening present?"

Wade shook his head and waved absently at Wiggins, who had come in with a handful of prints. "I don't know, Koppel. She might take it very well and she might not. She's not such a bad sort."

Koppel smiled. "We'll see. I don't like the way she's shaping up in this story. The evening papers are carrying plenty of suggestion that a hidden love affair may have been the spark that set the flame that killed the boy that bound the books."

"Nuts," said Wade, and walked back to his desk. For a moment he stood moodily looking down at his typewriter. In spite of the habit of detached observation which had been drilled into him by ten years of newspaper reporting, he found himself troubled by the pernicious chances that the Bible Murder was holding for Marie Castillo. He knew by experience that her attitude was beckoning trouble. He put the cover on his typewriter and stood thinking. Wiggins came up and nudged his elbow.

"Say, you. I'm done—if you are I know a joint where we can get some good brew. Right out by the lake. Wanta come?"

Wade smiled and slowly shook his head. "Thanks, but I've got another date."

"Whereya going, pardner?"

"To finish up some work. I'm going to see Marie Castillo."

"Work!" Wiggins repeated with voluminous scorn. "Work! You're just itching for trouble. Say, why don't you lay off her awhile? Didn't you and Farrell give her the works tonight?"

Wade reached for his hat and shook his head at Wiggins' chivalry.

"Sorry, monk. But it's either me tonight or Murphy in the morning."

Wiggins gave a lugubrious sigh. "Well, you go. You better go. By tomorrow morning even that mick Murphy will have ants so bad he'd arrest Mother Machree, if he could find her in Orleans Parish."

CHAPTER SEVEN

NEW Orleans is a Janus-town, and any story of New Orleans must be a tale of two cities. Wade drove along the narrow white canyon of Carondelet Street, walled on either side by the unromantic modernity of skyscrapers; he crossed Canal Street, brilliantly lit and brisk with the evening crowds; then suddenly, before he had gone a hundred yards on the other side of Canal Street he entered into the old city, built two hundred years ago, and was driving slowly through the serene decadence of the Quarter.

With that curious distortion which darkness gives even to the most familiar places, the strange old houses seemed to Wade taller and closer together than ever, as if they were tilting over the narrow street on which he drove. The lanterns at the corners gave out a glow that served more to attract candleflies than to illumine the surroundings, and there was a soft, almost sinister quality to the darkness. As it was impossible to distinguish house numbers, when he had reached the approximate neighborhood he sought he parked his car and walked slowly along the curb, throwing the beam of his flashlight above the doors and the courtyard gates.

At last he found Marie's number over a gate of scroll iron that opened into a paved courtyard, where a fountain long innocent of water poked up in the darkness. A high wall divided the court from the alley of the next house, and as the gate opened with a whine of rusty hinges Wade wandered into the dark patio and found a door at the right. He pulled the bell at one side and waited.

The door squawked open and a woman appeared, her ample person enveloped in an apron. "You want somebody?"

"Yes. Miss Marie Castillo. She lives here, doesn't she?"

"Garret—four flights up," she grunted, and disappeared into the shadows.

Wade flashed his light along a wide hall, where a broad low stairway curved its neglected dignity into the shadows above, and began his climb. The stairs wound up and up, past the second and third floors, and narrowed into what had been a garret ascent in the days of the brocaded aristocrats who had built the Quarter. At the top of the steep last flight he saw a door, with a line of light under it, and as he paused an instant for breath the door opened and a square of light projected itself into the dark. In the square he saw Marie's shadow zigzag down the steps.

"Who is it?" she called.

"Wade."

"Oh—the *Creole* man." Her voice was cool and clear.

"That's right."

"Come in." There was a flicker of mockery in her invitation. He ascended the last few steps and entered.

Marie lived in an enormous garret that would have been bleak but for the gay carelessness of its furnishings—brilliant curtains and hangings, furniture picked up here and there in the antique shops, and great worn medical textbooks toppling untidily from chairs and tables. In all the cheerful conglomeration there was one corner that was instantly noticeable as the focus and the shrine of all the rest—a miniature laboratory, with burners and test-tubes arranged in shining order, and tiny jars of chemicals on shelves above the table. He saw the loving bareness of the corner and the insouciant brightness of the rest of the great room as he crossed the threshold, and he had a sudden consciousness that here was an adequate summarizing of the personality of Marie.

She dropped on a scarlet-covered sofa and carelessly indicated an ancient armchair opposite. "Be careful how you sit down—it has necrosis in one leg," she said, and leaned back surveying him with appraising black eyes.

"I'm sorry to be coming so soon after your indisposition," said Wade, taking the chair, "but frankly, Miss Castillo, I'm worried about you. I wondered if you could spare me a half-hour or so."

He spoke almost gently, for she was evidently tired, and he knew the day had not been easy for her.

"Of course," she returned easily. "I hoped you would come." She began to smile, a slow, creeping smile, and sat up.

"That's good of you." Wade spoke cordially.

Marie was sitting straight. She looked directly at him, and when she spoke her voice was like a hacksaw.

"Oh, no, it isn't. You see, I never before wanted to tell a man what a low, unspeakable, disgusting, degraded, guttersnipe specimen of humanity he was. And now I have both the time and the opportunity and I'm going to tell you."

He smiled. "Go ahead. *C'est la guerre.*"

Her hands gripped the edge of the red sofa; her eyes blazed in her dark face. "That's about the answer I expected. Perhaps this imaginary tin badge that Farrell conferred on you tonight could make a man lose his sense of decency, but I don't think so—not if he ever had any."

Wade did not answer. He waited quietly for her to go on.

"I confess," said Marie, "that I'm quite ignorant of the powers the law confers on its representatives. But I am certain that the sort of third degree you and Mr. Farrell staged this evening would not be considered ethical by anyone who had respect for justice." She paused. Her words fairly bit at him. "But it seems that democratic law is a system so rotten that only a sadistic hypocrite can revel in its processes." She got to her feet.

"I think I've worn out my patience. I don't want to look at you any longer. Good night."

Wade made no move to go. He smiled tolerantly at her.

"Have you done?" he asked cheerfully.

"Quite. Please leave."

His smile faded. He leaned toward her and spoke with convincing earnestness.

"Miss Castillo, I don't want to be boorish, but I did come here to tell you something and I'm not going until I have told you. Your attitude troubles me, and I mean to talk. Two hours ago Mr. Farrell and I were impelled to make sure of your reactions to a set of unpleasant circumstances. The reason was that we did not want to charge you with murder."

Marie sat down. There was surprise and anger in her attitude, but hardly a suggestion of fear.

"Is this another of your inspired devices?"

"Believe me, it is not. Let me outline the hypothetical case against you."

She reached to the table at her side for a cigarette. She said nothing, but he saw that she was listening. He went on.

"First, we know that you and Quentin Ulman were discussing, if not actually planning, marriage. We know that you are not unfamiliar with death, that you are preparing for a profession that deals intimately with it. We know that whether or not you were in love with Quentin Ulman, you had good reasons for resentment against him. This afternoon when I took the river ferry, on my way to the scene of Ulman's murder, I saw you leave the boat."

Marie drew reflectively at her cigarette. "Go on," she said.

"You were called before the district attorney tonight and asked a number of questions. From the moment I first spoke to you it was obvious that you intended to bar the inquiry in any way you could— the very line of your back said 'Try and make me say something'—and as the interview went on it became increasingly apparent that while you knew a great deal that might relate to our problem, you were utterly determined not to say it. But I knew that for some reason, as yet unexplained, you had crossed the river this afternoon, returning just after Ulman's body was found. When I told you I knew this you collapsed."

She smiled bitterly. "Silly of me, wasn't it? I'd never fainted before. But I hadn't eaten anything since morning and I had smoked about thirty cigarettes before you called me in. I had had—well, rather a hard day."

"Undoubtedly. But we knew, you see, that you had thought nobody was aware of your going across the river. You had told me that after leaving the library you went home. And we knew that you were facing a climax in your relationship with Ulman."

She looked at him sharply. "How did you know that?"

"We knew it because of this."

He handed her a photostatic copy of the note that had been dropped on Prentiss' desk that evening. She looked at it.

"Where—where did you get this?" she gasped. She had begun to quiver. He was sorry for her. As much as he wanted to be impersonal in his search for the murderer of Quentin Ulman, he wished that she would let him help her out of the tangle she had woven around herself. With a nervous gesture she ran her hand over her shining dark hair.

"Miss Castillo," he said to her, "neither Mr. Farrell nor myself is inclined toward the theory that you killed Quentin Ulman. The original of this note was tossed on the desk by one of that group in the office tonight, someone who came in after you were unconscious. Terry Sheldon, Dr. Prentiss, Gonzales, Mrs. Gonzales and Luke Dancy were there. Whoever dropped this note is not your friend. Because there seems to be a desire on somebody's part to involve you, I believe it's time that you told everything you know about the murder of Quentin Ulman."

Marie looked intently at the toe of her linen shoe. "Has this note been made public?" she asked.

"Oh, no, and it's not going to be."

Marie's eyes lifted. She studied him with thoughtful intensity, as if she was wondering how his cynicism of two hours ago could have been so completely effaced by his evident sincerity now.

"All right," she said finally. "I'll tell you what I know. I'll tell you about that note. I'll tell you about Quentin Ulman and why I can't be very sorry he's dead."

Wade did not interrupt her. She lit another cigarette.

"Damn you," said Marie, "you asked for it, and here it is."

She flipped the ashes on the floor. "I never was in love with Quentin, Mr. Wade. At first I suppose I was—well, dazzled is about the right word. He had an astonishing amount of culture, and a personality that can't be called anything less than glamorous. Some people are like that."

She paused, and gradually he began to understand why she had tried so hard not to speak. He saw how jealously Marie had striven to keep her personal life her own, hidden by the fierce challenge of her pride. He listened with growing sympathy as she went on.

"And I—I liked him tremendously," said Marie. "Before I knew him I'd had just Terry and Alfredo to talk to. Of course I knew plenty of other men—boys at medical school and others at the university—but those three were different. I suppose you know what I mean when I say there's not a lot of people one can talk to. Alfredo dabbles in chemistry and he knows medieval medicine as well as he knows medieval literature; Terry had rather talk anatomy than anything else except Greek architecture and Epstein bronzes; and Quentin had a flair for things. He was one of those men who seem to know something about everything. I don't mean he was a scientist, but he had ideas. When I first knew him I thought he was the most gracious and most entertaining man I'd ever known."

She stopped again and looked at him questioningly, then, as if assured that he understood what she was trying to tell, she went on.

"In the three years I knew Quentin I never found him maudlin—in fact, except for his constant kindness there was nothing very affectionate about our relationship. We weren't in love, and I never thought of love in connection with him until a week ago when he asked me to marry him.

"Of course I knew about Winifred. I'd lived with a frank and irreverent group at school—nobody would call medical students a gentle-speaking lot—and I'd heard all the stories you've heard about Quentin and Winifred and probably a lot you haven't. And I'm not quite a fool. I've known Winifred for years, and ever since I can remember she's had somebody dancing at her heels, and her camping on the library doorstep hadn't bothered me. I did think she was silly, but it was no business of mine. I liked Quentin, and as long as it amused me to talk to him I couldn't see that it was my affair to be a reformer. Terry Sheldon used to rave and tell me I really ought to do something to stop it, but Terry's extraordinary devotion to Alfredo rather warped his views."

Wade was listening closely. Marie was talking as if her last resistance had crumbled and as if she was glad to talk at last to a sympathetic listener.

"Quentin asked me to marry him. I was surprised and I was sorry. We had had a good time together. I didn't want to spoil it. Things are always bound to be strained between a man and a girl who have definitely said they aren't going to be married to each other. But I didn't want to hurt him, and I didn't want to plunge into the Winifred business. So I used the excuse of not believing in marriage and a career.

"I talked so hard that I almost got myself around to believing in it. Quentin told me he was proud of my work—all that sort of thing."

Wade smiled comprehendingly.

"As a friend he had been impressive, and as a lover his technique was flawless. He made only one mistake. He was too voluble. He was just a little bit too eager in defining the freedom we'd both have when we were married. I finally got exasperated and told him that I wasn't marrying anybody who was so infatuated with another man's wife that he couldn't keep away from her twenty-four hours at a time."

She crushed out her cigarette with a quick angry movement. "He told me he'd been trying to break with Winifred for a month, that he knew what an idiot he had been and a great deal more of the same sort of rot. All this discussion occupied several days. At last, this morning, he told me Winifred was coming to the library while Prentiss was out and that he'd wind up definitely with her. I told him if he did we might consider ourselves engaged."

She looked straight at him. "That, Mr. Wade, is the basis for this pretty little crime-culture. I've been seventy different kinds of a fool and I'm telling you before you can begin to think I don't know it. Now here's what you came to find out.

"Winifred did come to the library this morning, as you know. Quentin grabbed a book and they shut themselves up in the reading-room. They were there nearly two hours. Prentiss came in and told me to get Quentin. I went into the reading-room and as I opened the door I saw him kiss Winifred on the back of her neck.

"They both knew I saw that kiss. But I don't think either of them guessed what a fury boiled up in me at the sight of it.

"It wasn't so much that I loved Quentin. I didn't, though I did think we might have an amusing time if we married. I wasn't jealous, just hurt. I suppose it's self-respect. I've never fed on the roses and lain in the lilies of life, you know; I've had to work pretty hard to stay in school—I've done my own laundry and I've worked nights typing out case-histories for a lot of lazy doctors, but I've done it because I wanted to pay my own way. Nobody has ever given me charity and nobody has ever had any chance to be sorry for me. And suddenly today, for the first time in my life, I knew I'd let that Gonzales woman and that self-appointed Don Juan make me ridiculous before everyone who knew the three of us.

"When I came out of the reading-room Quentin slipped that scrap of paper into my hand. I read it. 'That was only adios.' About that time Winifred said she'd drive him to the ferry. He grinned like a Jack-o'-Lantern and said 'Splendid.'

"I'm pretty catty, I suppose, but all my ancestors were the kind that would kill three men while Quentin's Viking forefathers were making up their minds to fight. I knew Quentin was lying, but I wanted Winifred to know she didn't have the world with a little red fence around it either. So I laid that scrap of paper on the desk directly under Winifred's eyes. I saw her look at it. Then she and Quentin went off together."

She stopped abruptly and laid her head against the red sofa-back, wearily. Wade came over to her.

"Do you want to wait awhile before you go on?" he asked her gently. "It isn't necessary to tell everything at once, you know."

She smiled and shook her head. "Thank you, but I'd rather get it over."

He sat down on the sofa by her, but for a moment she said nothing. Wade felt sorry she had been dragged into this; ordinarily, he thought, she must have a frisky impudence about her, in spite of her stern adherence to her purpose. Marie took up her story.

"I had to be pleasant and calm, because Terry came in for his conference with Prentiss and me. That was when Prentiss told us the books were gone—you know about that. At that conference everything you suggested was mentioned, including Quentin's attentions to Winifred and his so-called attentions to me. Afterward Terry and I walked out on the steps. He was furious and gave me five or six minutes of hell for having let Quentin make a parking-space of my affections while he was running after Winifred. I walked off blazing. I had to tell it to myself with every step—that I'd never given a damn for Quentin and that all this didn't mean a thing.

"It isn't the kind of trouble you like to talk about. Alfredo has been a sort of confessor to me ever since father died, but of course I couldn't go to him. Prentiss has been kindness itself, but he was half distracted over having lost his Gutenberg fragment, and besides, he's been too cloistered these twenty years to realize the potentialities of a human equation. So I just walked—and after about six blocks I had decided that I was going to the bindery. I wanted to pitch all Quentin's declarations of love into his face. I took the ferry."

Marie was looking directly at him. So far she had told her story and had lost nothing by telling it. He found himself hoping desperately that he would be able to believe what she was going to say.

"Halfway across the river," said Marie, "I realized that Winifred had probably gone over with him. I didn't know whether I wanted to face them both or not. So I rode back, thinking.

"The boat went back and forth and I sat on the upper deck. It was cool. I felt as if I'd swallowed a lot of boiling lead. I wanted to see him. But I didn't, just then, want to see Winifred. I didn't want to hear that little icy laugh of hers. I stayed on that boat for an hour. Maybe more. I stayed there while my instincts fought with my dignity. And at last, I knew I didn't want to see him then. I didn't want to make an exhibition of myself. Particularly not in front of her. So I got off. That's when you saw me."

She dropped her head on her hand. So that, Wade thought, was her story. He hoped, more than he liked to acknowledge to himself, that it was true. But he had to own that for the first time since the riddle of Quentin Ulman's death had presented itself, he had heard an admission of motive and opportunity for murder. He tried to keep his voice simply conversational as he asked, "And where did you go from the ferry?"

"I walked home," she answered, "and made myself presentable to go back to the library at four. When I got there Prentiss told me Ulman was dead."

She lifted her head. Her eyes met his again.

"That was four o'clock, Mr. Wade. It's after ten now. Six hours. I've been thinking for those six hours that perhaps if I'd gone to the bindery what happened there this afternoon might not have happened. Sometimes I wish I had gone. But sometimes—as I remember how he kissed her and that nasty little smile of triumph she gave me—sometimes, Mr. Wade, I'm damned glad I didn't go."

CHAPTER EIGHT

PAUSING to strike a match against a lamp-post, Wade walked back to the corner where he had left his car. As he walked he examined what Marie had told him, morosely blowing clouds of smoke toward the balconies that hung over the street. He wanted to believe her; he did, in fact, believe her, but in spite of the cheerful reassurances he had given before he left he knew that he did not have and could not get proof of her story, and it troubled him. He came up to his car.

"Whatcha know, pops?"

Wade started, then saw the button-nosed countenance of Wiggins protruding from the roadster. "Passed up the date," Wiggins volunteered. "Thought I'd mosey down here and wait for you. Been doing some scouting on my own account, and did I get the air!"

Wade chuckled as he climbed in and shoved Wiggins out of the driver's seat. "Where've you been?"

"Out to the Gonzales ranch. I figured this way." Wiggins helped himself to a cigarette from the pack in Wade's breast pocket and snuggled down contentedly as the car started. "We ain't got a good picture of Mrs. Gonzales—the one in the society file got kinda messed up last time they made a cut—and I thought we oughta have one. So I thought I'd just go out and get it: I figured she's the kind that wouldn't like a quick picture and would rather give me one that had been fixed up all fancy by somebody in a smart studio."

"How'd you make out?"

Wiggins sighed. "*Out*. See, when I rang the bell this feller opened it—a regular moving picture butler, so I told him I was the man who had come to see Mrs. Gonzales about a portrait. So he shows me in, see, and while I'm kind of catching my breath in the middle of that swell house in she comes. And when she arrives and gets a look at me—say, did I get lit into? I did. No fooling. I burnt up. Didn't say anything, you know, but if she's a lady I'm a physical culture ad."

"Never mind. It isn't important. We can probably fix a picture up tomorrow." Wade was abstracted.

"I'll fix a picture, all right. Don't you worry. But you think it ain't important?" Wiggins squinted at Wade's profile. "I told you there was a dame in this case and she's it. I guarantee you—" Wiggins marked his words with a small and stubby forefinger—"before she gets through with this thing she'll be seeing so many pictures of herself she'll think she's been put on a postage stamp."

Wade laughed and brought the car to a stop before the criminal courts building. "I'm going up to see Farrell. Don't get worked up; I'll see about a picture in the morning."

"Never you mind," ordered Wiggins, scrambling out after him. "I'm the one that's seeing about pictures. I get sixty bucks every Monday morning for getting pictures, see, so you go ahead and play policeman. I'll get a picture of that female or I'll get bashed in the head, that's what."

"All right, demon immortalizer. I'm going up."

"Me too." Wiggins wriggled past the officers at the main door and went into Farrell's office behind Wade. The district attorney sat in his shirt sleeves puffing at a long cigar, and across the room was Captain Murphy, his normally good-natured face harshly belligerent. They both turned gratefully when Wade came in.

"Thank the Lord you're here," Murphy greeted. "Me and Farrell, we been arguing about you for an hour."

Wade grinned as he pulled off his coat and sat down. "Ain't murder grand?"

"Say, you sleuth," retorted Farrell, "except for that grisly thing in the morgue and Marie's fainting, I wouldn't know there'd been a tragedy. If the Gutenberg Bible could be found it looks as if everybody'd be agreed that the passing of Mr. Quentin Ulman was something of a boon to society."

"Maybe," Wade vouchsafed dismally.

"Well, take a look at this. Here's a telegram I got tonight from Haverhill, Massachusetts. 'Quentin Ulman affianced to my daughter Evelyn Lawrence marriage scheduled for October spare no expense investigation if possible would like body shipped here for burial in family vault. Signed, Asa Lawrence.'"

"M-hm! The girl he left behind him. Mormon."

"What'd I tell you?" exclaimed Wiggins triumphantly from his corner. "Another woman. This case is beginning to look like a telephone operators' convention."

Farrell gave him a quietening look. "I'll ask the Pinkerton office in Boston to check on this."

"Our wire service will run it down for you," offered Wade, reaching for the phone. "It's about time we started to let the newspapers turn loose on this. Begins to look as if Ulman had sweethearts all over the lot. Let's stop being so blamed considerate, Farrell—he was no Galahad, you know, and the more information people get about him the more chance we've got of having somebody crack in with what we need to solve this murder."

"Go ahead, then. Probably won't do any harm." Wade phoned a story to his office, to the accompaniment of grinning approval from Murphy. As he hung up the receiver Wade swung his chair around to face Farrell. "I've just left Marie Castillo."

"So that's why you've had us sitting up all night," nodded Murphy. "That lady say anything?"

"Plenty." Wade told his story. "I left her thinking she's out of the picture now—I had to. I reminded her that if she rode the ferry so long the deck-hands would probably remember her, and when I left she told me she'd take back all the names she'd called me and thanked me for being rather nice. I felt yellow, Farrell, because she's really all shot to pieces, but I didn't have the heart to tell her she could have made seven or eight trips on the ferry and still have managed to do the murder between times."

Farrell took a sheaf of papers out of his drawer and began to add quick notes at the bottom of the last page. "Here's our summary of motives. I had it drawn up this afternoon. Listen:

"Alfredo Gonzales: Left home for university about ten o'clock, taught till eleven-thirty. Lunched about noon with two other professors and visited university library, then worked in office till about four. Alibi substantiated by professors and students who saw him in library and also saw him as he left office. Was alone in office but hardly had time to leave campus and commit murder before two-fifteen. Possible motives: jealousy of Ulman's attention to Mrs. Gonzales; theft of Gutenberg fragment from Ulman; possibly to silence Ulman about Bible, which Gonzales may have stolen as he knew safe combination.

that would mean he wasn't doused, because the boy at the filling-station says Ulman didn't come there today to buy gas. I think whoever killed him set him afire in the middle of the road so as not to start a fire among all that bush round about. It's been pretty dry lately."

Farrell ruminated. "Possibly, in spite of Prentiss' protestations, Ulman took the leaves to the bindery and delivered them there to a customer who killed him rather than pay off."

"I hardly think so," Wade objected dubiously. "Prentiss was perfectly right about that, Farrell. Nobody with Ulman's knowledge would have folded those leaves, and they couldn't have been concealed anywhere about a man's clothes without being creased pretty badly."

Wiggins perked up. "Couldn't he have carried 'em in his hat?"

"They're too big," Wade explained.

"Huh!" Wiggins wriggled his hazelnut nose scornfully. "A guy with a swelled head like that could have carried an encyclopedia that way."

"Shhh!" warned Wade, and Farrell, giving Wiggins a look of tolerant exasperation, asked seriously,

"What do you really think of the Bible? Do you think it was the direct motive for the murder?"

Wade frowned. "There's enough curious circumstances to provide a motive for murder if there'd never been any Bible. But of course, it might be a lot easier to find the murderer if we knew who stole the Bible. That fragment is worth too much, if it's genuine, for me to believe it has been destroyed."

"Sure," assented Murphy, "that Bible's somewhere round. The temptation to keep it would be too grand even if it wasn't the reason for the murder. Me, now, I'm in favor of taking that girl doctor into custody. I think somebody knows she did the job and left that note in there. Doctors don't mind killing people—Lord, they do it every day and get paid for it. I'm in favor of busting that girl. She knows plenty. Now listen. If she didn't do it she's got a good idea of who did. This ain't no tea-party, Farrell. Bowing and scraping is all right in its place, but this ain't no place for it."

Wiggins looked triumphantly at Wade. "What'd I tell you?" he whispered grandly.

"Wait a minute, Murphy," Farrell expostulated. "You couldn't hold Marie twenty-four hours. Her story is straight, whether or not it's true. Remember, this isn't a gang of thugs—you can't sweat this kind of people." Murphy leaned back and crossed his big legs. "They're entirely too close-mouthed for me, all of 'em. Course, I'm only an old cop, I don't know anything about Bibles except that none of these people act as if they'd ever read one. What this crowd needs is a little real grilling."

Wade had been staring out of the window into the darkness. Suddenly he wheeled around.

"Murphy, the best way on earth to shut this crowd up for good is to start using strong-arm methods. They won't be scared by that. I heard Marie's story tonight and I think it's true. I'm sure no grand jury would indict anybody on what we've got now."

Murphy was unconvinced. "Believe me, Mister," he argued, "the best and safest thing to do with that whole bunch is to slam 'em in jail as material witnesses and keep 'em there till somebody opens up. There ain't one of 'em I'd trust around loose."

Wiggins nodded as though in full agreement and then winked at Wade. "Murph's burning up bad as Ulman," he whispered.

"Be quiet," said Wade, then he turned back to Farrell. "Wait a couple of days," he urged seriously. "I've a little idea of my own. Farrell, I'm probably going to exceed my authority, but I'm going to order you and Murphy home to bed. And tomorrow morning I'm going to play young man about town and furthermore I'm going to knock on Mr. Dancy's door at half past six and wake him up for breakfast."

"Well," said Wiggins expansively, "I hope you're the early bird that'll give that worm some trouble." He turned to the others. "You know, there's six people in this case I don't like, and Dancy's at least four of 'em."

PART II
THURSDAY

CHAPTER NINE

ON THE morning after Quentin Ulman's death Wade got out of his cold shower at half-past five, swore at the muggy dawn while he shaved, buttoned himself into a linen suit too stiff for comfort and set out for Mr. Dancy's rooms before that genteel person had had time to wake up and think about the attitude he was going to assume.

Mr. Dancy lived in one of the pseudo-artistic apartment houses that have sprung up here and there in the Quarter during recent years. Wade looked up at it disapprovingly as he parked his car by the entrance. As he stepped out on the sidewalk the morning exploded above him with the suddenness typical of daybreak near the tropics, and Wade blinked sleepily at the brightness as he confronted the janitor. Mr. Dancy, he was told, lived on the second floor, and Wade trudged up the stairs.

He had to knock three times before a sleepy and disgruntled voice from within demanded,

"Who's there?"

"Wade," he said cheerily. "Wade from the district attorney's office."

"Righto. Just a minute." The voice was startled; Wade grinned wickedly at the keyhole.

"Please hurry, won't you? I've got to be back at the office by seven."

The door opened and Mr. Dancy appeared, frowsy with sleep, his crumpled pajamas buttoned up to his Adam's apple and his rust-colored hair sadly at odds with itself. He gave a look of bewilderment and distaste at Wade's immaculacy, and Wade suppressed his naughty grin.

"You must pardon me, Mr. Dancy, for coming to see you at this unseemly hour. But I have to be at the district attorney's office at seven, and it was imperative that I see you before any definite steps are taken."

"See me? What's the row?"

Mr. Dancy was conscious of the pale stubble on his chin and the confusion of his usually well-ordered hair, and he was also considerably taken aback. Wade walked in.

"In here, Mr. Wade—the flat hasn't been made up yet—"

"Hardly." Wade got a glimpse of a disordered bedroom as he passed the door, but Dancy hurried him into the front room, a frippery little parlor that had probably never known disarray during Mr. Dancy's tenancy. "Won't you—er—sit down?" Dancy invited without enthusiasm.

Wade established himself in a chair and lit a cigarette. Dancy was frankly disturbed.

"Mr. Dancy," Wade began, "you were among the last persons known to have seen Mr. Ulman alive. Frankly, I came to see you because it has been suggested that you were planning to leave town."

"Leave town? That's nonsense."

"Cigarette?" Wade offered.

"Not before breakfast, thanks."

Wade lit his with an airiness suggesting that he had had breakfast hours ago. "Well, I'm glad you aren't planning to leave us. You see, I was impressed yesterday by your willingness to help in the investigation, and I didn't want you to make any rash move if you could avoid it."

"But Mr. Wade—I—"

"Fine. Fine. I'll tell the district attorney, then, that there is no need to hold you as a material witness."

Dancy's eyelids flapped. "Hold me—?"

"Oh yes, he was thinking of it. But you could doubtless have been released on bond."

"But why—I don't see why—" Dancy was thoroughly bewildered. Plainly it was the first time in his well-ordered life that he had found himself called upon to act without precedent, and he was puzzled. Wade leaned forward and spoke impressively.

"The point is, Dancy, you are the only person we have yet found who has had intimate opportunity to observe the situation at the library and who at the same time has no personal interest in withholding information. Nobody could have worked there day after day and be ignorant of all the personal relations of these people who were so closely connected with it."

Dancy put on his bathrobe and his dignity in one movement. "I say, Wade, I don't talk about people. I don't approve of gossips."

"Of course you don't. Your delicacy is admirable. But we are looking for a murderer, and we know you want to help us find him." He looked impressively at Dancy, as though recognizing his importance in the scheme.

"I'll do whatever I can, Wade," Dancy said with restraint, as though not quite sure of the details of this important part he was being called upon to play.

"Good. I thought a man of your intelligence must realize that this isn't an ordinary situation." Wade gave him a man-to-man nod, and Dancy answered eagerly.

"I wouldn't want the police to get the wrong idea of me. But you know, I wasn't asked anything last night."

"I understand. It was most unfortunate that Marie Castillo should collapse. However," he added knowingly, "the poor girl has had a good deal to put up with." Dancy smiled sagely. Having discovered that his own arrest was not imminent, he was regaining his *savoir-faire*. "Oh, rather," he returned with the air of a man who might say a great deal more than that if he only would. "Maybe the murder of Quentin Ulman wasn't such a cropper after all, Wade." And from his grim smile Wade knew that Mr. Dancy had just said something very daring.

"Perhaps. I suppose you never talked about this side of Ulman's life, though?" He gave Dancy an appreciative look. If Dancy could be made to think that he was impressing Wade as the worldly man he yearned in his soul to be, he could be induced to tell what he knew as one sophisticate to another. Dancy was bland.

"Oh, no—except very casually with Terry Sheldon."

"I see. Terry didn't like Ulman, did he?" Wade reflected elaborately with knitted brows. "Dancy, you've good sense—I think I can trust you with some private police information."

"Thank you, I'm sure." Dancy was ponderous, but he was fairly shining with anticipation.

"What would you say if I told you—" Wade dropped his voice confidentially—"that while this game of hearts was being played in the library, Ulman was secretly engaged to a girl in Massachusetts?"

"He would be, he's just the type." Dancy was very much the man of the world now. He chuckled. "And all the time acting as if he was gone on Mrs. Gonzales—my word, that's too good, Wade."

"Absolutely." Wade rocked back and forth as he thought a member of the Pall Mall club might do. He did not think it necessary to add that Asa Lawrence's telegram was the kind of police information that would be in all the morning papers. "Mrs. Gonzales too, eh?" he added lusciously. "You bookish chaps are a gay lot."

Dancy smirked deprecatingly, as if to suggest that he didn't want to boast, but—

"Oh, Ulman and Mrs. Gonzales used to spend hours shut up in that reading-room pretending to be looking at French bindings." Dancy broke his pre-breakfast smoking rule and took a cigarette, putting the match to it with a distinct air. He sat back in his chair quite like a young man about town who knew a thing or two about the goings-on. "But it wasn't all beer and skittles for old Quentin at that," he continued. "He had his amorous difficulties—" he lifted an eyebrow as if to say "but haven't we all?"—"and I never thought he managed women very well, although he thought he had quite a way with them."

Wade tapped the ash from his cigarette into an ash-stand by his chair. "His sort always do, don't you think?"

Dancy pursed his lips and nodded, smiling thoughtfully. Wade watched him, hoping that some day this perfect secretary would get a really legitimate excuse to carry a shiny cane and wear spats. Hurriedly his mind fumbled for English novels and the sort of phrases that would represent conversational dash to his gay companion. "Amusing, eh?" was the best he could do.

"Quite," said Dancy, and Wade mentally slapped himself on the back. "You know, Wade," Dancy went on, "I've always thought that the French woman is the only one civilized enough to conduct an affair of that sort with discretion."

"With aplomb?" suggested Wade.

"Precisely," agreed Dancy confidentially. "I'm sure Quentin was quite fed up with Mrs. Gonzales. They quarreled quite a lot."

"Really?" Wade prodded in his best Mayfair. This was what he had come for.

"Rawther," came back Dancy. "I was in a very peculiar position one day—last Thursday I think—but it was amusing. I really tried not to hear them, and at first they spoke so low I couldn't."

Wade nodded, hoping there was a naughty twinkle in his eye.

"But later, she really dressed him down," Dancy elaborated. "Put him on the coals for true. I couldn't come out and let them know I'd heard the start of it, and I couldn't very well leave, because I was in the geology aisle and that's quite a way from the east door. So I just stayed there."

"Fancy!" said Wade hopefully. "Raked him out, did she?"

"Rawther! 'I'm not going to let you make a fool out of me!' she said. Then Ulman tried to be logical with her." He said this as if being logical with a woman was decidedly middle-class. "'Now be reasonable, Winifred,'" he quoted Ulman. "'We're getting ourselves talked about and I don't want Prentiss to decide it's his duty to fire me. This is a jewel of a place to work, and whether you understand it or not, I'm interested in my work as well as in you.' She blew that up, though," Dancy went on. "She told the blighter, 'If it was just your work, you idiot!' and he got whimsical and said something about after all, it was his conscience that had to carry the burden, and she laughed. 'Your conscience be damned—believe me, if you don't do something and do it quick you'll have more than your conscience to worry about,' and she stormed out."

"My word!" Wade sighed, trying to arrange himself in the proper pose for this kind of chit-chat. "Well, you know how that sort of thing is," he added, as if it were all very distasteful and very familiar. "It either ends with a breakup or in a mad dash to Florence."

"Oh, quite," said Dancy.

"My thought exactly," put in Wade, as though now they understood each other perfectly, which he sincerely hoped they didn't. "Do you think he could *possibly* have taken the Gutenberg thingumbob to finance a little flat in Paris?"

Dancy started. Evidently this was beyond the borders of tattle again and he didn't like it. Wade wildly wished he knew more about the pattern of Dancy's gossiping and how it was brought to the point. But Dancy seemed suddenly to have grown wary.

"Perhaps." But here was something about which Mr. Dancy had no tidbits, so Wade tried to recapture the London clubmen atmosphere. He dismissed the Bible with a twitch of his eyebrows and regretted that he had no monocle.

"I only thought you might have seen it coming," he suggested, but Dancy didn't take the bait, so Wade grabbed at another. "You're a Britisher, aren't you?"

"No," Dancy confessed, "though I've often been taken for one. My grandmother was from Devonshire."

"At any rate, you probably have the Anglo-Saxon attitude toward crime. I suppose you know that at Scotland Yard they say the lower classes go dumb when a crime is committed, the middle classes do a great deal of weeping and running about, while the people of the better walks of life seem to be really sane—"

"Quite," said Dancy.

Wade hoped that was what Scotland Yard said, and went on.

"—realizing that a murderer should be eliminated mercilessly for the good of the—people," he finished. He had nearly said "the Empire."

"What I'm interested in is a civilized person's observations on the general background. Now I wonder, Dancy, if you saw anything unusual yesterday morning at the library."

Dancy nodded without speaking, sepulchrally.

"Oh—you did?"

"Yes," said Dancy with a wise smile, "and deuced unusual it was, too."

"Really!"

"It was like this. When I came out of the library Ulman and Mrs. Gonzales were just getting into her car. I wanted to ask Ulman about finishing a monograph he'd been working on, and I walked down to the car. They didn't see me. Mrs. Gonzales was just starting the motor. They were having a row, and I heard her say, very distinctly, 'Drive you to hell!'"

Wade desperately hoped his face betrayed nothing but a mild interest. "Regular viper, eh?" he observed.

"Typical of her kind," nodded Dancy. "Then Ulman saw me, and when I asked him about the monograph he said he'd tell me about it the next day. Of course I didn't let him suspect I'd heard anything."

"Decent of you."

Dancy shrugged as if to say, "Oh, it might happen to any of us." He reached for another cigarette. "The peculiar thing about it was—" and Dancy was very earnest now, as if just a little bit frightened by the thought he was trying to express—"there wasn't any next day for Quentin, poor fellow, and wherever it was that Winifred drove him, he didn't come back, but she did."

"Horrible, wasn't it?" said Wade. He paused, while Dancy seemed to reflect on Quentin Ulman and his various lady friends. At length Wade thought it time to venture another question about the Gutenberg fragment.

Dancy's reverie ended. "I don't know a thing about it, Wade," he said sharply.

"Not even the combination of the safe, do you?"

"Not even that."

"Mrs. Gonzales doesn't know it, I suppose?"

"Not unless Ulman told her."

"That's a thought." Wade got to his feet. "Thank you very much, Dancy old fellow."

"Not at all. Hope you come through top-hole."

"Hope so." Wade managed to make a sober getaway, and went down the stairs with Dancy's owlish gaze behind him, but once in his car he fairly embraced the steering-wheel as he gave vent to his merriment. "Drive you to hell, eh? So that's what happened? Drive you to hell! It certainly is a shame, Mr. Dancy, it's a blooming, rotten shame, Mr. Dancy, how you do hate to talk! And I'll see you later about the Bible. Rawther!" After breakfast he reported jubilantly at the district attorney's office to find Murphy engaged in a pessimistic monologue.

"Now that we're all gone soft-headed," Murphy was saying in Farrell's direction, "I just thought I'd kinda drop around and see if there was anything particular on my engagement book for this morning. And do I wear a tail-coat now and have my name engraved on a card, or do I still make my calls by just showing my shield?"

Farrell laughed at him good-naturedly. "Don't get too excited, Murphy. The Bible Murder isn't twenty-four hours old yet."

"Yeah, but I'm older than that even if I ain't allowed to act like it. Have you seen that lambasting the *Star* gives the department this morning?" He sighed lugubriously. "However, it ain't murder that's bothering me just now, it's etiquette. I want to make a few little inquiries myself, just delicate-like, and I wanted to ask if I'd have to do same by appointment or if I just kinda went out and looked for somebody who'd been committing murder." He scowled at Wade, who stood in the door wearing his habitual empty grin. "Everything's got to be so polite. Mister Wade, will you please be so kind as to explain how we happened to find your cigarette-lighter at the scene of the crime?"

"My what? Don't be an egg. I never had one."

"Well, we ain't found one, either. I'm scared to send anybody over there—hear it ain't being done this season, visiting scenes of crimes."

"Be quiet, Murphy," said Farrell. "Wade's been making a social call himself. He's been talking to the secretary."

"So? What'd that clothes-horse have to say?"

Wade lowered himself into a chair and recounted his interview. "Of course," he ended, "if I'd had more broad a's about me I'd have felt more at home. But it went pretty well, except that he won't say a syllable about the Bible. That's the one place where he shuts up."

Murphy hoisted himself to the desk. "Say, you. Bibles ain't half this story. All these birds had reason to hate this Ulman and it looks as if they've all been busy doing it. Personally, I think it's time we got down to elementals. Now you listen. I had a few little lines of my own out—not very society, Farrell, but they worked."

"Yes? Get anything?"

"Sure. It's the old police system of working without any orchids in their buttonholes. There's always servants around to know when things happen. I put my little pipe-line out myself, Mr. Wade, and I discovered that this morning for the first time in five years the professor went into his wife's bedroom and raised almighty hell."

"Somehow," said Wade, "I can't picture Gonzales raising almighty hell."

"Well, it seems he was pretty mad, because when he left the bedroom he stood outside the door and swore to himself in Spanish till the air got blue." Murphy slid off the desk. "And you look here, Farrell. I'll wear a gardenia if I have to, but I'm going up this morning and have a nice confidential chat with that lady, and if you want to come along, Detective Wade, you can."

CHAPTER TEN

THE morning was still young when Mr. Wiggins of *The Creole* parked his catarrhal little roadster by a disdainful uptown curb, and having extracted a camera and a handful of plates, made his way around the corner to the great white-columned house where Mr. and Mrs. Alfredo Gonzales lived. Not that Mr. Wiggins was so naive as to fancy that the lovely and irritating object of his quest would be available at nine o'clock in the morning. It was just because Mr. Wiggins knew she wouldn't be about that he was here.

In front of the house he peered about to make sure his telltale car was parked out of sight, then, with the camera under his arm, he walked with leisurely assurance toward the steps, looking with disapproval at the satiny lawn, the palms and the repelling grandeur of the house. "Huh," said Mr. Wiggins to himself. "Snooty."

He was not abashed. He had frequently encountered the sort of women one met in houses like this—great ladies who favored the papers only when they married, died or had people in to dinner, and it delighted his spirit to put one of them into *The Creole* when she was involved in something socially less correct than marriage, death or entertainment. He surveyed the scene of his campaign.

The parlor at one side of the entrance had wide windows reaching to the floor, skirted with Spanish window-guards of wrought iron. The fact that the design of the window-guards was a costly adaptation from the reja of a Castilian cathedral would have impressed Mr. Wiggins not at all if he had known it; he simply looked at them, nodded with relish, and slipping across the lawn he lifted himself by the iron scrolls, shoved aside the long lace curtains, deposited the camera on the floor inside, hoisted himself across the window-guard and looked around.

"Huh," reflected Mr. Wiggins. "Looks like a theater lobby."

Having thus disposed of the golden magnificence of Winifred's Spanish parlor, he looked for a place wherein to stow himself away. In another moment his eyes were delightedly measuring the vast fireplace, which in winter burnt logs, but which now was shielded by a great three-winged wooden screen, carved, like the panels of the wall, with rhythmic Moorish scrolls. Mr. Wiggins did not stop to examine the carving or to estimate the place of the screen in the decorative scheme of Winifred's perfect interior. He merely gave a low chuckle and ensconced himself in the fireplace. Adjusting the screen so that he had a crack between the wings to see through he forced the lower hinge of the other wing with a bronze poker until he had an opening large enough to let his lens catch part of the room, then he sat back to see what was going to happen. The camera was ready for a time-exposure. It was one he used at trials when a ban had been put on courtroom pictures. If Winifred should choose this room in which to read the morning papers, good; if she shouldn't, Mr. Wiggins would have lost nothing but some time for which the stockholders of *The Creole* were paying him anyway.

He waited. The room was cool and the fireplace had been cleaned of soot after the last fire of the winter, so Mr. Wiggins, reflecting how much easier this was than climbing up to photograph a flagpole sitter, his last assignment before the murder, was well content. He pulled a pencil and a wad of copy paper out of his pocket and began to inscribe a letter to his girl at Pointe-à-la-Hache.

It was a quarter of eleven when the doorbell rang. Wiggins perked up his ears and heard a voice asking for Mr. Gonzales. The butler answered that Mr. Gonzales was out.

"Mrs. Gonzales, then," said the voice. "Tell her I'll wait in the parlor."

Wiggins blinked, and through his crack he beheld Terry Sheldon.

Terry was angry. He stalked in, leaving the door open, and planted himself on a sofa out of sight. Wiggins waited. Three minutes later Winifred appeared in the doorway.

For a moment she stood quite still, cool and exquisite in a sleeve-less dress of dark green voile, with white rufflings at her throat and shoulders. She leaned against the door-jamb, one slim white arm stretched out to support her, surveying Terry with a smile of cynical amusement. Wiggins snapped his shutter, tremblingly counted five and snapped it again, drawing a long breath of joy and accounting well spent the exceedingly stiff price he had paid for a noiseless camera. Winifred had not moved; she still looked at Terry with cool irony. He seemed not to have noticed her entrance, for it was with a suddenly startled voice that he exclaimed, "Oh, hello, Winifred."

She still smiled, as though he had been the three-legged man in an exhibit. "Don't bother to get up, Terry; it's much too hot to bother about being polite."

"Have you seen the papers?" he blurted at her.

Winifred crossed to a deep wicker chair and took a cigarette from a smoking-stand at its side. "I don't read newspapers, Terry."

"For God's sake start, then. It's awful."

"Yes?" Winifred was absorbed in blowing smoke rings.

Terry thumped a sofa-cushion. "Have you seen any reporters?"

"No. The butler has orders not to admit them."

("Oh, he has, has he?" thought Mr. Wiggins gleefully as he refilled his camera.)

"It's just as well," said Terry.

Winifred stretched her arms above her head. "Dreadfully hot, isn't it?"

"Where's Alfredo?" Terry asked shortly.

"He said he was going to walk."

"He's not at the university. I went by there."

"He meets the class only once a week."

Terry spoke again, slowly. "Gee, Winifred, I feel sorry for him. He's—proud."

Winifred said nothing. Wiggins heard Terry get up, and he came into view as he walked restlessly over to a window and ran his finger along the wrought-iron screen. Winifred smiled lazily.

"You won't find any dust, Terry. I'm a good house-keeper."

"Wonder where Marie is."

"Really, Terry, I haven't seen the little darling this morning."

Terry looked out at the nodding palms. "Do get me something to drink, will you? This damn thing has got me all shot to pieces."

"So I observe," Winifred said evenly as she went to the cellarette at one side and took out a decanter. "Early morning drinking is a bad habit, Terry—how many have you already had?"

"Plenty," he retorted, as he nervously poured whiskey from the prism-cut bottle. He gulped his drink in one quick swallow and poured another, while behind the screen Wiggins marveled at any man's drinking straight whiskey on so hot a day.

Winifred's face was in full view of Wiggins, and as he snapped his camera again he could see that she was frowning as Terry swallowed his second drink and poured a third. "Have you been questioned yet?" she asked with faint concern.

"Not yet, but I know that damn Wade will be after me before long." He turned the decanter in his hand, watching the light glance on its sides.

"Any reporters?" Winifred asked, more as if she was trying to make conversation than as if she cared about knowing, but Wiggins thought there was a hint of apprehension in her voice.

"Hounding hell out of me. I have no butler to keep them out, you know." Terry gave a sarcastic shrug. "That's why I left the studio."

"What did you tell them?"

Terry poured another drink. "Oh—'nothing to say.' How's Alfredo taking this?"

She lifted a slim hand in an all-disposing gesture. "Disdainfully—as Alfredo might be expected to take anything."

"What do you want him to do—have fits? Prentiss is the only one getting any kick out of this," Terry went on bitterly. "It's given him a chance to act superior towards Alfredo for the first time in his life."

"Oh, Terry," she said with exasperation, "don't be an idiot."

"And why? Maybe Prentiss killed Ulman. Maybe Ulman found out the Bible was a fake. Maybe Prentiss isn't as aloof as we think he is. There's a chance, you know, that this is going to make a public scandal out of your affair with Ulman—Prentiss might have done the job with that in mind."

"You're absurd. The papers wouldn't dare—"

"Well, there's a nasty lot of innuendo in the *Star* story. I hope Alfredo doesn't see it." Wiggins saw that Terry was feeling the effect of his liquor.

Winifred tilted her thin arched eyebrows. "But he will. There are always kind friends like yourself to see to that."

Terry was pacing restlessly about. "Has Wade been here?"

"No—has he seen you?" Winifred poured a generous drink of whiskey into a highball glass and shot a dash of vichy into it.

"Not yet." Terry took another drink.

She was playing with the corner of a silk scarf that lay across the chair. "Do you suppose he'll bother you?" she asked without looking up.

"I guess so. He'll be up here to see you too. Lord, I feel rocky."

("And rye-ey," commented Wiggins to himself.)

Winifred flung Terry a smile that was almost insolent. "I don't see why it should affect you so deeply, my dear. You didn't like Quentin Ulman." She tasted her drink and looked narrowly at him across the top of her glass.

"Hell, no." Terry picked up the liquor.

"You'd better be careful with that whiskey if you're looking forward to a police interview," she suggested coolly.

"I'm not scared. I've got nothing to hide." He defiantly took another drink.

"No?"

"Of course not. What the hell are you driving at?"

"Not a thing, darling." Winifred stretched herself luxuriously in the big chair. "Quentin Ulman didn't mean a thing in your life."

Wiggins, behind his screen, was ignoring his camera and taking speedy notes. Winifred's butler might be earning his wages, but Wiggins doubted it. Terry put down his glass, and it rattled unsteadily as he answered.

"Not a thing. I don't give a damn who killed him or why."

"Then why bother about it?" she challenged smiling. "Why don't you go down to the studio at Isle Bonne for a couple of days and get away from all the hubbub?"

He turned abruptly on his heel. "What? And have them thinking I'm trying to hide out? Oh, no. I'll stay in town. Why don't you take a run down to Cuba?"

Winifred smiled patiently as she lit another cigarette. "Mainly, dear, because Cubans bore me so."

Terry glowered at her. His face was flushed and his eyes glittering balefully.

"So I've noticed. You've done everything you could to establish the theory of Nordic supremacy."

"Really?" She took up her own glass and added another shot of vichy.

"Yes, really!" Terry watched her angrily. "I suppose it'll be Dancy next—he thinks he's a grand Anglo-Saxon, with a nice long skull and a handkerchief up his sleeve."

"Oh, Terry, don't be uncouth." She crushed out her cigarette and stood up. Behind his screen Wiggins stifled a chuckle and wondered if a guy like Dancy really had nerve enough to kill anybody. Winifred turned toward the door. "You're a little bit drunk, darling, so I think I'll run upstairs. You can wait here for Alfredo."

Terry gave an ugly laugh. "Don't hide your loveliness just because your great romance turned to ashes."

"Terry! Stop!"

Wiggins was scribbling appreciatively in the dark. His pencil fairly shivered across his wad of paper.

Terry laughed derisively. "Oh, I can't stop now. I'm infatuated with the subject. Becoming a regular criminologist." He took an unsteady step toward her. Winifred stood quite still. Terry went on rapidly, his words tumbling over one another in ugly confusion. "I've decided it might be amusing to do a plaster study of a murderer, so I've come here to get the right perspective." Winifred's hands were fisted at her sides. "I should not like to have to ask you to leave my house, Terry."

"*Your* house!" He laughed loudly.

"Yes, Terry, my house." She was white with anger. "I am glad to have my husband's friends call here, but I insist that they be respectful."

Terry was almost shouting with drunken enjoyment. "Respectful! Great idea. Be respectful and see the house, be disrespectful and see the garden. Ain't I respectful? I never said anything to you about how that big blond bon-bon was making a fool out of you. I'm a gentleman and a Sheldon. I never even told you there's a story in the paper today that says Ulman was going to marry a girl in Massachusetts in October and that she wants what's left of him sent up for burial."

Winifred stepped backward to close the door to the hall. "Terry—that's not true!"

Terry was weaving from side to side in front of her. Wiggins hoped that if he fell he wouldn't fall on the screen.

"Sure it's true. If you see it in *The Creole* it's true. South's greatest newspaper. All the news while it's news. Fi' cents a copy. Death and dirt and the comics—"

"Damn—damn—*damn*—" Winifred stood against the closed door; her voice died away in a whisper.

Terry thrust himself toward her. "Didja love him, Winifred? Didja really love him?"

She straightened herself with an effort and put a firm hand on his shoulder. "Terry, I think you'd better go."

"Lissen. I'll go when I'm ready." He shook himself free with a rough twist of his shoulder and with drunken insistence repeated his question. "Didja really love him? Didja kill the thing you loved?"

The idea seemed to charm his fuddled imagination; he began to recite, swaying in time with the meter.

"'For each man kills the thing—'"

"Terry!" It was almost a scream.

"Well, you did kill him, didn't you? Of course you did." He bent over and whispered hoarsely. "And I didn't tell. How did I know? Simple little problem in logic."

Winifred stood watching him with a queer fascination. Wiggins could hear her short angry breaths. Terry had begun to declaim.

"'Where were you between noon and four o'clock yesterday afternoon?' says the district attorney. 'Playing with matches,' says Mrs. Gonzales. 'What about it?'" He gave the answer with a lifted eyebrow in mimicry of her. "Pardon me while I have another drink."

He emptied the decanter and waved his glass. "To Senora Alfredo Miguel Gonzales y Castillo! May she get off with twenty years! Cuba libre!"

Winifred struck the empty glass from his hand, and it rolled over on the rug. "Terry, *will* you leave?"

"I'm waiting for Alfredo. 'Playing with matches,' says Senora Gonzales. 'Playing with matches is the defense of Senora Gonzales, gentlemen of the jury! And why not? And why not?' Weren't you the last one with him?"

Wiggins was feverishly taking notes and congratulating himself. At last, the woman in the case.

Winifred gripped Terry's wrists and spoke with desperate self-control. "Be still, you fool! Quentin Ulman is dead. That's finished. You'll put yourself in jeopardy by drinking like this."

Terry pounced on the word. "A jeopardy never changes its spots!" He wrenched himself loose and bowed deeply. "I'll fight it out on this line—"

"For God's sake, stop!" she cried. Then she added with piercing emphasis, "I want you to get into a car with me and drive down to Isle Bonne."

"What?" retorted Terry. "Get into a car and drive with you? No, thanks. It's too hot—and I'm afraid the longer I'd drive with you the hotter it'd get." He chuckled at this remark.

("Gee," thought Wiggins, "he's getting nasty.") He looked up from his notes to see Winifred standing with her back against the side table, her hands clenched as if in a furious effort for self-control.

"Not after Ulman, I won't," Terry went on. "Wouldn't take any rides with you, pretty lady, not unless we took 'em on a fire-engine."

She fairly flung him into a seat. "Stay here until I can get out the car. I'll have some coffee made to clear up your head."

He leered up at her. "Coffee and confessions for two?"

"Terry, pull yourself together! You can't answer questions when you're as drunk as this. You must be able to think—"

He shook his head. "For what?"

"Terry, *can't* I make you understand that I've got to get you sober?"

He stared foggily. "Why?"

Winifred stood looking down at him. Her lip curled. "Stop this nonsense, Terry." She lowered her head till it was on a level with his, and spoke again. But Wiggins, though he nearly knocked down the screen in his effort, could not hear what she said. He only saw her raise her head, smiling bitterly. Terry shook himself and sat up like a man suddenly started out of sleep. He struggled slowly to his feet, and looked straight into her eyes.

"So—that's—your—game!" he said thickly. "You—filthy—cheating—liar!"

Winifred moved back a step, her amber eyes glowing with such fury as Wiggins had never seen. He clutched his copy-paper and stared.

("It won't be long now," he thought. "Here's where a drunk gets the bum's rush from a perfect lady.")

Terry stood just back of the cellarette. His face was set in a snarl. He seemed to be fumbling for words. His hands clenched and opened.

Winifred had jerked open the drawer of the table. "You—damned—beast," she said, her voice quivering with desperate rage, "this—will be all—from you."

Wiggins almost whistled aloud. For she was facing Terry with a long-muzzled blue steel automatic pistol.

Terry stared from the gun to Winifred's eyes and waited, startled into swift understanding. His nostrils quivered in a sneer. Winifred spoke again.

"I said that was all, Terry. Will you get out?" Her gun motioned toward the door. "There's something else I'm going to tell you. Outside. When you're in your car. Maybe you'll understand it better there."

Terry was silent. Winifred's automatic did not waver.

"Don't stand there, damn you! Now go. I'm going to see you safely away from the house, and after you turn the bend I hope you drive into a tree and break your neck."

Terry made no answer. Winifred's voice was normal again. Wiggins was disappointed. He had expected to photograph the second Bible Murder. He swore softly at the screen and the need for secrecy, for he had wasted three plates trying to get Winifred and her gun in focus.

Terry had walked out of the line of vision and Winifred was following. Her green dress flashed past the side of the screen. She had snatched up the scarf from the chair and had flung it across the hand that held the gun.

Wiggins heard their footsteps die away. He grabbed his camera, shoved his notes into his pocket and walked quickly over to the

French window. In another instant he had jumped, his sacred black box hugged to his breast.

CHAPTER ELEVEN

"I'LL wager," Wade had said to Murphy, "that when we get there we'll find Wiggins behind one of Winifred's ormolu clocks."

Which was not quite accurate, for as their car slowed down in front of the great house Mr. Wiggins of *The Creole* emerged turbulently from behind a hydrangea bush. He leaped on the running-board, his camera in his hand.

"Drive around the corner!" he ordered in a wild whisper. "Get off before she sees you. I've been here all morning."

The car had obediently swung around the corner before his speech was over. Wade slipped the clutch, pressed the brake and turned severely as the car came to a stop.

"Now what have you been up to? Did you get her picture?"

"Picture? Say, I got an art gallery. And that ain't all. These pictures are talking pictures. Turn off the motor and listen to me!"

He wriggled triumphantly over the side of the car and wedged himself between Wade and Murphy. Perspiring and eloquent, he repeated what he had heard from the fireplace and at last sat back, blinking happily like the cat who has just finished licking up the cream. Murphy grabbed his knee.

"Go on, you! What did she say to him after he got in the car?"

Wiggins gave him a superior look. "How do I know? She stood there with the gun under that scarf and said something quick and dirty-like, and I parked behind that big bush and got a swell picture of her and Terry while she was saying it. Then, Terry, drunk as a lord, drives off like he's really got places to go, and in she walks, while I sit very still behind the bush and pray she won't go picking flowers. Then I see you coming. And that," said Mr. Wiggins grandly, "brings us up to now. And if you'll just let me out, thank you, I'll take myself down and see what I got on these plates."

He whisked himself out of sight, and Wade and Murphy, exchanging appreciative surmises, drove back to make their call on the troublesome Mrs. Gonzales. Murphy was warlike.

"That's the trouble with these society murders," he complained magnificently as Wade rang the bell. "Everybody is so high-strung you can't tell the good from the bad. That woman with the gun might mean anything. Some folks would think Terry justified her using it. For myself—"

The butler appeared to interrupt Murphy's conclusion, and Wade asked for Mrs. Gonzales. They were asked to wait and were shown into the golden, foreign room lately vacated by Wiggins. Wade sat down in its inviting coolness, looking with an appreciation Wiggins had not vouchsafed on the background Winifred's mocking checks had built for her husband. Winifred's house outside was a typical Southern manor, but the room in which they were waiting for her was like a misplaced entity from Spain. Wade had time to admire the carving of the walls and Wiggins' screen, and the copy of a Goya tapestry that hung over the fireplace, before he glanced at Murphy, who was standing uncertainly in the middle of the room, a bit bewildered by its gracious magnificence.

"Say," Murphy observed softly, "this is quite a place, ain't it? No wonder Farrell got gardenias on the brain."

Wade was thoughtful. "I'd like to know what its mistress could tell about this affair."

"Don't you worry. I'm not so hopeless. I'll bust this pretty lady this morning if I'm not too unlucky."

Wade gave him a warning look and stood up as the door opened. Winifred paused on the threshold, a trifle too pleasantly unconcerned to please the old police captain, to whom murder was a serious business. Wade rather admired the way she had recovered from her stormy session with Terry.

"Good morning, gentlemen. I'm so sorry Mr. Gonzales isn't here," Winifred said, as if the professor had been counted on for a fourth at bridge. "He went out to take a walk through the park—I'll send the car for him if you like." She crossed to where Wade and Murphy stood.

"That won't be necessary, Mrs. Gonzales," said Murphy, who seemed to have mastered his previous awe of his hostess and her surroundings. "We wanted to see you for a few minutes to clear up one or two points that aren't quite straight. We can see the professor later."

"That will be quite satisfactory." She spoke with the courteous condescension she would have given a salesman. As she sat down on the sofa facing them Wade noticed that she gave an infinitesimal glance toward the cellarette as though observing with relief that the evidences of Terry's visit had been removed. "You'll forgive me for not being informed on the latest developments," she added—"I came down rather late this morning and haven't had a chance to see the papers."

She took a cigarette from the stand at her side and Wade held a match for her. "Oh, there's nothing you don't know," Murphy was saying, "except maybe that Mr. Ulman had a fiancée up North waiting for him. Her father wired the district attorney last night."

"Indeed?" She looked up with well-simulated surprise. "That's rather hard on Marie, isn't it?"

"She seems to be bearing up very well," Wade answered dryly.

"By the way," said Winifred, "what made her faint last night? You must be terrifying, Mr. Wade." Her voice was playfully accusing.

Captain Murphy, who had no patience with shilly-shallying, spoke bluntly. "Well, ma'am, I think perhaps it was that note you put on the table."

She lifted a puzzled eyebrow. "Note? What note? I'm afraid I don't understand."

Wade produced the photostatic copy of the note he had found on Prentiss' desk and handed it to her. Winifred studied it carefully and then looked back at him. "Why, I never saw this before. What does it mean?"

"We don't know yet, ma'am," said Murphy stolidly. "Are you right sure, now, that you never saw it before?"

"Quite sure, captain."

"We thought, you see, that you might've picked it up in Dr. Prentiss' office when you were helping the young lady."

Winifred shook her head. "I'm sorry." Her words were not apologetic—they seemed rather to connotate "I'm sorry you're such a fool."

"Well now, Mrs. Gonzales, that's a disappointment. We thought you might be able to tell us what it meant—it being Spanish and all that."

She smiled patiently. "I know very little Spanish, Captain Murphy. But the word means 'goodby,' if that helps you any."

"I see, ma'am. Maybe, now, you could tell us if Mr. Ulman wrote it?"

Winifred glanced amusedly at Wade, who was listening to the dialogue in silence. "Why, I suppose he wrote it. It has his name signed to it."

"Would that be his handwriting, ma'am?"

She looked at the paper in her hand. "I—I really couldn't say. There's an old library report of his here somewhere that he sent to Mr. Gonzales—I think that has his signature, if you'd like to compare them."

"I hardly think that's necessary, Mrs. Gonzales," Wade put in serenely. He held out his hand for the copy and she returned it. "If you never saw the note before, you can't possibly know what it means. What we wanted to ask is a question or two about yesterday's events."

"I'll be very glad to tell you anything I can, Mr. Wade." Her cool little voice had not quivered, but he caught a challenge and at the same time a hint of fear in the way her eyes searched his face.

"Well now, ma'am, that's fine," Murphy said unexpectedly, with expansive friendliness. "Can you tell us what time it was when you left Mr. Ulman at the ferry?"

"About twelve-thirty, I believe. Possibly a little before."

"And what did you do then, ma'am?"

"I started for the country club to see some friends of mine who I knew were lunching there, but after I had gone part of the way I changed my mind and drove back to the French Quarter."

"And how did you happen to change your mind, Mrs. Gonzales?"

She smiled tolerantly on the policeman. "I suppose I may as well be perfectly frank with you, Captain Murphy—I'm sure I can trust you and Mr. Wade to keep what I say confidential: I went to see Marie Castillo. It appears there has been some silly gossip linking my name with that of Mr. Ulman, gossip that naturally irritated me when I heard of it. Marie had mentioned it yesterday morning at the library, and I was annoyed—so much so that I spoke rather harshly to her.

After I had left it occurred to me that I hadn't been quite fair, for you see—" she looked at Murphy naively—"you see, after all, Marie was in love with Mr. Ulman, and girls in love are likely to be silly."

She was talking directly to Murphy, her great amber eyes regarding him with a half-amused, half-confiding candor. Wade noticed that she was avoiding his own scrutiny as though to shut his presence from her mind; but he guessed nevertheless that she was acutely conscious that he was there, a part of her own world judging her as her world was judging her, and that her defense was meant for him. He smoked in silence.

Murphy nodded blandly. "Yes, ma'am."

"I was thinking about this while I drove out toward the country club. I'm really very fond of Marie, and I realized that I had spoken to her more sharply than I should; so I thought I'd look her up and try to clarify the situation a little. I felt very apologetic and I thought she ought to know it, for I should not like to have our friendship spoilt by the foolish chatter of foolish people."

"So you went to see Miss Marie," Murphy prompted when she paused.

Winifred nodded.

"Did you see her?"

"No, I didn't. I was very sorry. I stopped at a cigar store and called up Charity Hospital, where she does some of her work, and when I found she wasn't there I looked in at a restaurant where she often takes lunch, but I didn't see her. So I went by her apartment."

"You left your car parked down in front?" Murphy asked.

"No. Royal Street is so narrow that I dislike parking there if I can help it. I parked the car by Jackson Square, on the cathedral side, and walked over." She spoke now as if she were reporting a shopping tour.

"You said you didn't see her?"

"No. She wasn't at home, but as the door of her apartment wasn't locked I went in. I was really very eager to see her, so I waited there a long time—it was nearly three when I left."

"You drove home then, did you?"

"Yes. I was at home the rest of the afternoon."

"When did you learn about the murder, ma'am?"

"One of the maids told me when I came in. She had a copy of *The Clarion* in her hand when I saw her." Murphy surveyed his cigar for a moment in silence. Wade looked reflectively at him and then at Winifred. She had still not turned her eyes toward Wade; she sat very still, looking small and trusting on the big sofa in her sandals and her ruffled sleeveless dress. One hand was in her lap, holding a tiny wisp of a handkerchief, the other, on the arm of the sofa, held a cigarette with the smoke hovering over the tip. Wade studied her, the shining brown ripples of her hair, her faint make-up, the sophisticated simplicity of her dress, and suddenly he realized as he had not done in the ascetic surroundings of the library the day before what a beautiful woman the wife of Alfredo Gonzales was. He looked at her and she looked at Murphy, while Murphy contemplated his cigar.

Suddenly, as though there had been a flash of daylight within him, Wade knew that this was precisely what she was intending that he should realize; that her careful avoidance of his gaze had been to give him the opportunity to see her preoccupied with something other than himself, that the picture of Winifred Gonzales on the great sofa between the lace-draped windows had been designed by Winifred Gonzales for the purpose of projecting Winifred Gonzales. Murphy was no fool—she must know that; but she also knew that Wade was an opponent who could meet her on her own ground, and she was using against him the cool chain-mail of her charm. He was silent, and Murphy, apparently satisfied with his rumination, spoke.

"Then, ma'am, as I understand it, you left the late Mr. Ulman at about twelve-thirty, drove toward the country club, changed your mind, got back downtown and looked for Marie. You rang the hospital, visited a place where you thought she might be having her lunch, then went to her apartment and waited there for more than an hour."

"Yes. I must have reached her apartment about one-thirty or shortly before."

"Where'd you eat lunch?"

"I didn't have lunch. I seldom do."

"Did anybody see you go to Marie's?"

"I'm sure I don't know, captain."

"Did you maybe leave a note—a calling card, perhaps?"

"Why, no. My call wasn't as formal as that."

"Did you leave Mr. Ulman—let's make sure we understand this, ma'am—did you leave Mr. Ulman on this side of the river or at the landing on the other side or did you drive with him to the bindery?"

"I left him on this side—at the Canal Street station."

"Did you park your car and walk to the boat with him, or did he leave the car and walk to the ferry entrance by himself?"

"I walked with him to the ferry entrance. I wanted to get a magazine at the newsstand there."

"Did you get your magazine?"

"No, they didn't have it."

"So you left Mr. Ulman at the ferry gate, walked back to your car and drove out toward the country club?"

"Yes."

"Which country club was it?"

"The Vincennes Club."

"You didn't go to the railroad station next to the ferry house for your magazine?"

"No."

"Did you maybe stop anywhere to buy it on the way to the country club?"

"No, I didn't."

"You didn't look around for it in the Quarter, did you, to have something to read while you were waiting for Marie?"

"I didn't know I was going to wait so long. But I made no other attempt to buy any magazines except at the ferry news-stand." She said this tersely, as if annoyed by Murphy's insistence on so trifling a subject.

"I see. Do you remember what magazine it was you tried to buy?"

"It was an architectural publication."

"Was it by any chance," asked Murphy, "the July *American Architecture*?"

"Why, yes, that was the one. The July number has an article about one of the lovely old houses on Dumaine Street that I wanted to read."

"I think it's only fair to tell you, ma'am, that a copy of the July *American Architecture* was found in the pocket of Mr. Ulman's coat that he left hanging in the bindery."

Murphy had watched for the effect of his words, but Winifred was unperturbed.

"I don't doubt it. Mr. Ulman had a copy with him when we drove to the ferry. In fact, it was on the way to the ferry that he called my attention to the article."

Murphy uncrossed his legs and leaned forward. "Mrs. Gonzales," he said sternly, "isn't it a fact that when you came in yesterday afternoon you were excited and in a great state of nerves, that you carried a copy of a newspaper in your hand and that you went straight from the front door to your room and did not come out of it till you started for the library to meet the district attorney?"

Winifred regarded him coldly. "I don't like your attitude, Captain Murphy. I told you what I did yesterday afternoon. I have nothing else to add."

"But you did know Ulman was dead before you got home, didn't you?"

"I did not." Her voice was venomous, and Wade wondered how far the butler could be trusted in the statements he had made to Murphy.

"You didn't bring a newspaper with you when you came into the house?" Murphy persisted.

"Certainly I did. If you will be good enough to frame your questions with less accusing implication, Captain Murphy, I can satisfy you more directly. We happen to subscribe for *The Telegram* as well as *The Clarion*. When I reached home *The Telegram* was lying on the porch and I brought it in and put it on the hall table where Mr. Gonzales would see it when he came home. The paper was rolled into a cylinder, as it usually is when delivered by the carrier, and I did not unroll it." She spoke with indignant contempt. Murphy's persistent hammering at her was having its desired effect of beating through her self-possession.

"Mrs. Gonzales," went on Murphy, "did you by any chance go over the Napoleon Avenue ferry?"

"Certainly not—not over it."

"What do you mean—not over it?"

"I drove out Napoleon Avenue as far as the river, but I didn't take the boat." She was answering with defiant exasperation.

"You did drive at a great rate of speed up St. Charles Avenue at about ten minutes of one, didn't you? And you did turn left at Napoleon Avenue, didn't you?"

"I always drive pretty fast, Captain Murphy," she returned coldly.

Murphy stood up. "Do you always break the rule against left turns?"

"Of course not!"

"Do you know that a traffic officer took your number yesterday—"

"I didn't—"

"—and turned in a complaint ticket marked one o'clock, saying you came up St. Charles avenue at fifty miles an hour and turned left toward the Napoleon Avenue ferry?"

"I can explain—"

"Do you know that?—And that Ulman was killed on the other side of the river between twelve-thirty and two o'clock—"

"What are you trying—"

"—that he had told you yesterday morning he was going to marry Marie Castillo—"

"What do you mean?"

"—that the two of you quarreled in the library?"

"We did not—"

"—that when he got into your car you told him you were going to drive him to hell?"

Winifred had gripped the edge of the sofa in a panic of terror. As his words shot at her she had slowly risen to her feet, and now she stood quivering before him, her hands groping vaguely at her sides for some support, her eyes wild with fright.

"You can't—you can't think—"

Murphy lowered his head on a level with hers.

"Do you know that? *Do* you know that you did drive him to hell?"

The back of her hand went to her lips as if to smother the faint little jerk of sound that came into her throat; suddenly she turned from Murphy, her hands held out to Wade as if reaching to him through desperate chaos. "Mr. Wade—for God's sake don't let him talk to me like that! I didn't kill Quentin Ulman!" Her voice rose to a scream. "I didn't kill him!—I don't know anything about who did—but I didn't kill him! Isn't there anybody who believes me?—"

"But of course, my dear, I believe you."

The quiet, compelling voice of Alfredo Gonzales came from the door. Winifred's arms dropped and Wade sprang to his feet as the professor, suave and smiling, advanced into the room.

"I am sorry I came so late, gentlemen. The butler told me you were waiting for me."

CHAPTER TWELVE

WHEN Professor Gonzales stepped from the hall into the great golden room it was as if an empty alcove had been completed by the master-piece for which it was designed. He came silently across the carpet, a slight smile on his thin disdainful lips; with his entrance he had become absolute master of the situation, so that Captain Murphy turned brickish and even Wade felt like a little boy caught with his hand in the jam-pot. Gonzales slipped a supporting arm about his wife and regarded the two men with devastating courtesy.

"I am sure Mrs. Gonzales' position can be explained, gentlemen. Won't you sit down, Mr. Wade? And you, Captain Murphy?" He turned gently to Winifred. "Take this seat, my dear."

Winifred crumpled back on the divan and fumbled for a cigarette and a match. Gonzales solicitously adjusted a cushion at her back before he took his seat at the other end of the divan. He lit a cigarette and looked at Murphy through a cloud of blue smoke.

"Surely, captain, you are not suggesting that Mrs. Gonzales was in any way responsible for the death of Mr. Ulman?"

It was a rebuke so gently and yet so destructively administered that the belligerent policeman had nothing whatever to say. Wade answered.

"There are some facts in Mrs. Gonzales' account of how she spent yesterday that aren't clear, professor. We are trying to get the discrepancies ironed out."

"I understand." The professor bowed slightly. He did not look at Winifred, who was smoking in hurried little jerks and watching him apprehensively. "I am sure, Mr. Wade, that Mrs. Gonzales will be glad to give you any information that is essential to the successful pursuit of your inquiry. Shall I be permitted to remain, or would you perhaps prefer to continue your conversation alone?"

The question was crushingly punctilious. But Wade had recovered his own self-possession.

"If it is quite agreeable, I should like to ask Mrs. Gonzales a few questions privately. Will you and Captain Murphy be good enough to excuse us?"

"Certainly." Gonzales rose at once. He still hardly glanced at Winifred, but Wade had noted the almost visible stiffening of her nerves. "Perhaps," suggested Gonzales, "Captain Murphy would take a highball with me? When prohibition threatened, captain, I stocked the cellars to last the rest of my life, so it will be—" he smiled—"quite legal."

Murphy got to his feet. "That being the case, sir, I could enjoy a drink to perfection."

"Excellent." The professor stepped to the door and held it open. When it had closed behind them, Winifred looked questioningly at Wade. She had twisted her bit of a handkerchief tight around her fingers as if to stop their trembling.

"I want to ask you a few questions if you feel quite well again," he said casually, rising as he spoke and opening the door of the cellarette. "I believe there's a drink here somewhere—it might help you."

"Yes, please." He poured some heavy rum into a glass and she drank it hurriedly as if it were medicine. Then she said, almost lightly, "Give me another cigarette, will you? Thanks. Stupid of me to get panicky, wasn't it?"

The little handkerchief ripped in her fingers. She thrust it between two cushions and chattered on, as though she could not stem the rush of words.

"But yesterday was so dreadful—and last night I was all geared up for your examination. I'm sure I could have answered all the questions clearly—and then Marie fainted, and I knew I'd have to get up my nerve all over again today."

Wade wondered if it was natural that any woman should have that icy little flute of a voice. He felt himself shiver inwardly; he had seen hysteria often, and his experience had been that when rigid women cracked it was ghastly. Winifred rattled on.

"I do want to be questioned and get it over, but I seem to have made an idiot of myself this morning, and no woman likes to be anticlimactic, Mr. Wade. I've always heard about the relentless machinery of the law, but I never thought I'd have experience of it. Fancy that left turn's being important."

She was smoking fast; he recognized the nervous necessity for little movements that are characteristic of one who is fighting for self-control. The hand that had held the handkerchief was clenched in her lap.

"I must have broken that rule a dozen times before, and I never thought anything about it—I'd much rather pay a traffic fine than go around the block when I'm in a hurry." She said the last words naively, like a child sharing a secret.

He was watching her with surprise. Winifred did not wring her hands nor strike her forehead; she sat rigidly, chattering in an even little voice like a robot that had been wound up too tight.

"The police can be very brutal, can't they? I'm frightened now, for no reason at all—they can't possibly involve me in this horrid mess. But how in the world did Captain Murphy know about that magazine?"

She looked inquiringly at him.

"But you told him yourself," said Wade smiling.

"So I did—and he put things together? I see." She stood up and went to the table, where she straightened a pair of book-ends. "Funny, isn't it, how anything as absolutely innocent as that can sound so damning when a smug person begins talking about it!"

He noticed the nervous flutter of her hands about the books on the table. ("It's going to be terrible when she cracks," he thought.) He watched her closely as she crossed to a window and lowered the shade an inch or two.

"But I had no business losing my nerve. Now of course he thinks I've got all sorts of dreadful things to cover up. But I haven't, really. What on earth makes him so suspicious, Mr. Wade?"

She was drawing the lace curtains.

("All right," he thought, "here's the break. I might as well hurry it up.") So he said aloud,

"You made a mistake when you didn't tell him the truth about that note, Mrs. Gonzales."

She turned from the window suddenly. But she did not seem frightened.

"That note you showed me? But why do you say I didn't tell the truth when I said I didn't know anything about it?"

Wade took a chance. "You didn't wear gloves in the library, you know."

"But that's idiotic. I didn't touch it." Before the words had left her she was laughing, a thin tinkling little laugh of concession. "There, I've done it again!" She shook her head regretfully. "I did see it yesterday. Marie had laid it on the desk. But I don't know what it means, and I don't want to start tattling about her."

"I see." She was clever, he thought as he looked at her, silhouetted against the bright noon beyond the curtains. She had even thought to stand so that her face would be in shadow. "But it's advisable, Mrs. Gonzales, to tell the police the truth. If you don't you're likely to put yourself in a bad light."

"As I've already done." She shrugged. "There'll be a lot of talk, of course. I hate it. I wonder—the police are cruel, aren't they? And stupid too. But you aren't of the police, Mr. Wade, so maybe you can understand how I feel."

"Yes," he said, "I can understand that."

"I feel so weak, and somehow so guilty. I can't explain it." She talked in a low, confiding voice, like a little girl. Wade began to understand how harrowing her interview with Terry must have been.

"Have you any idea who might have committed this murder?" he asked her gently.

She looked out of the window. "Mr. Wade, it doesn't seem as if anybody I know could have done a thing like this."

"You saw Terry Sheldon this morning, didn't you?"

"Yes," she said without surprise. "Poor boy—he seems quite upset."

"You quarreled with him, didn't you?"

She turned incredulously. But he was inexorable. "You ordered him out of the house with a gun, Mrs. Gonzales. You told him you hoped he'd break his neck—"

She drew back against the window. "Who told you that? Is this another police trick?"

He spoke quietly. "No, I know you quarreled. But I want you to tell me why. Do you think Terry killed Quentin Ulman? Does he think you killed Quentin Ulman?" He went to her and looked down at her earnestly. "Mrs. Gonzales, you'd do a great deal better by telling the truth. Please don't try to hold out any longer."

She sat down, her clenched hands pressed against her temples, her eyes wild with fear and bewilderment.

"Oh, I don't know—I don't know! I can't tell you what he thinks. I'm not sure what I think."

Wade drew a chair close to hers and sat down, speaking to her with considerate sincerity.

"Why don't you tell me about it? You think it's bad now, Mrs. Gonzales, but you don't know what a police inquisition means. And you don't know how far the person you are trying to protect will go if he is pressed."

"But I can't tell you anything," she insisted in a desperate whisper. "I don't know anything."

He took out his watch. "Very well. I know this much. Twenty-four hours ago Quentin Ulman's body was found. Twenty-four hours from now somebody will probably be in jail charged with his murder. Then the whole story of Quentin Ulman will be told, and it will be too late for you to be cautious. If you'll tell me now what you are holding back I promise you that I'll do everything in my power to keep you out of the case. If you don't tell me, I can't know what it is you are fighting and I can't know how to give you such protection as I might be able to give."

Winifred looked up at him, seriously. "Mr. Wade, I can't tell you anything now. Terry Sheldon was drunk this morning—he was not accountable for what he said. I was nervous and over-wrought, and I said things I didn't mean, too."

"Mrs. Gonzales," said Wade, "do you think that your husband was responsible for Ulman's death?"

She laughed, a delicate normal laugh.

"Thank you," she said.

The mention of Alfredo seemed to have restored her balance. She went on, laughingly. "It all seemed so personal a minute ago, but really, trying to put Alfredo on one side of the eternal triangle shows how ridiculous the whole thing is. I can't believe anyone I know did the murder. Some gangster must have killed Mr. Ulman for something you and I know nothing about." She gave out this theory as if to indicate that it was all settled in her mind, and that Wade was being very silly and Murphy very bothersome.

He stood up. "I'm sorry. But by tomorrow or the day after Captain Murphy will have somebody in jail, and perhaps someone you do know. Then every newspaper in New Orleans will be drawing its own conclusions as to the murder and its reason, and no matter how ridiculous it may seem to you, the people who read it will believe it."

"Tomorrow," she said archly, "is another day. By tomorrow I may change my mind and have something to say, but today, Mr. Wade—I know nothing about the murder." She became serious again. "Call me up about ten tomorrow morning. I may be convinced by then that you're right."

Abruptly she stood up and went again to the window, drawing the curtains apart and looking out to where a great palm waved in the sunshine. He saw how slender she was, with a figure many younger women might have been proud of. For a moment she stood there, the wind rippling her dress, then, without turning, she asked,

"Did you see the body?"

"Yes," said Wade.

Her hand gripped the curtain till he thought she would tear the lace apart.

"What did he look like?"

Wade rose and went to her. He did not try to see her face, but stood by the window-frame looking at her averted head.

"Please do not ask me to tell you, Mrs. Gonzales."

Wade hardly knew what he had expected her to answer. But what she said astounded him, and he knew that whatever it was he had expected it had not been that. For a moment he stood looking at her, as she kept her face turned away from him and her eyes on the waving palm-branches, and when she turned she was smiling, the gay querying smile of a pretty woman to a pleasant young man. Her hand loosened itself from the curtain and laced lightly with the other hand in front of her, and she lifted her great amber eyes to him and said,

"Why don't you call me Winifred?"

It required a lightning leap, but ten years of newspaper assignments had made him a connoisseur in the art of adjusting his own mental attitude to that of other persons, and it was without any perceptible hesitation that Wade smiled back at her and answered,

"It's an idea—but it might be habit-forming."

He knew what she was doing, but he had no defense against it. With catastrophe on her own doorstep she still refused to believe in it, trusting that here too she could conquer with the only weapon she had ever needed. Wade habitually viewed life with the paid observer's attitude of careless detachment, so he found himself amused at how well she had achieved changing the tenor of the interview.

She wanted to be sure of her victory. Having taken the conversation in her own hands she meant to keep it to a pattern made familiar by years of effective coquetry. Crossing to the table, she lit a cigarette and asked coolly,

"What habits might it form?"

He leaned his arms on the back of a chair and smiled—he hoped, regretfully.

"We'll never know—Mrs. Gonzales."

CHAPTER THIRTEEN

WINIFRED sat down in front of him, her brown hair brushing across his elbows as they rested on the back of the chair. She drew her filmy skirt over her knees, crossed her hands in her lap and looked primly up over her shoulder as if to say, "So, Mr. Wade, I've been put in my place, have I?"

He walked to the chair opposite her and studied her for a moment, half appalled by her confidence in the rôle that she wanted him to believe she had never played before. Innocent or guilty of murder she might be—he could not tell, but he was both amused and exasperated at the cool and delicate offer of her charm as the price of his championship. He was suddenly reminded of waitresses who wanted to be bathing beauty queens, and a great many other analogies that were out of place in the world of Mrs. Alfredo Gonzales; but at the same time he found himself forced to acknowledge that her appeal was nearly as powerful as it was assured. He wanted to be done with the interview, and because he felt her challenge he wanted to be the one to bring it to an end.

"So tomorrow, then," he suggested, "you'll tell us what you think we should know?"

"Tomorrow," she returned with a malicious little smile, "if I think there's anything to tell."

Wade went to the door feeling that perhaps this last joust had finished in a draw. When he returned with Gonzales, Winifred had stretched at full length on the divan, a cushion tucked under her head.

"Captain Murphy," her husband told her as he entered, "expressed a desire to speak to the servants. He will be here in a moment. He told me of his interview, and asked me to convey his regrets that you were disturbed by his necessary questions."

Winifred did not answer. As Gonzales sat down she glanced warily at him, a glance that somehow conveyed to Wade a sense of inscrutable hostility, definitely present between those two and yet behind which they were uniting against himself.

"Then I'll get back to my part of the inquiry," Wade said. "I wanted first of all, Mr. Gonzales, to ask you about the Gutenberg Bible fragment."

Gonzales' answer was faintly bitter. "It is a pretty sample of parchment, Mr. Wade, but it is not Gutenberg."

"If it's so obvious a fake," Wade went on, "isn't it surprising that Dr. Prentiss should believe in it?"

"He has made mistakes before," Gonzales returned acidly, "in trying to build his own reputation at the expense of the library."

"Your trusteeship doesn't give you the right to protest when books are bought?"

"No, only at the time of the regular reports." Gonzales looked with enigmatic attention at the tapestry over the fireplace.

"Then you are never consulted?" Wade asked incredulously. He was beginning to understand the extent of the bitterness provoked by the Sheldon will.

"Never. And yet, I am in a measure responsible for every item in the catalogue. It is a peculiar condition, but—" he gave an expressive Latin shrug.

There was a flicker of amusement on Winifred's face, but Gonzales was not looking at her. He was standing before the great controversy of his life, and was intent upon it. "Dr. Prentiss believes that these nine leaves were discovered in the rubbish of a Bavarian monastery," he went on with a touch of derision. "He forgets that the industry of producing rare old books thrives as briskly as the industry of producing beds on which Napoleon died. While I have not made an exhaustive examination of this fragment, I am convinced that it is a made-to-order Gutenberg."

"Could you tell me why?"

"Certainly. The Gutenberg Bibles, as you know, were printed about 1450. Now the parchment used for Dr. Prentiss' leaves is old—over a hundred years old, I should say, but not five hundred. There seem to be other differences as well."

"Such a bother," murmured Winifred, "about nine moldy pages of a book."

"Leaves," corrected her husband crisply. "Nine leaves are eighteen pages."

"What's the difference?" she asked lazily.

Wade, not sure whether she was playing the fool for his benefit or from a desire to laugh at Gonzales' earnestness, hastened to put a question of his own.

"You have been in New Orleans nearly all your life, professor?"

"Since I was thirteen. I came here after my father's death."

Winifred glanced up. "His father was a professor of literature at the University of Havana. Alfredo inherited his taste for learning. He speaks French and German as well as English, and he reads Anglo-Saxon and medieval as well as classical Latin."

Her chant was interrupted by the sound of the door's opening as Murphy came in. "I see you've started already," he said as he sat down. Winifred, not turning her head, rambled on—

"And you should take a look at the monograph he published last summer on the types of bindings found in the library of Diane de Poitiers."

Wade wanted to laugh; Gonzales' face showed unmistakable signs of exasperation. Murphy, however, plunged into business.

"If my friend Wade is through, there's one or two questions I'd like to ask, professor."

"Certainly."

"Well, we didn't go into this before, and a man with your own brilliant mind will understand why we've got to go into it sometime." Murphy presented a perfect picture of geniality. "Now this murder," he went on affably, "is a puzzle, and we've got all but one piece. That one piece is the murderer. We could make out a pretty good case against two or three people, but we don't want two or three possible suspects. We want one murderer, and until we get him everybody's going to be ill at ease."

"Including Captain Murphy," said Winifred dryly.

"Yes, ma'am." Murphy gave a profound nod.

"Believe me, captain, I am most eager to assist you," Gonzales said with a suggestion of well-bred impatience. "Just what is it you want me to do?"

"Well, sir, in the language of the ordinary policeman, which is all I know how to speak, what we want to see is just the things that are being hid. We want to know everything about Ulman and every-thing about your relationship with him. You see, we've got reason to believe that he was kind of a cavalier, and that he admired Mrs. Gonzales a good bit."

Gonzales answered with terse politeness. "Captain Murphy, I cannot countenance this sort of conversation in my wife's presence. Will you permit her to retire?"

"No—let me stay," said Winifred quickly. "I may never get another chance to see a real third degree."

Gonzales assented silently. Murphy spoke.

"We always like to oblige anybody who's interested in seeing the force operate, ma'am," he said with large sarcasm.

Wade grinned in spite of himself. Gonzales was politely irritated; Wade saw it and spoke directly to him.

"You must understand, Mr. Gonzales, that to Captain Murphy this is a problem in what people were thinking about Ulman before Ulman was killed."

"That's it exactly," agreed Murphy. "We're all sorry for the poor young gentleman, even the person who killed him might be sorry. So what we want to know is not who's mourning for the dead man, but who hated the live one. Maybe you can give us some ideas on that." Gonzales had become coldly analytical. "Do I understand that whatever we say here is confidential?"

"We're speaking entirely in confidence," Murphy told him. "Nothing for the papers."

"Very well," said Gonzales. "I am assuming, then, that we are all civilized persons, discussing a deplorable circumstance in which we are somewhat involved."

"That's right," encouraged Murphy.

"Then," said Gonzales rising, "I am going to give you a very simple hypothesis for your case."

He was standing by a window, his back to the light, so that his face was subdued by his own shadow. He was completely at ease, and as he began to discuss the murder of Quentin Ulman in his rich, even voice, Wade understood why Gonzales was one of the university's most popular lecturers. Even Murphy had settled back into his chair—a singular tribute—and Winifred, who still lay carelessly along the divan, listened negligently at first and then with growing concern. Gonzales spoke with effortless detachment.

"I believe," he was saying, "that the police have agreed with the coroner that Ulman was shot, or killed by a blow, and the body burned afterwards?"

Murphy nodded, to Wade's surprise, for the coroner himself had been dubious as to the method of Ulman's death. But Gonzales, apparently satisfied, went on.

"Dr. Julian Prentiss may have killed Quentin Ulman."

The statement brought Murphy up to the edge of his chair and Wade's eyes moved from Winifred to the professor.

"Here is the case against him." Gonzales was speaking with careful deliberation. "First, his position as a collector and his post at the Sheldon Library are all of his life's interests. He buys the Gutenberg fragment and I say that it is spurious. This he denies, but later Ulman points out an obvious flaw that proves my contention, even to Dr. Prentiss. He refuses to admit the flaw, but he sees his prestige and his position endangered, for Ulman has told him that he will not be a party to the fraud."

Wade looked back to Winifred. She was listening intently.

"But Prentiss has a way to silence his assistant. His narrow mind, made brittle by his years as a recluse, sees in Ulman's friendship for Mrs. Gonzales a sinister thing. He threatens to expose this affair to me unless Ulman is silent about the Bible flaw. Ulman, not wanting Mrs. Gonzales embarrassed, says he may have been mistaken. But then Prentiss hears that his hold is in danger because Ulman is planning to marry Marie. There is only one way to keep Ulman quiet—murder."

Winifred gasped audibly. Murphy was sitting very straight, as if about to make off to have it out with Prentiss. Wade himself, impressed by the suggestion, was wondering if he could complete the outline of the case with the necessary details. But Gonzales was looking at all three of them with a flash of satiric triumph.

"But you see, Captain Murphy, in order to believe this theory you must believe that Dr. Prentiss did not take lunch at the library and was not seen shortly thereafter by his housekeeper, or you must believe that he paid someone else to kill Ulman. You have to believe too that Ulman knew of the Bible fraud, and if you believe that, you will find it difficult to understand why Ulman should have stolen the Bible. Suppose we look at our next hypothesis."

Murphy's jaw dropped, and Wade grinned.

"Then," suggested Gonzales mildly, "let us consider Luke Dancy.

"Dancy heard Dr. Prentiss tell Ulman to go to the bindery. If Dancy was Ulman's confederate in the theft of books from the library, Dancy might have gone across the river to discuss a division of their spoils. If he did this, it is easy to understand that they might have quarreled."

Murphy had started to scribble in his notebook. Gonzales, addressing nobody in particular, spoke with the smiling confidence of a professor sure of the interest of his subject.

"Ulman was a powerful man, and Dancy no match for him. If their quarrel began in the bindery, however, Dancy may have snatched up one of the long knives used for trimming leather edges on full-size bindings and used it as his weapon. There are several conceivable reasons why Dancy might have wanted Ulman out of his way, but—"

he smiled gently—"why discuss them? For if Dancy is to be proved a murderer it must also be proved that he was the accomplice of a man whose secrets have been dead with him for more than twenty-four hours."

Murphy sighed and started to put up his notebook, but Gonzales had not paused. Murphy turned to a clean page.

"Or, we might consider my charming young cousin, Marie Castillo."

Winifred slipped to a sitting posture as though in sudden fear, but her husband still had not looked in her direction. He was speaking as though his academic interest in somebody else's crime afforded him a faint and subtle amusement.

"Marie," said Gonzales, "is engaged to be married to Quentin Ulman. But she discovers that he is flagrantly deceiving her."

Winifred started slightly, but Gonzales noticed her not at all.

"Ulman is planning," he said calmly, "to be married to a girl in New England. Marie goes to the bindery and there charges Ulman with his duplicity. She is a quick-tempered girl, of the same hot Latin race to which I myself belong. Ulman may laugh at her, but in the next instant is dead. Marie is not horrified at the sight of death—she has been calloused by years of intimate experience of it. She thinks quickly: the surest way to remove the traces of her crime is to destroy the body of her victim.

"This is a nice theory, gentlemen, but in order to believe it you must prove that Marie, a girl with a girl's strength, dragged Ulman's body from the bindery to the spot where it was found, and you must show also why there are no traces of blood anywhere in the bindery or along the road."

He paused an instant. Wade saw that Winifred was watching Gonzales with narrow, furious eyes, and he guessed that she like himself noticed that Gonzales had not said that in order to prove jealousy as Marie's motive it would be necessary to show that she knew of Ulman's fiancée in New England.

Gonzales, however, seemed oblivious of any reactions to what he had suggested. "And there is Terry Sheldon," he said. Murphy held his pencil hopefully.

"Terry," said the professor, "may have gone to the bindery and quarreled with Ulman because of Ulman's deception of Marie, or because—" the professor gave another enigmatic smile—"of some other difference with which we are not at present acquainted. He might have killed Ulman and burned his body, and he had time and opportunity to do it—but to prove that he did, gentlemen, you must prove too that Terry was himself in love with Marie, or that he was so delightfully old-fashioned that he considered it his duty to wipe out an insult to a girl by taking the life of her faithless lover, or that he was implicated in looting the library—all of them strained hypotheses, for Terry has given no indication of unusual affection for Marie, he is an essentially modern young man, and he has ample means and does not collect books."

Winifred relaxed and reached for a cigarette as though relieved to think that her husband's troublesome lecture was at an end. But Gonzales still stood as though explaining a problem to a class of not-too-brilliant students, and he continued.

"Or we might, gentlemen, consider the possibility that Mr. Ulman was murdered by Mrs. Gonzales."

Winifred froze, a match halted halfway to the cigarette between her lips. Gonzales kept his eyes straight ahead.

"Mrs. Gonzales has manifested friendship and admiration for Mr. Ulman. He rides to the ferry with her and recommends an article in a magazine. When Mrs. Gonzales is unable to buy the magazine she decides that she will follow him to the bindery and read Mr. Ulman's copy while he is working, then drive him back to town. She goes to the bindery, but Ulman, who has misinterpreted her innocent friendship, takes advantage of their seclusion to make improper advances."

Winifred suddenly threw away her match, which had burnt down to her fingers. She was watching her husband with a venomous fury of which he seemed entirely unconscious as he continued his suave, smiling and faintly supercilious reconstruction of the crime.

"Mrs. Gonzales is stunned at this sudden affront to her character. She repels him with all the force of her outraged dignity. She leaves the bindery and goes to her car, but Ulman follows her, snatching the key of her car from her hand. Beside herself with terror, she sights a stone by the side of the road and hurls it at his head. He falls, his skull crushed by the blow.

"She is appalled at what she has done. While her action has been entirely justified she realizes that there were no witnesses to his unprecedented conduct. With some nebulous idea of protecting herself by destroying the body of her assailant, she pushes the body into her car, takes it some yards down the road, pours upon it gasoline she has found in the bindery, and sets it afire." He bowed ever so slightly, as though a trifle proud of his own logic. "An extremely plausible theory, gentlemen, but to make it tenable you must prove that Mrs. Gonzales did cross the river yesterday."

Winifred dropped into the ash-tray the torn and twisted fragments of the cigarette she had never lit.

Gonzales smiled tranquilly. "It would not be sportsmanlike for me so carefully to seek motives for my friends without suggesting an equally strong case against myself. I too might have murdered Quentin Ulman. I might have gone to the bindery and shot him with deliberate purpose. I might have dumped his body on the road and set it afire. I might have thought it a good day's work.

"But to believe that I did, you must also believe that I knew of his being there at that time, and you must believe as well that those with whom I lunched and walked yesterday on the university campus lied to protect me."

Gonzales had finished his game of hypotheses. For an instant he stood regarding the others with an impersonal serenity suggesting that as far as his interest went the affair of Quentin Ulman was dismissed. But Wade, who had been more impressed by Gonzales' manner than by his words, sat thinking a moment, while Murphy bustled over to have the professor clarify some of his notes. Winifred had found another match and another cigarette and was blowing peaceful spirals toward the ceiling. Wade was not sure whether her husband's irony had been assumed to draw attention away from Winifred or to remind her that he did not intend to forget Quentin Ulman—a sort of cruelty that somehow did not seem incongruous in the analytical coldness of Alfredo Gonzales. She studied her smoke rings for a moment with a puzzled air, then suddenly she asked in a voice clear enough to carry to where Murphy and Gonzales were standing,

"Is the class in murder over now, Mr. Wade?"

"I think so," he told her. "Are you done, Murphy?"

"All done," said Murphy, coming back from the window. "All I've been able to find out this day is that college professors are smarter than I thought they were. Mr. Gonzales ought to be on the force."

Wade stood up. "I'll call you tomorrow, Mrs. Gonzales," he said deliberately. "Mrs. Gonzales," he explained, "has already told me that she will tell us something relative to the murder tomorrow—if she thinks we ought to know it."

Winifred smiled vacuously, and Professor Gonzales' cool voice asked her,

"Can't we have your hypothesis now, my dear?"

Winifred turned to look at him steadily. "What I have to say," she responded with calm insouciance, "isn't a hypothesis. It's merely a fact."

CHAPTER FOURTEEN

AT HALF-past eight Wade climbed the crooked stairway leading to Marie's garret and knocked with grim resolution. A moment later she stood in the doorway, her scarlet smock flecked with soapsuds and her hair tousled into a confusion of black tendrils around her ears. "Oh, it's you," she greeted. "Come in. And don't blush. This is only me and the laundry."

He laughed, relieved at the gay normalcy of her attic, where various items of lingerie flapped in limp immodesty on a crisscross of clotheslines. "Don't let me stop you."

"Nothing left but one pair of stockings. They can wait. Sit down." She curled up on her red sofa and offered him a cigarette. "Why the magnificence? Don't tell me a dinner-jacket is the new police uniform."

He glanced down at his expanse of shirt-front and back at her. "No. I'm going to the Chinese ball at the Vincennes Club. I want you to come with me."

Marie raised a pair of hard black eyes. "Don't be an idiot."

"I know you don't want to go. I don't blame you. But it might be a good idea."

"Can't see it," she answered. Then she looked at him with a sudden reluctant appeal for understanding. "Please don't think I'm not glad you asked me. I know I ought to show people that I can find another escort the day Quentin's fiancée gets her name in the papers. But I can't go."

"It's more important than that, Marie." He spoke with urgent sincerity. "I want you to prove that you aren't heartbroken. You aren't, but perhaps you don't realize how many persons might enjoy saying you are."

She nodded bleakly. "Winifred."

"Not only Winifred, though she'll do for an example. But others you know will be there tonight, and if you're with me they'll have less reason to say Ulman left you high and dry."

"I can't." She shook her head. "Please—don't you understand I'm not like Winifred? She'll be there tonight—beautiful as ever and not giving a damn. But I haven't got the sort of courage it takes to be frivolous in a crisis."

For a moment he looked at her without answering, involuntarily elaborating the contrast she had suggested—Winifred, from her perfect house to her perfect marcel an achievement of expensive and consummate artistry; Marie, washing her own clothes in her garret, too conscious of reality even to pretend that she could ignore it; and he went to her abruptly and took her hands in his. "Then I can't persuade you?"

Marie smiled as his eyes met hers. "No. But thanks just the same." She stood up. "Run along to your party. I won't have a bad time, for I'm all ready for my own kind of quiet evening—a couple of chocolate bars, a new pack of cigarettes and a lively treatise on volumetric analysis."

He left her regretfully, wishing that she would let him help her, but in spite of himself feeling a slow admiration for her independence. But he was troubled, nevertheless, for he knew how precarious was her chance of maintaining it, and when he met Farrell and Murphy for a prearranged conference in his own courtyard Murphy's fist words emphasized what Wade had dreaded.

"So the Gonzales gentleman was explaining how the whole shooting-match might have done the job," Murphy was saying to Farrell.

"And the only one he couldn't clear was that girl doctor. The only alibi he could make for her was that she couldn't have dragged the body down the road, but he took pains not to remind us that she could have been walking with Ulman when she stuck the knife in him. That knife, now—"

"That knife, Murphy," Wade cut in belligerently, leaning on the rim of the fountain, "was not found with bloodstains on it."

"Well, she coulda wiped it off, couldn't she? She's a chemist, remember—she's no amateur in knowing how to do things like that. Me, now, I'd lock her up."

"Well," said Wade decidedly, "I wouldn't."

Murphy leaned back in his chair, clasped his hands over his ample middle and gave Wade a condescending scrutiny. "Just what is this party you're going to tonight?" he asked. "I'll have to keep better informed on the doings of the fashionables now that they've gone in for murder."

Wade looked meditatively at the chuckling fountain. "It's quite a party, Murphy. The only big in-town affair that can be counted on for the summer. They started having a costume ball some years ago for the university summer population, and the smart people who happened to be in town began taking it up, till now the summer-school students are pretty lucky to get in. I gather that some of the stars in our show will be there—Gonzales has to go out of duty, Mrs. Gonzales has the leading part in the pageant that's the high spot of the evening, Prentiss heads the list of patrons, and Terry designed the decorations. What I wanted to see you boys about was to ask if there's anything I should keep in mind tonight."

"Keep a watch on Mrs. Gonzales," said Farrell musingly. "And Terry. She might bring that gun with her." He looked up suddenly. "From what Murphy's been telling me, that Gonzales is a pretty fine fellow. Smooth, but it was damn decent the way he came in and stood up for his wife."

"That woman," said Murphy ponderously, "is no good, or I never saw a tommy in my life. I thought he'd spill on her when he got talking, but all he did was give us a pretty fair lead about Prentiss."

Wade made a wry face. "He made us stop bothering her, but he took plenty of pokes himself a little later."

"You remember Prentiss," Murphy advised. "He mighta got rooked on that Bible and planned to fix it so he could stay shut up in that mausoleum with all them dead books. Or he might have had an eye on Winifred. That dame can't be so young, can she?"

"I figure she's thirty-six," said Farrell. "The professor said she was sixteen when they married. No flaming youth."

"Look here, Farrell," exploded Murphy, "don't you talk about nothing flaming to me. I'm yearning for one of these nice sloppy killings where a guy gets stuck in the gizzard and a lot of fingerprints on the knife. You better light your own cigarettes tonight, son. Don't let none of them firebugs hold a match near you."

Farrell stood up. "It's time you were getting along, Wade. If Winifred won't talk to you tomorrow morning I'm going to send for her again and show her what a police quizzing can be like. We can pick up that gun she shoved at Terry and hold her as a material witness, but I don't want to do that unless she absolutely won't talk."

They walked out of the courtyard to the street. Wade paused with his foot on the running-board of his car.

"Say, Farrell, I'm not cut out to be a policeman. I never felt so low in my life as this morning when Gonzales walked in."

Murphy sighed. "Well, he don't bother me with his fine talk. He may be one swell intellectual, but I think he's just a man that can't keep tab on his own family and a bit of a gigolo; probably dances a beautiful tango."

Wade laughed as he drove off, but on the way to the club he became morose again. For two days he seemed to have been doing nothing but hitting his head in blind alleys. He was tired. Sweeping down the long curve of road between the dusty palms, he remembered Alfredo and Winifred, and he wondered what had happened in their great quiet house after he had left it.

The morbid undertone of the Chinese ball rushed heavily upon him as he entered the great ballroom. But he was forced to own to himself that whatever else Terry might be, he was certainly an artist. His exotic screens and hangings, and the colored lanterns that dipped from the ceiling, formed a brilliant background for the guests who danced there. Most of them were in costume, though professors who had come from a sense of duty were in simple evening dress.

Wade glimpsed Dr. Prentiss for a moment, and saw what looked like Gonzales' back, but before he had time to speak to either of them the curtains were drawn aside on the stage at one end of the ballroom and the pageant began.

It was a glamorous spectacle, for Terry's work had been done with a practised eye for effect. Wade found himself fascinated by the cool self-assurance of Winifred, as he watched her in her mandarin suit of gold and scarlet with lurking undertones of green; she wore only the trousers and a sleeveless silk vest, which left her arms and shoulders bare against the luminous background. When the curtains closed Wade found that Dr. Prentiss was at his side, watching the stage intently. He started when he saw Wade and put a perfunctory question as to what Wade had thought of the pageant. It was evident that he was avoiding the attention that any reference to yesterday's tragedy might have brought on him. Wade smiled.

"I liked it very much. The decorations were splendid." Prentiss agreed. "Terry's work. He is gifted."

"Very. Is he here?"

"I haven't seen him." Prentiss glanced again at the closed curtains. "Mrs. Gonzales did extremely well. I've never seen her more charming."

Wade nodded. "Her costume is a masterpiece."

"It is indeed. The full suit includes a coat, but she hasn't worn it. It is one of the treasures of my Oriental room."

Wade looked up thoughtfully, tired of the amenities. "May I ask you a question that doesn't concern the pageant, doctor?"

Prentiss smiled without fervor, as though trying to conceal a justifiable annoyance. "Certainly, Mr. Wade."

"What was Ulman's opinion of your Bible fragment?"

The doctor gave a slight shrug. His face hardened. "I do not recall that he ever expressed an opinion. He was not an authority on fifteenth-century printing—he specialized in the work of French bookbinders of the days before the revolution."

"Has it occurred to you," Wade asked, "that Ulman might not have been the man who robbed you?"

"Yes, I've thought of that." Prentiss passed his hand over his eyes wearily. He looked a trifle haggard, as though the events of the past two days had corroded his placid life more than he cared to admit.

"But at any rate, Mr. Wade, the Bible is gone. Several representatives of Mr. Farrell's office spent a large part of today at the library, searching."

Wade was about to answer when two acquaintances of his joined them, and Prentiss moved to another group with evident relief. Wade looked after him, thinking. Prentiss was taking part in the sprightly inconsequentialities of the evening with a formal amiability that betrayed nothing of what his thoughts might be.

Professor Gonzales, when Wade found him, was gravely cordial. Wade pitied both men for the social necessity that had forced them to attend the ball, bringing with them as they must their auras of unwelcome prominence. He could not find Terry, and he had to look a long time through the brilliant rooms before he found Winifred. At last he saw her, gorgeous in her green and gold and scarlet; she stood just in front of an arch of lanterns, like a lady on a Chinese fan, and though she was chattering with a group of nondescript people it was as if by some law of attraction she had gathered to herself all the many colors of the lanterns behind her and stood out alone. For an instant Wade let his doubts slide out of his consciousness while he granted himself the relaxation of simply looking at her, then she caught sight of him and waved gaily. In another moment she had crossed the room to where he stood.

"Good evening! How goes the chase? Are we here for business or pleasure?"

"Pleasure," he smilingly prevaricated. "One can't keep man-hunting forever." He saw that she had on a necklace of crystals and topazes, which though out of place with her costume gave her the piquant air of a woman lovely enough to dress to please herself.

"Really?" She looked slantingly up at him, and he saw that the subtle quest of the morning still held. "I thought detectives were supposed to be at it all the time, ceaseless as a tom-tom, beating things out of people—oh, but I mustn't be personal. It's much too pretty here."

"You were charming in the pageant," he told her.

"You liked it? I thought it was rather nice. Don't you love this mandarin suit?"

"Beautiful."

"Prentiss lent it to me. I thought I'd never get it, for Terry had borrowed it and Prentiss had to send Marie down to pry it out of Terry's studio. That idiotic little secretary with the fish-colored hair brought it up to me this afternoon. He brought the coat, too, though I hadn't asked for it. I wore it instead of a wrap tonight—it's in the car. The whole suit is devastatingly beautiful, but rather hard to wear. It's so heavy, and the stiffest brocade I ever saw." She made a tantalizing gesture with her slim hands. "If I weren't going home this minute I'd ask you to dance with me."

He smiled non-committally. "But you're not leaving?"

"Yes, little boy, I'm going home. I've had rather a hard day, in case you've forgotten, and I'm tired. So I thought I'd slip out and leave Alfredo to do the honors for the family."

Dr. Prentiss joined them, and complimented Winifred on her part in the pageant. She thanked him merrily. "Everybody's been envying my costume, doctor." Prentiss looked at the exquisite texture of the embroidery with a gaze that was almost caressing. "Magnificent, isn't it? An amazing race, the Chinese. Only a strong and vital people could produce anything so perfect in all its aspects." He turned to Wade. "I've always had a vivid admiration for the Chinese. They have the courage to demand that they be let alone."

"What time is it?" asked Winifred suddenly. "Eleven-thirty," said Wade, glad not to have to answer Prentiss' last remark.

"Then I must be going. I'll send the suit back tomorrow, doctor. I wore the emperor's coat instead of a wrap tonight. Goodby, both of you."

"Chinese Cinderella," observed Wade.

She laughed. "Yes, with Dr. Prentiss as fairy godfather providing the finery. I hope my car will behave less as if it's guided by white mice than it did yesterday." She flung him a mischievous look, waved lightly over her shoulder to them and went off.

A moment later Dr. Prentiss was buttonholed by a brisk young woman who urged him to come and be introduced to a visiting celebrity, and Wade made his escape to a side balcony, where he sat down grateful for the solitude, and looked moodily out into the dark. The night was soft as velvet, a clinging night of warmth and fireflies, and though there was only a thin-looking moon slightly worn down at one edge, the magnolia leaves beyond the balcony looked as if they had been brushed with silver. From inside, the dance music tapped a rippling strain in odd contrast with his thoughts. He leaned back wearily. The bright ballroom and the forced lightness of the guests in whom he was interested had roused in him a depressing sense of futility. He thought of Winifred, enigmatic and troublesome behind the wall of irreverence she had built between herself and the world, and he did not know—he doubted if even those most intimate with her could know—what she was capable of doing. He started when he heard a step behind him.

"Hi, pardner."

"Hello, monkey. What are you doing here?"

Mr. Wiggins of *The Creole* put his camera on the floor and deposited himself upon it. "Here to get the pictures, pal. Kinda grand in there, ain't it? I can't find the society reporter. Say, I sure do hate that Gonzales dame."

Wade laughed. "She get away from you?"

"Hell, yes. I've been looking all over for her and just now that old Prentiss tells me she's been gone home half an hour."

Surprised to discover he had been sitting so long on the balcony, Wade resolved to finish his talk with Prentiss and then go home. Wiggins perked up suddenly.

"Where's the snappy little Cuban?"

"Marie? She's not here."

"No? I kinda wanted a shot of her. Haven't got a good one yet, and she's got a nice nose for a profile.

"Say." Wiggins edged closer. "You know who I think did this killing? I think Murphy did it."

"*What?*"

"Sure. Listen. He's all hot and bothered, wanting to lock up everybody, but he ain't found out a thing. He's just running around in a circle getting in everybody's way. I think maybe Murphy went out to arrest that guy for having that Bible, and then got the notion that he could sell it for a million dollars or something, and just bumped Ulman off in a hurry. Get me? I think—"

An attendant came out on the balcony. "Mr. Wade?"

"Yes?" Wade stood up, chuckling.

"Phone call," said the boy. "Phone's just inside the door here."

Wade told Wiggins to wait and went to the telephone.

"Hello? Wade?" The voice sounded strained, almost ghostly.

"Yes," he said. "What's up?"

"This is Farrell. Listen and don't say anything at your end. They've just found a car on fire with a body in it. It's on the Metairie Road between town and the club. The license plates are K-87053. The record shows they were taken out by Mrs. Alfredo Gonzales."

CHAPTER FIFTEEN

GONZALES spoke only once on the long drive back to town. All the way he had sat in silence at Wade's right, staring through the windshield at the dark. When the car had turned into the drive to the house he spoke without turning or lifting his head.

"What a hideous end for such an exquisite woman!"

Wade, bending stonily over the wheel, did not answer. For not at that moment nor when he thought of it in the desperate days that followed could he tell whether Gonzales was gloating or heartbroken.

As the car drew up in front of the house Gonzales turned to Wade.

"Will you be good enough to come in with me?—I cannot be alone yet."

Wade slipped from under the steering-wheel without speaking. The horror of what they had just seen was on them both too forcibly for many words.

Gonzales led the way inside and opened the door of the room they had been in that morning, and Wade shuddered involuntarily as he caught sight of the great sofa where Winifred had sat. Then he started, for in a corner of the room he saw Terry Sheldon.

Terry was curled up in a deep chair under the dim circle of a floor-lamp, looking as if he were asleep. With a smothered exclamation Gonzales clicked on the ceiling light and Terry opened his eyes. "Where's Winifred?" he asked.

Gonzales' expression had become hard, almost brutal. With deliberate slowness he walked over to Terry's chair.

"Winifred is dead."

Terry started violently; he put his hand to his forehead and stared, as if he were trying to grasp that this was not a phantasm of sleep. Gonzales stood in front of him, his jaw set as though in a fury of self-control. His voice kept its terrible evenness.

"Winifred is dead. Her car was found in flames an hour ago on the Metairie Road. You did not know it?"

Terry's backward step was almost a stagger. "Good God, Alfredo, no!"

For an instant Gonzales said nothing. Wade looked at them from the doorway—the cold menacing fury of Winifred's husband and Terry's horror-stricken face. Then Gonzales added, "Did you come here to see me?"

Terry glanced at Wade. "I'd like to talk to you alone, Alfredo."

Gonzales turned to Wade, and his manner became almost gracious. "Mr. Wade has my fullest confidence." He indicated a chair. "He is here to discover the author of Winifred's murder, and whatever you have to say may be said before him."

Wade sat down; Terry looked uncertainly from him to Gonzales.

"I—I don't know how to say it, Alfredo. I came to talk to Winifred."

"Yes?" Gonzales had not moved.

"She told me she'd get out of the ball before midnight." Terry's fist beat a fitful tattoo on the chair-back. "I'd been down at the studio on Isle Bonne all afternoon—I drove up tonight and got in about a quarter to twelve. I suppose I went to sleep. She was to meet me here."

"Is that all?" Gonzales inquired.

Terry looked at him strangely. His assurance had melted.

"Why—I suppose so. We had an appointment—" his voice trailed off.

Gonzales crossed to the door and held it open. "The dead can keep no appointments. Good night."

For an instant Terry stood quite still. Then, slowly, he went toward the door. On the threshold he paused.

"I don't quite hate you for this, Alfredo. Not yet. But in another couple of days, I think I will."

He turned with a flare of his old arrogance, but Gonzales coldly shut the door and walked back to the cellarette. "Mr. Wade," he said, taking out a bottle of brandy, "I asked you in because there was something I was thinking of telling you. But while I was not sure I would speak before, Terry Sheldon's being here tonight has made me determined. How long can you stay?"

"As long as you need me, Mr. Gonzales." Wade took the glass the professor held out.

"Then I can say all I had intended." Gonzales filled his own glass and sat down. "This morning I outlined for you several facetious hypotheses. Tonight I shall talk to you about what is more in the nature of evidence." He stood up and walked the length of the room before returning to his seat. "Mr. Wade, if my grandfather had experienced the emotion that I felt when I entered this room and saw Terry Sheldon before me, Terry Sheldon would be dead."

He paused and Wade did not urge him to go on, for he was trying to analyze Terry's last remark. After a moment Gonzales went again to the cellarette, picked up the brandy and set it down again as though resolved to finish his story without even the interruption of a drink.

"This afternoon," he began, "Mrs. Gonzales and I had the first serious conversation we had had in a good many years. You can understand her realization that a crisis confronted her, and that she needed me, perhaps for the first time in our married life. There is no need for me to try and preserve the illusion I sought to create in this room when you were here last; I must speak to you frankly now.

"You know that Terry Sheldon was here this morning. Mrs. Gonzales told me you knew of their meeting. Terry was very drunk, and he accused her of having murdered Quentin Ulman. Goaded by his charge, she told him there was reason to believe he knew more of Ulman's murder than he was admitting, and she ordered him out of the house."

"Terry? Did she tell you the reason?" Wade was watching Gonzales closely for a possible indication that the professor was inventing a story. But the answer came back instantly.

"She did, and I was amazed that she had not told you. But she had promised Terry a chance to clear himself."

"So this," exclaimed Wade, "is what she was to tell me tomorrow!"

"Yes. If she had told you today it might have saved her life." The words were spoken so calmly that Wade felt almost as if he were being shown an abstract bit of logic to prove a minor premise.

He did not answer. He was thinking that there was no way of proving what Gonzales was going to tell him, unless Terry could be made to admit it. Winifred had been silenced.

"You asked her about the drive to the ferry," Gonzales was saying. "She did not tell you that she was trying to overtake Terry Sheldon."

Wade started. "Did he cross the river?"

"She did not see him take the boat, because when she reached the ferry house the boat was already moving away. When she told him she believed he had crossed the river, Terry did not deny it, but answered that he could explain his errand. She gave him till midnight to do so, saying that if by midnight he had not come here to offer an apology for his conduct of this morning and to give her a satisfactory reason why he was so near the scene of Ulman's murder, she would inform the police of what she knew." Gonzales made a weary gesture toward the chair Terry had been occupying when they came in. "Mr. Wade, you saw—Terry was here when we arrived. Mrs. Gonzales was dead. And unusual as it may seem, I was her only confidant."

Wade stood up. "If she had only told us!" he repeated. "May I call police headquarters?"

Gonzales directed him to the telephone in the hall and Wade rang Captain Murphy. He gave a quick direction that Terry's apartment be covered and that he be arrested if he made any attempt to leave town. "Otherwise," he ended, "leave him alone. All we have against him is hearsay testimony. Give him some rope and see what he does. I'll explain later."

He hung up the receiver and returned to Gonzales, who had stood in the hall waiting. "Can you tell me why Mrs. Gonzales followed Terry up the Avenue?" Wade asked.

"I can tell you what she told me. She wanted to speak to Marie, and at the library yesterday morning Marie had said that she intended lunching with Terry. Mrs. Gonzales saw Terry's car near St. Mary Street, and seeing him alone she assumed that the luncheon engagement had been broken, so she tried to overtake him to ask where she could find Marie. When Terry's car turned into Napoleon Avenue she followed, toward the ferry, and reached the landing just in time to see the boat leave the slip. That was, as nearly as she could reckon, about one o'clock on the day Quentin Ulman was killed."

For a moment Wade stood looking into the professor's dark, sardonic face. Gonzales went on. "She gave Terry time to regain his reason. When he did—" Gonzales broke off, and there was a slight trace of emotion in his voice. "Before you go, Mr. Wade, I want to offer you any assistance in my power, and I want to tell you why. The murder of Quentin Ulman could not take on the proportions of a personal tragedy to me. But the death of my wife is an attack upon my house. Good night."

"Thank you," said Wade gently. "You will tell the district attorney what you have just told me?"

"If you think it necessary."

"He will let you know. Good night, then."

He went out, his head lowered in chaotic thought. Only tonight had he suddenly been stricken by the depth of the evil against which he was fighting. He had seen it when he saw the smouldering wreck on the Metairie Road and had found Winifred's little necklace of crystals and topazes, the links half melted, among the ashes. As he drove downtown now a sense of futile exhaustion crept upon him, but he shook it off resolutely, for though it was more than two hours past midnight ,there was someone else he must see. He turned his car into Royal Street and drew up in front of the house where Marie Castillo had her attic.

There was no line of light under the door when he climbed the stairs, but at his first knock the light flashed on and a moment later he heard her turn the key. She stood in the doorway a moment in her bright flowered pajamas, looking at him with frightened bewilderment.

"Wade! What's happened?"

"May I come in?" he asked.

She laughed. "It's hardly respectable, but I suppose I'll have to let you in. Wait till I get something on." She took a kimono from the foot of the bed. "What under heaven is the trouble?" she asked again as he sat down. "I can't afford liquor, or I'd offer you a drink—you look as if you need one."

Wade rested his forehead in his hands, suddenly aching with weariness and defeat. "A drink might help." He raised his head. Marie stood watching him with a troubled face. For a moment he looked at the gay defiance of her cotton pajamas and the cloud of black hair on her shoulders, and he fairly quivered when he remembered what he had come to tell her. "Marie, Winifred has been murdered."

She staggered back as though she had been struck.

"Winifred—oh, tell me—where? Tonight? Was it—was it like Quentin?"

He nodded. For an instant she simply stood there, staring at him, then he went to her and put his hands on her shoulders.

"Sit down, Marie. This is going to be hard as hell, but I've got to do it."

She allowed him to lead her to the sofa. He sat down by her and gave her a cigarette. She inhaled deeply, looking at him with a steadiness that nearly disarmed him. But he forced himself to his question.

"Marie, where were you tonight?"

Evidently she had expected it, for she did not flinch. Slowly she leaned forward and rested her hand on his knee.

"Wade, do you think I killed her?"

"No," he said earnestly, "I don't. But—don't hate me for this—I'm working for the district attorney. I know you disliked her intensely. I came here and asked you to go with me to the ball, and you wouldn't go. I came here again two hours after her body was found, the same sort of smoking wreck we found on the river road Wednesday, and you were not asleep. Don't you understand that I've got to ask you?"

She nodded, looking away from him. Her voice was expressionless as she answered.

"I was here till about ten o'clock. I was reading. But I couldn't read very well. I was all torn up. I didn't sleep more than four or five hours Wednesday night, and I'd worked hard all the afternoon, trying to make myself so tired that I'd be sleepy now. But I couldn't get sleepy. I felt like—oh, if you can't imagine what I felt like there's no use trying to tell you. About ten I went to the movies. I thought if I could watch a picture it might give me something else to think about."

"What theater was it?"

Marie still looked away from him toward the wall. "The State." She reached for another cigarette and smiled ironically. "It was the official picture of the Antarctic expedition, in case you're interested—but of course I might have read that in the newspaper."

"When did you come home?" Wade asked, feeling like a medieval inquisitor.

Marie pushed back her tumble of hair. "About one-thirty."

Wade set his jaw. He somehow found this harder than he had thought it would be.

"The State Theater closes at twelve, Marie. It's not more than a twenty-minute walk from here."

"Yes, I know. But I walked around. The picture hadn't done me any good. I wanted to find somebody—anybody I could talk to. I went by Terry's apartment, but it was dark. I went by the French Market and walked through the coffee stalls, hoping I'd find somebody I knew. But I didn't. So I walked down on Esplanade Avenue."

"Alone?"

She jerked back her head. "Good heavens, I'm no ingenue. I've gotten up at three in the morning and walked to Charity Hospital when I wanted to see an interesting case—dozens of times." Suddenly she turned to face him with a look that was at once a plea and a challenge. "I know how hopeless all this is! But for some reason I did think you'd believe in me. You—you've been so decent all through this—oh, for God's sake, don't sit there looking as if you already saw handcuffs on me! I can't stand it!"

She sprang up and took a step away from him. He caught her hands and forced her gently back to the sofa.

"Marie," he said, "you don't think I'm enjoying this, do you? But if I don't get it over now it will be the district attorney's office in the morning—and I had to come and have it out tonight. I don't want you dragged into this horror any further than I can help. Can't you understand that?"

He felt her tense muscles slacken. "Thank you," she said in a low voice. "You're being better to me than I deserve—but I know what they're thinking—two persons I hate meet violent deaths in the same week, and I'm either under the palms all by myself at one o'clock in the morning, or else I'm taking the air on a ferry boat. And I suppose the policeman on this beat has orders to keep an eye out and be sure that I don't try to run away tonight, hasn't he?"

"I suppose so," Wade admitted. "But don't you see why I had to come and put you through this?"

"Yes," she said suddenly, "it's because you're kinder than I had any reason to expect." She put her hand on his. "Please—please understand that I know that."

Wade shook his head. "I came for another reason, Marie. There is someone who seems intent on wiping out your immediate circle. The murder of Quentin Ulman was an isolated case that might have had any of a number of reasons that had nothing to do with you. But the murder of Winifred, executed in just the same way, evidently by the same hand, shows that these murders were done with one thought, by a killer who knows the movements of your intimates and who hates them—a killer whose hate is so violent that it demanded not only the deaths of those two but their deaths in a form that did not simply destroy their lives but left their bodies so hideous that the very mention of their names must arouse a shudder. That kind of a hate is what we're fighting. Marie, I'm afraid for you."

Her eyes met his with a gaze so clear and level that he was amazed. "Wade," she said quietly, "I'm not afraid."

"But I am," he insisted. "Marie, what do you know about these murders?"

"Less than you do," she answered. She absently began to make little folds in her kimono. "Wade," she begged, "can't you realize that if there's danger, you're the one to fear it?"

He took both her hands in his and sat a moment looking at her in silence. Then he said, "No, Marie, I can't."

She smiled, and her teeth were startlingly white in her dark ivory face. He saw her throat quiver faintly above the open collar of her pajamas.

"Very well," she said at length. "But I'm afraid for you. Not for myself. Not as long as you believe me."

PART III
FRIDAY

CHAPTER SIXTEEN

AFTER a turbulent conference in the district attorney's office the next morning Wade and Murphy went to see Terry Sheldon. He lived on St. Ann Street, in an apartment that looked over Jackson Square and the ancient gray cathedral of St. Louis, the heart of the French Quarter; and Wade listened with an indefinable sense of paradox to the cadence of the cathedral chimes as Murphy pounded his warlike fists on the door.

Terry opened it. "Here you are," he said dully. "I've been expecting you."

They went in. It was a gay, teasing little place with green and lavender walls on which were hung paintings of the Vieux Carré courtyards and of ladies in various stages of undress. Here and there modernistic bronzes and reproductions of Greek statues cluttered against one another in incongruous comradeship, and an easel and several experimental clay models suggested Terry's own interrupted work. "What a cool place you have!" Wade remarked as they entered and the breeze from the square fanned his face. "Do you work much here?"

"No," said Terry shortly. "I work at the studio on Isle Bonne." He kicked ungraciously at a pencil that lay on the floor. "Why don't you talk about what you came for? I'll tell you anything I can." He was pacing about restlessly, one hand thrust into his pocket and the other rumpling his light disordered hair.

Murphy sat down cautiously in one of Terry's fantastic chairs. "Well, let's understand this, Mr. Sheldon. You tell us you'll do all you can to help us, and we sure hope you will—we think it's about time somebody did. First thing, I want you to tell us why you've been so almighty careful to hide the fact that you were over at the bindery the day Ulman was murdered."

Terry stopped. His free hand jerked at his hair.

"I didn't go near the damned bindery."

"Oh, you didn't, didn't you?" retorted Murphy. "Then I guess there's no sense in us wasting a lot of time here. You'd just better come down and tell that at headquarters?"

Wade shot the policeman a warning look. "Wait a minute, Murphy. Let's talk about this first. Sheldon, exactly where did you go after you left the library Wednesday?"

Terry looked grateful. "Why, I rode around awhile and then went to the studio at Isle Bonne. You have to take the Napoleon ferry to get to Isle Bonne, you know."

"That," said Murphy bluntly, "ain't what you said after the murder, and I think it's only fair now to warn—"

"That whatever I say will be used against me, eh? You needn't remind me. I know it already."

Wade interposed mildly. "Terry, why didn't you tell us when you made your first statement that you'd been down to Isle Bonne that day?"

Terry looked down at the floor. "Oh, I don't know. I suppose it was because I didn't want to own that I'd crossed the river at the crucial time."

Murphy scrutinized him. "So you took the ferry, did you?"

"Yes, about one o'clock."

"Thanks for nothing," Murphy growled.

"How did you go to your studio?" asked Wade. "Why, the regular route," said Terry. He was standing in front of them, and his harassed face had taken the set look of a man who has nerved himself to swallow a bitter dose as fast as possible. "I crossed at the Napoleon ferry and drove directly away from the river—it's State Highway 30, I think—and turned off the road just this side of Lafitte. You ought to know where Isle Bonne is, down there where the three bayous meet."

"Yes, I know. Did you do any work while you were there Wednesday?"

"Just made some clay bases." But Terry had hesitated a fraction of a minute before answering. "I've been pretty busy lately," he hurried on, "working on a statue for the winter exhibit. Classical subject. I like to work, and I was pretty upset by what Prentiss had just told me about the theft of the Bible, and I thought if I worked awhile it might do me good."

Wade nodded abstractedly. Murphy grunted a question.

"Now you might explain your doings of yesterday, young man, and what you were doing in Mrs. Gonzales' parlor last night."

Terry was facing them defiantly. "I went to see Mrs. Gonzales yesterday morning. After I left I came back to this apartment, got some sketches I'd made, took the Napoleon ferry—" he shot a challenging look at Murphy—"and drove down to Isle Bonne. I had an appointment with Mrs. Gonzales at midnight, so I worked down on the island till nearly ten, drove back and got to the Gonzales house about eleven forty-five."

Murphy nodded ponderously. "You're sure you weren't to meet Mrs. Gonzales some place besides her house? Sure you weren't to meet her some place on the road, you in your car and she in hers, to talk about whatever you had to talk about?"

"I told you where she had said to meet her. At her house."

"You're right sure of that?"

"Certainly." Terry flung out the word angrily.

"Well, now, did you tell anybody you were supposed to meet her at the house?"

"Yes, I told Dr. Prentiss."

"And where did you tell him this?"

"At the library, before I left yesterday afternoon. We were talking about the costume Mrs. Gonzales was to wear last night. I had just returned it to him."

"Who was in the library and could hear what you were telling him?"

"Nobody but Marie and Dancy."

"We'll see them," Murphy mumbled, scrawling in his notebook.

"Tell us how it happened, Terry," Wade suggested.

Terry answered without hesitation. "Well, Winifred was to be in the pageant. In the Oriental wing of the library Dr. Prentiss has a collection of garments and knives and screens and such stuff that he brought with him from China three years ago. Some of the things are very fine, and he's been generous about lending me something now and then to use as a model. I'd borrowed this robe Winifred wanted about a week ago—I was thinking of doing a sort of fantastic study of a scene from Marco Polo. Dr. Prentiss had promised the robe to Winifred for the pageant, but all this mess had gotten me so unnerved I forgot all about the blamed thing till Marie came by yesterday morning—said Prentiss had called her and asked her to get the robe and bring it when she went to the library. Yesterday afternoon on my way to the Napoleon ferry I dropped in at the library to ask if I could borrow the suit again after Winifred was done with it. I told Prentiss I was going to see Winifred last night after the pageant and that if it was all right with him I'd like to get her to give it to me then. He said it was o.k."

"You didn't mention what it was you were going to see her about?" Wade asked.

"Yes, I did. Marie asked me, 'Since when did you and Winifred get so clubby?' and I said Winifred had some idiotic tale she was going to take to the police and I had to find out what it was. You see—oh, I guess you know it already—I got lousy drunk up there yesterday morning, and I didn't remember just what either of us had said."

Murphy was rocking dangerously back on the hind legs of his chair. "That's a mighty pretty story, Mr. Sheldon, mighty pretty. You and Mrs. Gonzales were regular pals, weren't you? Meeting each other at twelve o'clock at night. Borrowing dresses off each other."

Terry gave him a stormy look. Murphy leveled his chair and sat forward on the edge of it. The room was suddenly quiet.

"So you were great friends. Weren't you now?"

"There was certainly nothing unusual about my going to the Gonzales house," protested Terry. "I've been there a dozen times in the past month."

"Sure you have. Just dropped in any hour of the day or night. I know how it is. Sure. Great friends. Related, in fact."

"We aren't related. My uncle Michael married a cousin of Alfredo's."

"Sure, sure. And under old Mike Sheldon's will you come in for a good slice of money, too, if fate and her many agents that seem so busy these days work out a little problem of succession for you."

Terry glowered wrathfully. He stood quite still.

"If old Dr. Prentiss can't find his Gutenberg Bible to prove it's real he might lose his job, mightn't he?"

Terry did not answer. He stood stiffly, glaring at Murphy, but there was a sudden flash of fear across the desperately controlled impassivity of his face.

"As I understand it, me that don't know much about Gutenberg Bibles and such, Mr. Ulman never did express his opinion, did he? If he'd made up his mind that the Bible was real he got himself killed off before he could tell folks that Prentiss was right. The Bible is all gone. So's a lot of other books. If Dr. Prentiss can't take any better care of things than that, he might get kicked out, mightn't he? And if he gets kicked out you stand to get about three-quarters of a million dollars, don't you?"

Still Terry had not moved.

"I think I understand everything, except one little bit," Murphy proceeded. "As you've said you want to help us all you can, I know you won't mind telling us about it."

Terry's jaw was set. "What do you want to know?" he demanded thickly.

"Well, if you don't mind confiding in an ordinary cop like myself, I'd like to know what you think Mrs. Gonzales meant by saying you murdered Quentin Ulman."

Terry took a step nearer. His whole body seemed to dilate with rage.

"She was lying. You know she was lying. You can't hang that on me."

"Well, young fellow, I'm going to try to hang it on you. Or you on it." Murphy pointed a threatening finger. "I think I've got you cold, Sheldon. All I want is an excuse to arrest you. You'll save yourself a lot of trouble by telling the truth. We know that Mrs. Gonzales thought you killed Ulman. We know she was going to tell that story to the police this morning. We know you took the Napoleon ferry and were on the other side of the river when Ulman was killed. And within forty-eight hours we'll know the rest of this pretty little puzzle and if there's anything you can say or do to help yourself you'd damn well better do it and do it quick."

Murphy got up. "Mr. Wade, you stay here with this young fellow and talk it over with him. I'm twenty years a policeman and I've never seen anybody yet that held out information on a crime of this sort that didn't hold it out to protect himself.'"

He went out. They heard him clattering down the steps. Terry stood rigid, looking at the door.

Wade took a peep at his wrist watch and smiled at Murphy's dramatic exit, recalling that at two o'clock the captain was due to go over the effects of Winifred Gonzales. It was now ten minutes of two. After a pause Wade rose and went over to Terry.

"Terry," he said to him, "I don't want to talk to you unless you want to talk to me. I let Murphy howl at you without interrupting him because I wanted you to see how the police work when they start, and what you'll be letting yourself in for if you aren't careful."

Terry looked squarely at him. "Lord," he said, "it's horrible!"

"It is. Now sit down. I'm going to talk to you, but you don't have to answer."

Terry seemed to appreciate Wade's manner. He allowed himself to be led to a chair. Wade sat by him and went on.

"I'm not a cop, Terry, and I can't seem to get a cop's psychology. But I warn you that if you're arrested what Murphy gave you a minute ago will seem like a Sunday School picnic."

Terry dropped his head in his hands and looked at the floor.

"Murphy wants action," Wade went on, "and so does Farrell. So does the public. In the *Creole* office this morning the city editor told me that unless something happens pretty soon there's going to be plenty of panic in town. Now frankly, I do think you're holding back on us. If you're shielding somebody else, you're foolish. If you've got anything to say, this might be as good a time as any to say it." He spoke persuasively. Terry lifted his head.

"Why couldn't Prentiss have sold his own books and killed Ulman so he could lay the theft on him?"

Wade stretched out his long legs and looked narrowly at Terry.

"On the face of it, that's a reasonable theory. I've, thought of it myself. But it won't work. Prentiss is a literary miser; books are the only things on earth he wants, and as long as he is custodian of the Sheldon Library the collection is virtually his. His judgment of books is his only vulnerable spot; the reason for his dislike of Gonzales is that Gonzales attacks him there. He doesn't need money for his personal affairs—his income is amply large, and if he had more money he'd simply spend it on books. It's foolish to suggest he'd sell his treasures. No, Terry, that won't go."

Terry clenched his hands on his knees. His face wore a puzzling expression of impatience and fear.

"Terry," said Wade, "why do you want to pin this affair to Prentiss?"

Terry shifted his eyes uneasily.

"What do you mean?"

"I can tell when dust is being thrown in my eyes."

"You told me if I had anything to say I should say it."

Wade looked at Terry—his lowered eyes, the dejected droop of his shoulders, the lines of weariness on his face. "Terry," he said firmly, "do you know who did this murder?"

Terry did not move.

"What you said," Wade went on, "is not what you're thinking. Whatever it was that inspired the murders of Ulman and Mrs. Gonzales, it's possible that there are others who stand in the way of the murderer's purpose. The creature who could perpetrate two crimes like these would not hesitate if it seemed advantageous to commit another. Don't you understand why I want you to speak?"

Terry suddenly sat up and faced him. "Wade," he said tensely, "I don't know who did it. And I won't speak until I do. Why don't you get out?"

Wade was silent. Terry went on desperately. "Look, Wade. I didn't get to sleep till seven o'clock this morning. I'd struggled over this terrible business all night. I understand my position, and I think I understand Murphy's. But—I've got a glimmer of an idea on these killings and you can help me. Hold off Murphy and Farrell for forty-eight hours. Give me a chance to do a little investigating of my own." He spoke with fierce earnestness. "I've been foolish, and I can't tell you now everything that I possibly should tell you, but for God's sake give me time to think this through. I know what everybody's thinking. I know how it looks for me. But I want to go down to Isle Bonne today. Today's Friday. If I can't offer you a solution by Sunday you let Murphy go ahead and do his damnedest."

It was a challenge. He looked squarely at Wade and waited for his answer.

Wade put his hand on the arm of Terry's chair. "You won't say more than that?" he asked.

"I can't, Wade. I can't." Terry sprang up and walked to the end of the room and back again. "I won't suggest who might have done this thing until I'm sure. Maybe I can explain what I mean." He sat down and talked rapidly. "I think with my hands, Wade. When I'm working in clay or marble or any other medium, my hands do not only the work but the thinking. Sometimes when I've been working with what seems like the intensest concentration, I discover suddenly that I've put something there that I didn't intend to at all—a change of line or adaptation of color that alters the whole tone of the statue or the picture, put there by my hands without the conscious direction of my brain. Don't you understand?—it's an experience common to all persons who realize their medium through their hands. Do you do touch typewriting?"

"Yes, I always have." Wade was listening with interest.

"Can you tell me in what order the letters come on the keyboard?"

Mechanically Wade's fingers felt along his knees. "A-S-D-F-J-K— no, that's wrong; H and G come between the forefingers."

"See!" Terry exclaimed. "You can't see the keyboard in your mind. You can only feel it. Most expert typists can't look at a blank keyboard and find the letters. Their hands know. I've read that highly educated blind persons sometimes develop at their fingertips gray cells that are like those of the brain. It may not be true, but it illustrates what I mean about thinking with the fingers. That's what I do. I can't think with my hands in my lap. Now I went down to Isle Bonne yesterday afternoon and thought with my fingers."

"Go on. What did you find?"

"I can't tell you." He shook his head. "I thought I'd found it yesterday. When I came here from Gonzales' house last night I paced the floor, trying to capture what it was. I think I've got it. But I can't tell. It's too dreadful, as long as I'm not sure." His voice carried an impassioned eagerness. "I've been working on a statue for the winter exhibit—it represents a mythological character."

"Yes. What else?"

"I wanted it to be beautiful, to be better than anything I've ever done. I've studied the background for months. It's a fearful subject, horrible almost as the Laocoon, and it has the possibility of representing, as that does, the acme of tragedy, the utmost horror of physical and spiritual suffering. And Wade, my hands were thinking—and suddenly, as I worked, they thought of something so hideous, something so unutterably and incredibly evil—Wade, I can't say it now. It can't be said unless I *know*."

Wade had listened avidly. Terry's sincerity seemed obvious, and it had caught Wade with an impelling power. "And you won't, you simply won't, tell me what you suspect, Terry?"

"No!" The word was like a bang. "You can arrest me if you want to. But I won't say what I think is true till I know it. Suppose you had known and liked somebody—and then suddenly you got a glimpse of such brutality as would have shocked the Indians in the days of scalping? You couldn't speak until you were certain. In God's name give me two days, and if I can't tell you something Sunday you can go ahead."

Wade spoke slowly. "Suppose the murderer should strike again while I waited?"

"I don't think so. I think there were two murders planned and two executed. There's no reason for any others."

"Have you told anybody else you had a theory?"

"No. I don't want it known. Just say I'm down at Isle Bonne working on my statue."

"What does your statue represent, Terry?"

"I haven't told anybody that either. The statue gave me my theory." He shuddered. "Wade, it's the most atrocious conception that ever warped my mind. To think that somebody I've talked to—and shaken hands with—and liked—will you give me two days?"

"Yes," said Wade suddenly. He stood up. "Terry, come down to the district attorney's office and make a statement of where you were last night. I'll tell him to give you the time you want. You have a phone at the studio?"

"Yes." Terry went to the door with him. "I'll get a shave and come down. It's mighty good of you, Wade."

"That's all right." Wade opened the door and turned back. "Terry, you won't give me any idea of your theory—something that doesn't give away the person you suspect? Won't you let me put my wits on it too?"

"Maybe if I did you'd prove me wrong," Terry returned with a bitter smile. "I wish you would."

They walked together to the head of the stairs. "I'll be down to see Farrell in an hour or so," said Terry. Suddenly he put his hand on Wade's arm. "Wade," he said, "did you ever read Euripides?"

"*What?*" Wade stopped short. But Terry was already re-entering his own apartment. The key turned in the lock.

CHAPTER SEVENTEEN

IN THE anteroom before the district attorney's office Wade encountered an impudent gathering of reporters, lounging over the table and chairs with the boredom of their trade. He grinned upon them.

"What's new, fellows?"

"Try and find out," retorted Kennedy of *The Telegram*. "Gee, if you don't know how do you expect us to? Aren't you supposed to be the bright little newsmaker?"

"Say, Sherlock," put in McFee of *The Star*, "they're two up on you now. Why don't you quit this detective job and come back to the fold before Nero turns up with his fiddle?"

"Suppress yourself," said Wade genially, helping himself to a cigarette. "What are you guys doing here anyway?"

Churchill of *The Clarion* made a face at the closed office door. "Waiting for a statement! Lord, how the trade's going to pot! In my young days we'd have busted in the door and collared the d.a. and there'd have been plenty of action. Now look at us! Sitting around like we're waiting for the dentist."

Kennedy sidled up with an air of mock confidence. "Sure enough, Wade, do you know anything?"

Wade drew up his loose-jointed person and answered ponderously.

"Gentlemen, I have nothing to say."

"Except," finished McFee with a bow, "that you used to be a newspaper man yourself and you know what we boys are up against. Whew!"

Wade turned toward the door. "Farrell inside?"

"Yeah. Waiting for you so he can put out that statement."

Wade was about to open the door when up from nowhere bobbed the chimpanzee figure of Wiggins the photographer. "Say, Wade!" He confronted Wade and stood on tiptoe to peer into his face. "Honest, who burnt up the lady?"

"I don't know, half-pint, and if I did I shouldn't be standing here talking about it. Who sent you here anyway?"

"Koppel said there might be a chance for some art." Wiggins reached up and grabbed a lapel of Wade's coat. "I think—" his voice lowered sepulchrally—"I think it was the old librarian with the face like a duke because he was the only one she hadn't been cheating with and he got jealous because he was left out. Now you listen to my theory—I been thinking about this all morning and I think that these old codgers who act like they hate women always have complexes and suppressed desires lying around somewhere so they—"

"Look here, mosquito. You stick around and look for pictures. I've got work to do, see? Inside. Where you aren't allowed." He waved over his shoulder and went into the office. Farrell sat behind the desk, the telephone receiver at his ear. Before him a collection of typewritten statements littered the desk-top. He glanced up, nodded to Wade, mumbled "Chief of police—report," and turned back to the phone.

"All right, chief. I'll tell Murphy about it. See you after I've had a chance to look through these reports. Gonzales and Prentiss and the girl will be down in a minute or two to sign the statements. Dancy's phone doesn't answer. And listen. I'll need three men assigned to this office to work under me for the next couple of days. Want to put a tail on some people." He hung up and swung around.

Wade, who had hunched his unwieldy length over a chair at the back of the office, got up and came to the desk. "Who're the shadows going to play tag with?" Farrell grinned. "They aren't exactly shadows. But I don't want to leave any of these people without—er—protection."

"Bright idea."

"So I've ordered a man each to cover Prentiss, Dancy and Gonzales. I'd like to keep the girl covered too but I don't precisely relish the idea of sticking a cop into her apartment—she might think we were presuming too far. I could send her a police matron."

Wade leaned across the desk. "See here, Farrell. She's all right. I saw her last night."

"Where'd you find her?"

"At her apartment."

Farrell shook his head doubtfully. "Wade, I'm not sure about her. A couple of men from headquarters went by her place as soon as we'd gotten word of what happened last night. She wasn't there. They left word with the man on the beat to watch the house, and he called a little before two to say she had come in alone. His report this morning says she didn't go out again. What's her alibi?"

"She hasn't any." Wade began to walk uneasily. "But for heaven's sake, Farrell, let her alone."

"Don't be a fool, Wade. I'm not trying to pin murder on anybody, but she's the only one of the bunch who's confessed to a pretty strong motive for both these holocausts and who has had a good chance to do them both. Oh, sit down, damn you!"

Wade acquiesced drearily, noticing the tired lines in Farrell's face. Farrell was speaking with more sympathy than sternness. "I've spent two hours with the coroner and the automobile expert from headquarters. This thing last night wasn't an accident. It was murder, Wade—and that means hell's loose in town." He looked at Wade with weary earnestness. "We can't get mushy because Marie Castillo is young and a girl."

Wade was sitting with his head in his hands. "I know. But she didn't do it. And she's stood about all she can."

"So," retorted Farrell, "have I." He smiled ruefully. "But we're not through, son. What happened when you went to see Terry?"

Wade lurched his chair further forward and leaned his elbows on the desk. "Well, I had quite a talk with him after Murphy left to go through Mrs. Gonzales' bureau. Terry's in a bad spot and knows it. But I've got something to tell you—if I were you I'd delay his arrest for awhile."

"Isn't that a bit dangerous?"

"You mean from the standpoint of policy?"

"I mean from the standpoint of murder. But tell me what happened."

Slowly and with considerable detail, Wade described the interview he had just ended. "Honestly, Farrell," he concluded, "the boy looked sincere. I think he's got a clue. I've talked with too many crooks in my time not to have a fair idea of when a man means what he says, and either Terry is simply screwing up his courage to confess, or he has an idea of what's behind this. I don't think he's seriously involved."

"Well, I've just gone over all the reports the men made last night." Farrell pushed at the jumble of papers in front of him. "Terry takes a prominent place."

"Prominent enough to convict him?" Wade asked pointedly.

"No." Farrell was discouraged.

"That's one of the main reasons I'm for giving him his two days off. Does anything at all show in last night's investigation?"

"Prentiss and Gonzales were both at the party—dozens of witnesses to attest that they didn't leave the ballroom after Mrs. Gonzales went out. Dancy was at home in bed when our man got there about one o'clock; says he'd been there all evening. Marie seems to be your part of the story. What did she tell you when you saw her?'"

"That she'd been out walking," said Wade grimly. "Alone."

"Hm. Just another of those solitary souls who does things by herself and so makes murder interesting."

"Anyhow," insisted Wade, "I believe her."

But Farrell was not convinced. "Headquarters checked all the places that rent cars," he went on, "and couldn't discover that she'd had one out last night, or Dancy either. The man on the beat says he didn't see Marie at all till she came in about one-thirty. He knows her pretty well—seems she makes a habit of chatting with policemen and the garbage man and people like that. I *would* like to know what she was doing last night." There was a knock and Farrell's secretary put in her head. "Miss Marie Castillo and Mr. Gonzales are here to sign their statements, Mr. Farrell."

"Bring them in." Farrell lumbered wearily to his feet. Marie and Alfredo came in and Wade drew up chairs for them.

Gonzales was evidently holding a desperate leash on his self-control. He sat down stiffly, keeping his eyes fixed on Farrell, as if he was welcoming this chance to assist the state in wreaking its penalty on the murderer of his wife. Marie turned an apprehensive look at the district attorney and then at Wade. He smiled at her reassuringly, but before he had time to speak Dr. Prentiss was shown in. The librarian gave a curt nod toward the desk and then, before he took the chair Wade had proffered, he shook hands with Gonzales, as though offering a gesture of silent sympathy toward his old antagonist. Prentiss' face was worn and tired, and in spite of his distant courtesy it was easy to see that as on his first interview he resented the American legal system as a colossal mistake of human understanding. Of the three, he was the only one who appeared ill at ease when he sat down.

As eager as they to have the interview over, Farrell began without preliminary.

"I shan't keep you long. If any of you knows a single fact that might assist this investigation I wish you'd tell me at once, for last night should convince you that there is no time to stall. This fiend may be planning to strike again. Frankly, I'm worried for your safety, and I am going to detail one of my men to act as a bodyguard for each of you, beginning today."

Marie and Prentiss did not speak; Gonzales gave a slight shrug. "My house, Mr. Farrell, is overrun with detectives now. I hardly think that one more or less will make any appreciable difference."

"The routine of an investigation, professor," said Farrell considerately, "is not pleasant, but it is very necessary. I am sorry, but we must go over your wife's personal effects. It is just possible that we may find a clue there."

Gonzales bowed. "Forgive me," he returned with a trace of unctuousness. "I know. In my present state of mind, however—" he made a hopeless gesture.

Wade had been watching Marie. She had sat with an expressionless face, looking ahead of her; the professor's words seemed to affect her curiously. She gave him a strange look, compassionate, but conveying something else that Wade could not define. She moved restlessly and lit a cigarette as Farrell answered.

"I know it's hard, Mr. Gonzales. Most people don't realize that the process of enforcing the law is unpleasant even for those of us who have to do it." He paused and pushed a stray lock of hair off his forehead. He was tired; his own apparent helplessness before the fury of his hidden challenger had told heavily on his spirits. But he continued briskly. "I have the statements Dr. Prentiss and Mr. Gonzales made last night to men from headquarters." He pressed a button. "Will you give Mr. Gonzales a copy of his statement?" he said to his secretary when she entered. "If it is not correct, professor, make any changes you like, and then sign the completed document."

Gonzales rose, bowed slightly toward the others, and followed the secretary out of the office. Farrell spoke to the librarian.

"Dr. Prentiss, I have a man who will report to you at the library at four o'clock this afternoon. I want him to stay there. If you will step outside my secretary will give you a copy of your last night's statement."

Prentiss stood up, an effortful smile on his harassed face. "Very well, Mr. Farrell. I'll try to make your man comfortable."

"Just a minute before you go," Wade interjected. "Have you seen Dancy this morning?"

"Mr. Dancy? No."

"We'd like to talk to him," Wade explained. "He's not at home, and we thought he might be due at the library today."

Prentiss shook his head. "He has not been to the library today. The library is closed to the public, of course, as it has been since Mr. Ulman's death; curiosity-seekers have been storming the door, and I shan't open the library again till this dreadful affair is cleared up and the morbid interest has somewhat subsided. Yesterday morning I telephoned Mr. Dancy and Miss Castillo here to ask them to come down for about two hours, for I thought that going over some routine work would be good for all three of us, but as none of us was in any mental condition to work I told them both that they need not return unless they were called. I have not seen Mr. Dancy since then. Did you see him last night?"

"Yes," Farrell returned, "one of the men from headquarters saw him at his flat. But we'd like to speak to him again today."

"If he comes to the library I'll tell him to get in touch with you." Prentiss was impatient to be gone; it was evident that he regarded Wade and Farrell as only slightly above the pests at the library door. "Is that all?"

"Just a minute, Dr. Prentiss," said the district attorney sharply. "Our office is not omniscient, and it is possible that there are some details of these two crimes that we've overlooked. Is there no suggestion you can make?"

The doctor hesitated an instant, standing halfway between the desk and the door, then he turned and faced Farrell as though finally determined to say what he thought.

"I have no suggestion to make," he responded acidly, "to an investigator who employs the bullying tactics that you have exercised on this young lady. I shall see to it that persons of influence in the city will have my views that you have bungled this thing execrably, so far as to let this maniac commit a second murder almost under your very eyes."

Marie had started indignantly, as if she did not entirely appreciate being defended by white-haired old gentlemen. Wade answered with a patience that he did not feel.

"There was no way to foresee the second murder, Dr. Prentiss."

"Permit me to disagree with you, Mr. Wade. Murder is the most elemental form of elimination known to the human race. It sometimes happens that two people share some secret that provides the murderer's motives, and in a case of this kind you might have taken into consideration that if the murderer thought his secret in danger he would not hesitate to strike again."

Farrell was scowling, but Wade had kept his habitual impudence. "Of course, Dr. Prentiss," he suggested, "this is all hindsight."

Prentiss shrugged. "No more so than your now providing bodyguards for the rest of us. That step might with elementary logic have been taken yesterday. The history of crime is full of mass murders." Prentiss spoke with polite sarcasm. It was plain that he considered all police officialdom of the same generic type as traffic cops.

"I have found," said Farrell quietly, "that the history and practise of criminal deduction are far removed, Dr. Prentiss."

Marie was drawing nervously at her half-smoked cigarette. Her eyes were on Prentiss as he answered.

"The history of criminal deduction, Mr. Farrell, is merely the record of its practise. Despite the methods employed in these two tragedies, it is quite obvious that the murderer was not concerned about hiding the identity of his victims. If the convenient cigarette case of Mr. Ulman's did not convince you of that, certainly the circumstances under which Mrs. Gonzales met her death should do so. If the bodies were not burned with the purpose of concealing the identity of the persons killed, it seems as if the murderer simply wanted to make them both a hideous memory."

He turned toward the door again. "A sound observation," Wade commented languidly.

His hand on the doorknob, Prentiss spoke over his shoulder.

"Probably," he ended, "you will find when you get the scoundrel who took the Gutenberg Bible fragment that you have your murderer. May I ask with all respect if the loss of the Gutenberg has been entirely overlooked in this most exciting man-hunt? Pardon me if I am unduly disturbed. Is that all?"

"Yes," said Farrell with ill-concealed impatience. "You may sign your statement in the outer office."

Prentiss went out, and Wade and Farrell were left alone with Marie Castillo. She looked at them with a touch of defiance as Farrell spoke.

"Miss Castillo, Detective Ferguson reports that you were not at your apartment at one o'clock this morning. Mr. Wade tells me you had returned by two-thirty when he went to see you."

"Yes," she replied quietly. "I had been out alone."

"Walking, Mr. Wade tells me."

Marie's eyes narrowed. "I didn't kill Winifred, Mr. Farrell."

"We aren't trying to prove you did," Farrell said to her. "But we do want to give you a chance to prove that you did not."

"I can't prove it." Marie went to the desk and stood facing them. "I can't prove anything, Mr. Farrell. I went to the movies last night, then I walked around the Quarter—that's all I can tell you. And if you want to arrest me, there's nothing I can do about it."

"Marie," said Wade earnestly, "Mr. Farrell doesn't want to arrest you. Nobody does. But he knows how little legal value an unsupported alibi has."

"Oh, I know it," she exclaimed desperately. "I know it's high time somebody was arrested in this case. I did hate Quentin and I despised Winifred, and I think there'll be more peace in the world now that they're out of it—but I didn't kill them!"

Wade stood up and put his hand on her arm. "Marie, is that why you're trying to shield the person who did?" She drew back and as her eyes met his he was suddenly sure that she was harboring something—if not knowledge, at least a suspicion that was torturing her and yet which nothing could wrench from her. But she did not quaver.

"Wade," she said, "I've told you all I can."

Suddenly, as if she had been leaning on a column that had gone limp as paper, Marie crumpled back into her chair, her forehead sunk on her hands. "I've tried to make you understand. I've tried as hard as I can to tell you that I'm not responsible for what has happened, that all I want is to be let alone. But you won't believe me." She lifted her head and smiled as though ashamed of her insurrection. "You see, I haven't as much courage as I thought. I'm sorry—but my nerves are whipped to ribbons."

Farrell waited as Wade went around the desk to her. "I know what it's like," Wade said. "Farrell and I are nearly as frantic over this horror as you. All we want you to do now is to sign a statement saying where you were last night, and then we're going to send a police matron to stay with you, if it will make you feel safer."

She looked up as though grateful for his sympathy. "Thanks, but you needn't. I think I'm going to be with Alfredo. He told me on the way here that he wanted somebody in the house besides the servants—somebody to talk to."

"I'm glad of that," Farrell put in. "It relieves my mind considerably—I'm putting a detective there to protect him."

"May I go now?" she asked.

"Yes, in another minute." Farrell opened the door to the office where his secretary was waiting. "Miss Blake, will you take a statement from Miss Castillo?"

Marie glanced questioningly at Wade and went out. As he closed the door behind her Farrell beckoned to him.

"Wade, I don't like to do it, but unless Terry Sheldon turns up something convincing and unexpected I'm going to turn Murphy loose on that girl."

"If you do," said Wade shortly, "I'll break his neck."

"Listen to me," Farrell exclaimed. "She could talk and you agree with me though you won't own it. For heaven's sake, Wade, come to your senses. I don't like to howl at her or to think of Murphy's doing it, but we're confronted with two of the most atrocious murders of my experience and you want me to sit still because you admire the shape of Marie's ankles. Well, this is my job and I won't."

Wade's hands, buried in his coat pockets, clenched tight.

"Farrell, she didn't do these murders."

"All right, who did? Gonzales and Prentiss have alibis. Dancy hadn't the ghost of a motive for either, so far as I know. It looked like Terry, and you tell me Terry's persuaded you of his own wronged innocence." Farrell stood up and glared savagely. "In God's name, do you want me to believe it was Wiggins?"

Wade stared at the desk in tired helplessness. He saw Farrell's argument with a clarity mocking his own sureness that Marie had not lied. But Farrell was a lawyer looking for evidence, and Wade knew he had none to give.

"I'm sorry for her too," Farrell added at length. "But I've talked to the coroner, Murphy and everybody else who's working on the case, and they all agree with me." Wade set his jaw as he turned to the door. "Well, you see before you the shouting minority. I don't." Banging the door behind him, he went into the outer office where Marie sat by the desk while the secretary typed the statement she had just made. He waited till she had signed her name.

"Do you want me to take you home?" he asked.

"Thank you, no. Alfred is waiting for me downstairs. He has the— the other car." She shuddered. As they walked away from the office she looked up suddenly. "Wade—will you tell the district attorney that I could hardly have walked out the Metairie Road last night, and that I don't know how to drive a car?"

"You don't?" he exclaimed. "I'm glad you told me, Marie; that does help."

She smiled with swift gratitude. "Wade, you do believe me, don't you?"

They had reached the elevator gate. He looked down at her with deep sincerity. "Marie," he answered, "I told you last night I believed you. I believe you still. But I can't give you useless encouragement. The district attorney doesn't believe you. If there is anything you can tell me that would help me to prove to him you are clear of all this, in God's name won't you tell me now?"

"Wade," she returned in a low voice, "I don't know anything. You have as much reason for suspicion as I have. And I'm not going to voice any suspicions that aren't based on facts—because I won't make anybody else experience the hell I've been through in these three days. That's all. Goodby—and thank you for being such a peach."

When the elevator had taken her down he stood gazing at the cage for ten minutes before he remembered that he must leave too, since his office was waiting for his report. After a hasty lunch at a pie-counter he made his way to the city room of *The Creole*. Koppel required placating; like the rest of the public he was itching for action, and Wade exasperatedly repeated to him that there was none to be had. He had plumped himself down before his typewriter to pound out a story when Koppel shouted for him.

"Wade! O'Malley's on the wire. I sent him out with Murphy. Swell new lead on the Bible story. Murphy just turned over a lot of Prentiss' lost books stuck under some pink silk doodads in Mrs. Gonzales' wardrobe."

"Lord!" Wade grabbed the phone. "Yeah, O'Malley?" His right hand fumbled eagerly for a pencil and a sheaf of copy paper on the desk. O'Malley's excited voice clicked over the wire.

"Seven books, I think—tucked off in the bottom of the wardrobe in her bedroom—hidden under a lot of lace and things—you know the things women wear under their clothes—"

"Yes! Go on—what books?"

"Murphy got Prentiss on the wire and the old man is prancing all over the library—they won't let him come to the Gonzales house—say the books will have to go to headquarters—evidence—"

Wade's right hand was scribbling wild hieroglyphics. "Yes?"

"A volume of French lyrics—sixteenth century—arms of Jacques August de Thou on the cover—"

"Spell it." Wade scribbled frantically. O'Malley ran down the list of books found. "That's all?" Wade demanded shakily. "Lord, O'Malley, that's not all! What about the Gutenberg fragment?"

He listened; his jaw dropped; and then, at the head of the mad scrawl on the copy paper he wrote in staring letters,

"NO BIBLE."

PART IV
SATURDAY

CHAPTER EIGHTEEN

SAUNTERING into the *Creole* office at half-past ten Saturday morning, Wade found O'Malley scribbling a note for him. "What's the bad news?" he inquired.

"So here you are at last!" O'Malley tossed the note into the wastebasket.

"At last? Tripe. Oh, poor suffering tripe! Me that's supposed to arrive at two P.M.! Until I started being a detective, young man, I wasn't out of my little white bed at this unearthly hour twice a year. At last? Me that was up half the night reading Euripides."

"Euripides?" O'Malley's face went blank with amazement. "Since when did detectives go in for Greek drama?"

"Oh, lately. Good for insomnia. But what's on your mind?"

"Phone call. Dancy has been ringing you since half-past eight."

"My God, what does he think I am? Did he say what he wanted?"

"Just said he had to talk to you."

Wade heaved a sigh. "Give me his number. Did Farrell finally get hold of him?"

"Yes, they nabbed him when he came home last night. He was all surprised and bothered, protested that he really had no idea, don't you know, that he was wanted—had been strolling about town all day on some innocent private business. Repeated his story of having gone to the movies with another fellow the night of the murder, home about ten and so to bed, where the headquarters man found him. The movie part checks, but of course he can't prove how long he'd been asleep."

"I'll give him a ring." Wade lowered himself into the chair behind his typewriter and reached for his phone. The city room was strangely quiet; to Wade, whose working day was normally from two till ten and who rarely saw his office at this hour, it was uncannily quiet and effeminately clean. The floor was bare of papers and cigarette ends, the desks were dusted, with the typewriters neatly put away underneath; the wastebaskets stood properly on end, the files were shut, and the stacks of copy paper stood rigid, with bristling corners. O'Malley strolled aimlessly about, stopping now and then to experiment with setting the fans at various speeds; the morning city editor, his collar and tie in place, was checking over the first edition of an evening paper, and a yawning copy boy ate peanuts in a corner. Otherwise the room was empty. Wade disgustedly dialed Dancy's number, reflecting meanwhile on the asininity of people who call morning newspaper offices before noon.

Dancy's voice, sharpened with eagerness, answered him. "Are you there?" asked Wade, with a wink at O'Malley. "This is Wade of *The Creole*."

"Hello, Wade!" Dancy sounded as if his relief had almost made him forget that his grandmother came from Devonshire. "I want to see you as soon as possible. Will it be convenient this morning?"

"Sure, I'll come down. You want me to come to your place?"

"Right."

"Be there in a couple of minutes. Important, you say?"

"Quite important, Wade."

"About the murders?"

"Exactly."

"All right. See you soon." Wade hung up and stretched himself joyfully. Maybe now things were going to happen. He wondered what it was that Dancy had to spill. Of course, it was impossible to tell what sort of news might seem important to Dancy, but at least it looked hopeful when Dancy was so eager that his accent moved all the way from Devonshire to Texas without his being aware of it. Wade went down to his car in high good temper.

His knock was answered with such alacrity that he suspected Dancy of having sat just inside the door to wait. Dancy was sleek and smooth as to grooming, and his rooms were so unutterably neat that Wade automatically looked at his own shoes for dust, but Dancy's manner belied his appearance and his apartment as well. He was fairly jumping with nervousness.

"Come in, Wade. I'm sorry to have troubled you."

"No trouble." Wade followed him into the little parlor, where the detective detailed to guard Dancy was smoking in a corner. He stood up inquiringly as they entered.

"If you don't mind," began Dancy with politeness that tried to be airy and wasn't, "I'd like to talk to Mr. Wade privately."

"I'm supposed to stay, mister."

"It's all right," Wade assured him. "You take a walk around the block and wait downstairs till we're done. I can look out for Mr. Dancy's safety meanwhile."

The detective departed and Wade stretched his length on a sofa. Dancy placed himself neatly in a chair opposite. "There is something," he began, flicking a speck off his knee, "that I really think you ought to know."

"Righto," said Wade, with an air that was much better than Dancy's for the moment.

But Dancy, though struggling up from Texas, was still too uneasy to do it well. "What I have to say," he began lamely, "is of such a nature that I—I hardly like the thought of saying it in an office full of people."

"Certainly. I understand," Wade prodded stoically.

"I don't think you do, Wade. It's really a sort of confession."

"Yes? What have you been doing?"

Dancy fidgeted. "You see," he parried, "it isn't entirely my affair, and for that reason I've said nothing about it so far."

Wade nodded encouragingly.

"And I thought—you see, it seemed that the other person involved should be the one to tell you—" Dancy hesitated.

"But he didn't," prompted Wade, feeling a strong need for a pitchfork.

Dancy lounged back in his chair, his eyes roving with elaborate nonchalance. Then he turned back to Wade with vague concern.

"I want you to know first that I feel like a rotter for not having said anything about it sooner."

Wade smothered what he felt like saying and answered patiently.

"I understand. It takes some thought to decide these things."

"You're damn right it does." Then Dancy plunged. "It's about the Gutenberg Bible."

Wade set his teeth for endurance. It was with an effort that he forced himself to remember that there had been nine leaves of a Gutenberg Bible, the loss of which had seemed important before the murders. He waited in silence for Dancy's explanation, while that ordinarily lackadaisical young gentleman, having nerved himself to talk, sat on the edge of his chair buzzing with excitement.

"I really don't know where to begin." By now Dancy's eyes were fairly popping with the sense of the spotlight.

"Just tell it in your own way," Wade urged with a gentleness that hid his consuming desire to administer a spank.

"Well," said Mr. Dancy, "it all started about ten days ago. We were in the library."

"We? That includes—?"

"Oh, Prentiss and myself and Marie Castillo."

"Yes. Go on."

"Wait before I go a bit further, Wade. If I tell you everything I know, you will guarantee that I won't be prosecuted?"

"Why—I don't know." Wade felt an insane desire to giggle. "Suppose we have the district attorney up here."

"I'd rather we didn't!" Dancy protested. He reached for his suavity. "You never can tell what attitude these professional jobbies might take—that's why I called you. All I want, Wade," he proceeded confidentially, "is your assurance that you'll give me—the breaks, I think they call it."

Wade sighed and managed to compose his face. "Well, it's customary in cases of this kind, that if the person guilty of a misdemeanor gives the state evidence affecting a major crime the misdemeanor is palliated by the service rendered the prosecution." He drew another long breath. "But I should worry about that. The worst you can expect is to be summoned as a witness, and of course you would have to testify."

"Yes, but—well, I've already given assistance to the prosecution, you know."

"Indeed?"

"Oh, yes." Dancy nodded with huge satisfaction. "I picked up that little mash-note from Quentin to Marie and left it in the office that night when Marie fainted."

"Oh—so you left that note, did you?"

"Why, yes. I thought you ought to have it. Now do you think I should be prosecuted?"

Wade sighed. "I hardly think you could be prosecuted for anything you are going to tell me about the Bible."

"Maybe not, maybe yes," Dancy answered with the swing of his former jauntiness. He edged closer like a man about to fire a fuse. "You see, I stole it—or part of it."

Every muscle in Wade's body seemed to jump in its own particular direction. Nothing but the trained impassivity of his craft kept him in his place, as he managed to respond with a calmness that distinctly disappointed Mr. Dancy, "Did you? How, and why?"

Dancy blinked; Wade deliberately walked across the room and stood by the window. He flung his cigarette over the sill and stood a moment looking at the lop-sided roofs of the Quarter, while he struggled to keep his features immobile. But there was a triumphant chant beating in his brain—*Dancy stole the Bible, Dancy stole the Bible.*

"And now," said Dancy from behind him, "will you prosecute me?"

"If you return the fragment," Wade answered, his eyes still on the roofs, "I'm sure the district attorney will give you a very reasonable hearing."

"Oh, but I haven't got the old thing!" Dancy's voice was almost jubilant. "I never did have it all, don't you know, and I haven't got any of it now."

"Hm," said Wade non-committally, but he turned his back to the window and looked at Dancy, who was plainly enjoying his rôle as a maker of surprises.

"That's what I wanted to tell you about. I didn't take it for myself, you see."

Wade grinned in spite of himself. "I never would have suspected you—never. But tell me what happened."

"Oh, it all started a long time ago. Prentiss doesn't rate my services very highly, but last year he had promised me an increase, and really I could have used an extra tenner every fortnight. He'd never miss it, for the old worm has plenty of money for salaries. He's really quite Scotch about it." Before the footlights now, Dancy was strutting with a satisfaction that eliminated all hope of his being brief. "I took this place at the Sheldon Library because it was a good chance to study rare books under such authorities as Ulman and old Prentiss—I collect a bit myself, you know, only I specialize in the modern writers."

"Suppose," said Wade desperately, "you tell me about the Bible."

"I needed money, of course," Dancy rambled, unperturbed, "and I was still waiting for my raise and rather churlish about Prentiss' not doing the sporting thing, so when a certain person came to the library about ten days ago and offered me a thousand dollars to take out one leaf of the Bible I took him on."

He paused to watch the effect of his story. "So you were paid to take only one leaf?" Wade urged.

"Righto. And that's all I took." Dancy lay back in an attitude of infinite leisure and crossed his legs. "I was to remove one leaf and substitute a forged leaf, so that it would not be missed. The person who asked me to do this swore that in forty-eight hours the original leaf was to be restored, and as the fragment isn't bound there didn't seem to be any danger of desecrating the original pages. I was told that the reason for wanting the leaf out was to make a careful inspection to see whether or not the fragment was genuine, and perhaps if it wasn't, that self-satisfied mogul Prentiss would be dethroned and somebody who really knew about books put in charge of the library."

"Sort of a revolution?" Wade suggested as Dancy paused.

"Quite. Its political complexion was what made me go into it. It seemed rather jolly then to be working for both sides at once."

"The man in the middle, yes. Go on."

"It was easy to justify, for if the fragment was genuine it wouldn't hurt to have one leaf out for forty-eight hours, and if it wasn't genuine certainly it wasn't cricket for old Prentiss to be passing it off—after some consideration, I decided it was my duty."

"Certainly, certainly. Go on."

"So as its return was absolutely guaranteed, and the receiver very responsible, I took the leaf—and the thousand dollars. I still have the money here in the flat." Dancy smiled triumphantly as if demonstrating a hitherto underrated cleverness.

"But how," asked Wade, "did you manage to get away with it?"

"Oh, it was easy. I was given the safe combination." Wade's eyes were thoughtfully on the matting. "When did you take out the leaf?" he asked.

"The day before Ulman was murdered," responded Dancy coolly. "I knew Dr. Prentiss was to go out early that afternoon—he was taking dinner downtown, and so I knew he wouldn't be examining the safe that night."

"Yes. Pretty easy, wasn't it?"

"Stupidly simple," Dancy said modestly. "You see, all one had to remember was that this person had to get the leaf in perfect condition—it would never do to crease it or let it get soiled. My arrangement was five hundred when I promised to do the job and the other five hundred when I delivered the leaf."

Wade drew a long breath and ignored Dancy's thrills at his own audacity. "How did you manage to pull it off so effectively? You were never suspected."

"Oh, I just tackled the safe after Prentiss went upstairs, when nobody else was in the library. I made the substitution and took the leaf I wanted into the reading-room, wrapped it up very carefully, with a piece of cardboard to hold it flat, and slipped it in between the pages of the *London Illustrated News*. When Prentiss came down again and told me I could go, I just carried it right out under his nose. I had brought in the forged leaf the same way. I always read the *London News*, so it wasn't strange that I should be carrying it around."

"Who made the forged leaf?"

"The same person who wanted the leaf out."

Wade ferociously kept his voice calm. "And so you delivered the leaf to—?"

"—to that person, yes," finished Dancy provocatively. "And I got the other five hundred. I came by the flat—I didn't want to deposit the money in the bank because I thought maybe it might leak out and my bank account would be checked."

Wade wearily lit a cigarette and glanced at his watch. "So you gave this person the leaf and that was all?"

"Hardly," said Dancy with teasing lack of emphasis. "You haven't heard half the story."

"Indeed? What else happened?"

Dancy's expression was one of rueful penitence. "I was very well satisfied with myself then—though I don't like to own it now in the light of later events, but I couldn't help thinking I'd gotten my salary increased this year in spite of Prentiss' parsimony."

With an inward writhe Wade looked again at his watch, but he looked up to give Dancy a nod that he hoped was merely interested. "Yes, yes, I see. But suppose you tell me the rest of the Bible story."

"Well, I made the delivery and was promised that if the leaf was false, and if it was found that Prentiss had really been putting a trick over, the new administration would retain me at a better salary."

"The fruits of victory, yes. Then what happened?"

"Well, everything seemed tip-top until the next morning and then you know what happened."

"Yes—Ulman was murdered."

"Right. And the rest of the Bible fragment was gone. You can imagine the funk I was in."

Wade swallowed a groan. "What did you do then?"

"Why of course I went right to the person that had the stolen leaf and we had it out—"

"Yes?"

"What do you think I was told?"

Wade felt goose-pimples of impatience run up his spine. But there was no shortening Mr. Dancy's time in the spotlight. "I haven't the faintest idea."

"I was accused," said Dancy impressively, "of having stolen the whole fragment, and I was told that if I didn't give up the other eight leaves I'd be turned over to the police. I knew that was a bluff, and countered by saying if I was arrested I'd expose the real traitor in the Sheldon camp."

Wade frowned stormily. "Did Dr. Prentiss open the safe after you substituted the forged leaf?"

"Yes, to put back some papers, and I got quite a thrill watching him. He just moved the leaves aside without even looking at them."

"Then the next day, after you were accused of the theft, what did you do?"

"When I intimated that I might go to the police myself, I was offered another thousand dollars to keep quiet. Needless to say, I didn't take it. I was worried—I wanted to get the Bible back, all of it."

"Well," said Wade casually, "after Mrs. Gonzales tried to pay you to keep quiet—"

"Oh, no, Wade, it wasn't Mrs. Gonzales."

"No?"

"No, and I can't tell you who it was just yet."

Wade prayed that his patience might endure for the requisite number of hours. Aloud he said, "Well, and what happened after Mrs. Gonzales' death?"

"Something very strange."

With visions of himself in a padded cell, Wade thrust his hands into his pockets to keep them away from Dancy's jaw. "What was it?" he asked.

"You'd never guess. I have been threatened with murder."

If Dancy had thought to produce an explosion he was gratified. Wade sprang to his feet.

"But this is a serious thing, Dancy! Why didn't you tell me before?"

("Cheers!" he was thinking. "Now maybe I can scare this egg into talking fast.") "You are probably in danger right now, Dancy," he added with delight.

"Rot," said Dancy airily. "I'm all right." He made a wide gesture as though to suggest the soldier who jests in the face of the cannon, and reached for a Virginia cigarette with a British name. "I'm rather a valuable witness now," he went on with a glance that barely missed being coy. "You chaps had better take good care of me."

"You're indispensable," Wade assured him. "Probably, Dancy," he added impressively, "you are going to solve the mystery of the Bible Murders!"

But it was too much to expect that Dancy would be so naive as to show how much he was enjoying all this concern. "I hope not," he said languidly. "It's all too messy. But I suppose I'll have to carry on."

Wade had resumed his seat. "But let's get down to cases. What about this theft?"

Dancy had become very much the witness on the stand, conscious that a crowded courtroom is admiring his poise in a breathless moment. "Yesterday morning at about ten o'clock," he said, "the person who planned the theft phoned and asked me to meet him at ten-thirty. Knowing that it might be a trap, I took this with me." And Mr. Dancy, opening his coat, displayed an automatic in a neat shoulder holster.

Wade bit his tongue. "You were wise to carry a gun, Dancy—you never can tell when it might come in handy."

"My thought exactly," nodded Dancy, with the manner of a man to whom rushing into a dangerous rendezvous is a matter of no moment. "So I went to this meeting and was told that I must tell what had happened to the rest of the Bible fragment. I answered that all I had taken was one leaf. Then the threat was made that if I didn't come clean and dig up the other eight leaves I was going to get my damn neck broken."

Wade made a face, then recollected himself and put his features in order.

"I was enraged, of course. I told this party that I thought perhaps others knew more about where the eight leaves were than I did, and if I couldn't be believed I never should have been trusted in the first place. Then I was told that if I really wanted to do something import- ant I could furnish the other eight leaves at the same price that I got for the first. I realized suddenly what it all meant. I was a common thief. It was rather a shock."

"Naturally. Then what happened?"

"I was given this ultimatum: if I didn't show up with the rest of the fragment in twenty-four hours I'd get myself in a great deal of trouble. My exasperation got the better of me. I slammed the door and walked out." Wade waited a moment, but this seemed to be all. "So that," finished Dancy, "is all that happened. I thought it over and decided I'd talk to you. What do you advise?"

"When did this interview take place?" Wade asked.

"With one interruption of about an hour, it took place from ten-thirty yesterday morning until late in the afternoon."

"So that's where you were yesterday while Mr. Farrell's men were looking for you?"

Dancy nodded.

"What did you do last night?"

"Nothing in particular. There was a bobby waiting for me when I came in, and I went to the district attorney's office and told them where I'd been the night Mrs. Gonzales was killed. Then I came home. That detective has been with me ever since."

"All right." Wade sat up and faced him. "Now suppose you tell me who bribed you to take that Bible leaf."

"Really, Wade, I'd rather not."

"I'm waiting, Dancy."

Dancy's hands expressed a vague protest. "You needn't insist. I can't tell you till I've made a little investigation of my own. It wouldn't be fair, y'know."

Wade's patience snapped. He was on his feet. "You listen to me, you sap. Don't talk to me about investigations. We'll do all the investigating necessary. You tell me who bribed you to steal that Bible leaf."

Dancy's jaw dropped. He squirmed further back into his chair. "Really, Wade, old chap," he exclaimed in an injured voice, "there are no witnesses to what I told you, you know, and my word is as good as yours in court."

But Wade was past placating him. He glared upon Dancy's outraged countenance.

"Dancy, you're a fool and a thief and a sneak. I told you we'd take care of you. All right. I'm going to put you in a safe place where no harm can come to you, and damn it, you're going now." He crossed to the telephone and jerked down the receiver. "I'm going to call police headquarters and after an hour with our friend Captain Murphy you'll probably be glad to tell all you know. Before I make this call there's something I want to remind you of. The theft of that Gutenberg Bible might in the eyes of an indignant grand jury be construed as the action of an accessory before the fact of murder. If the Gutenberg fragment had not been stolen Ulman might be alive today. If you had told this story two days ago Mrs. Gonzales might not have died. And by God, whether or not a grand jury looks at it as an accessory before the act it's a cinch it's an accessory after the act and you by holding out the name of this person stand liable to an indictment for murder!"

Dancy was furiously impassive. "I'll deny everything."

"Swell chance you've got. You're going to the Third Precinct in just a minute and you're going in a patrol wagon. You're going to be the first arrest in the Bible Murders. You're going to have your picture in the papers and five detectives are coming up here to search this flat for that thousand dollars, and everybody's going to believe, no matter what you tell, that you're not telling half you know. Somebody's going to hang for these murders and you'd better be damn careful. You've got one chance. Tell me who bought that leaf."

"You can't arrest me!" Dancy exclaimed angrily. "I'll denounce you—I'll say I never told you a thing—I haven't done anything you can prove!" He stood up defiantly. "You can't arrest me and you can't bluff me. I know my rights and I'll have them."

Wade hung up the receiver and strode over to him. "Is—that—so!" He ripped open Dancy's coat and a button fell off upon the matting. Dancy jerked back but not before Wade had grabbed his automatic from its holster. "All right, Mr. Dancy! You're under arrest for carrying a concealed weapon."

Dancy had put his shaking hand behind him. No longer the good citizen demanding his rights, he was quite plainly scared.

"All right—all right—I'll tell you now—"

"Hurry up, then." Wade took down the telephone receiver again and dialed two letters.

"I'll tell you!" Dancy squawked. "Don't arrest me! I'll tell you—" he ran forward in terror and jerked down the hand that Wade held over the dial—"I'll tell you! It was Terry Sheldon."

CHAPTER NINETEEN

WADE strode up and down the district attorney's office, his head thrust forward between his shoulders. He was raging; his fury shot from him in low, ferocious phrases that lashed at Farrell's ears and moved even the excited prosecutor to admonition.

"Take it easy, son," he urged. "You're really getting somewhere, you know."

"Damn!" muttered Wade.

Farrell smiled tolerantly. "Murphy will have Dancy so rattled that he'll spill everything any minute now."

"To hell with Dancy. I want that guy Sheldon and I want him quick." Wade took another furious turn down the room.

"The man we sent to check the ferry ought to report in a minute or so. Do you think Terry went to Isle Bonne?"

"I don't know where he went. God, when I think how I sat there yesterday like a sawdust doll and let him pump me full of a tale that wouldn't have fooled a sob-sister on her first day at the orphan asylum! Me, that's spent years grinning at crooks, let down by a blubbering artist with tears in his voice! Me, coming back here full of sweetness and light—'I really think he can be trusted, Farrell'—me, sitting there drinking in his lies while that featherbrained Dancy sat in the next room and giggled! And I fell for it! I let him go!"

Wade growled again at the thought of Dancy waiting in the next room while Terry told his story. Farrell made an effort to be cheering. "Well, he can't have gone very far. He didn't leave town till this morning."

"But he's gone—and I was reading a damn Greek play all night while he grinned behind my back! Lord!" Wade jerked his volume of Euripides out of his pocket and hurled it at the wall.

"There's one thing to be taken in our favor," said Farrell thoughtfully. "He can't have meant to go far. His apartment is in good order—he seems to have left most of his clothes."

"Well, we'll know pretty soon how many lies he told. If I don't get to Isle Bonne pretty soon I'm going to be nuts. And if he's not there—Lord, of course he didn't leave till this morning. He took it easy. I was thoroughly fooled—and he strolled around and made all his preparations at leisure. You wait till I find that Sheldon—I'll bring him back on two charges of murder and when Murphy turns loose his third degree I'll sit in the corner and cheer. Ten years I've chased this racket—and the first one to make a fool of me was a sweet-speaking sculptor!"

"Sit down, for heaven's sake!" exclaimed Farrell. "Do you think you're the only one in this office who wants to yell?"

"Oh, I'm sorry." Wade slumped into a chair and wiped his forehead. "But I feel like such an infernal ass!"

"Well, quit braying. We've got some work to do before we get the reports. For the first time we've got what looks like clear motive."

"Motive? It's as clear as plate glass. Listen. Terry Sheldon never did like the idea of his uncle's leaving his money for a library instead of to Terry himself, but there's three-quarters of a million coming to him when Prentiss dies, or when Prentiss is kicked out for incompetence. Terry suspects the Gutenberg fragment is a fake. He thinks he'll steal it and have it examined by competent authorities somewhere. If it's false, Terry can easily bring a charge of incompetence against Prentiss, who has so vociferously declared its authenticity; if it's real, he can bring the charge that Prentiss doesn't take proper care of the books, since the greatest treasure of the library has been stolen, or perhaps he might say that Prentiss found out the thing was a fake and destroyed it. If Prentiss is ousted Terry automatically gets the money. Maybe Terry thinks too that since he can't spend the rest of the six million he'd like his pal Gonzales to be head of the library—Gonzales would be the logical person to succeed Prentiss, since he's been head trustee all these years, and the will doesn't specify that Prentiss' successor has to be unmarried. But Terry wants to play safe, so he bribes Dancy to take one leaf, so that if the theft of the whole fragment is discovered Dancy will have to take the jolt.

"But suppose Ulman got wind of this. Ulman may have seen Terry at the safe. Now the discovery of books in Mrs. Gonzales' room makes it look as if Ulman had been filching the other books, but we don't know whether this is so or whether the books were planted there the night Winifred was murdered. Anyway, Ulman charges Terry with the theft of the Bible fragment. If Terry didn't know Ulman was already a thief, he'd have been scared to death; if he did know about Ulman he'd have threatened to spill what he knew. Perhaps Ulman figured that by telling on Terry he could hang the theft of the other books on him too. So Ulman and Terry arrange to meet at the bindery to have it out. Or possibly, when Terry was told by Prentiss that the theft of the Bible was discovered, he went to the bindery of his own accord. Anyway, he went there, shot Ulman and destroyed the body. Murder number one.

"Now about Winifred. Terry and Winifred had a red-hot session Thursday morning. Ulman may have told Winifred in the reading-room Wednesday that Terry had taken the Bible. Terry didn't know Winifred knew he took it, but Thursday morning she charged Terry with murder. She and Terry made a date after the pageant, but Terry, banking on the success of the first murder, duplicated it. He knew Winifred would be coming home from the pageant early and alone. Murder number two.

"He goes to the house so as to give the appearance of innocence, hears Gonzales and me come in, and pretends to fall asleep in his chair. Winifred evidently didn't tell Gonzales everything, but she told him enough to make him guess at once that Terry was responsible for her death. He tells me—if I'd only had the brains of a kitten I'd have arrested Terry that night.

"The only weak spot in Terry's plan seems to have been Dancy. He probably figured that Dancy, being a pretty weak sister, would eventually confess having stolen the single leaf and Terry could deny the transaction—this would cast suspicion of everything on Dancy."

Farrell nodded slowly. "That's a good theory. I think when Terry's confronted with it he'll break down."

"He'd damn well better break, or I'll break him. Lousy little worm! Playing me for a sucker with Dancy sniggering in the next room!"

"Well, don't worry now," pleaded Farrell. "You're next door to having Terry in your hands. He's probably down at Isle Bonne feeling safe."

Wade grunted mirthlessly.

"What do you think of this Dancy?" Farrell asked.

"Oh, he's a spineless little poser, face to face with the first excitement of his life. I'm not interested in him. Where the hell is Murphy? I want to start for Isle Bonne."

"Do you think," suggested Farrell, "that we should call up the boys from the press-room and give them this Dancy arrest?"

"If I were you I'd hold him incommunicado and keep back the news of his arrest till after we've nailed Sheldon. If he hears Dancy's been arrested he'll certainly make a break for the open."

"Good idea. If you nab Terry we'll break it all."

"Lord, where *is* Murphy?" Wade spread out his long hands on the desk and clenched them greedily. "I want my hands on Terry. I want him worse every time I think how he took me in by looking wide-eyed and telling me how bad he felt. I promise you—"

Murphy barged in. "Hello!"

Wade sprang up. "Where the hell have you been?"

"Busy. I'm going to keep Dancy safe till we're back. I told everybody that if word of his arrest leaks out before we tell it I'll send every cop in that station-house out with the goats."

Wade was jerking on his coat. "Ready to go?"

"Yeah. Just a minute. Chief just told me he got a report from that man at the Napoleon ferry. Sheldon's car or one just like it went over on the eleven o'clock boat."

"That's the way to Isle Bonne," nodded Farrell. "What else have you got?"

"Reports from the detectives stationed at the library and at Gonzales' house. Ferguson, the man at the library, says that Terry came over to see Prentiss about eight o'clock this morning and asked the doctor for some books. Then he made a couple of phone calls to the Gonzales house. Talked to the professor first and then to Marie. Then he told Prentiss he'd come back by the library on his way to Isle Bonne, but wanted to run up and see Marie and the professor a few minutes. He came back and got the books he'd asked for and borrowed one of them blue dusters—smocks, I think they call 'em—that they wear working around the library, and left in his car. Prentiss insisted on giving him some coffee—seemed to feel sorry for him, because he looked pretty upset. Ferguson says Terry was in kind of a hurry to get off."

"How does that check?" Wade asked.

"Oh, it checks all right. Boudreaux, the fellow up at Gonzales' place, says Terry got up there a little after nine and had a talk with Marie, and got a book from her and another one of them dusters. They had quite a confab. Went upstairs and gabbed for about twenty minutes. When they came down the professor and Terry passed a few words, but not many, but Boudreaux says they shut the door anyway so he couldn't hear. Pretty soon Terry comes back to the living room, where Marie is sitting side by side with his suitcase, which he grabs and makes out. Gets into his car and drives off. That must have been just before he got back to the library the second time."

"Very thrilling," said Wade, "but let's go. When we get back we'll see Gonzales and Prentiss and Marie and hear what they talked about, but right now I want Sheldon."

"Ready," assented Murphy. "I wanted to tell you, Mr. Farrell, I put two men at each one of these places instead of one. Terry's made elaborate plans to tell everybody he was going to Isle Bonne, and from all that alibi-making he might be planning some more fireworks."

"Fine. I'll be waiting by the phone, Wade."

Wade nodded grimly. "Come on, Murphy."

They went downstairs and out toward where a bright green police car waited for them at the curb. In the doorway they were stopped by the vociferous press contingent.

"Where's the body, Wade?" Kennedy demanded. "What the hell is happening?"

Wade smiled broadly. "Just stick around, son, and I promise you one beautiful story in time for the Sunday edition."

"What?" They were clustered upon him.

"Can't tell you now—but in confidence—" he bent his head and spoke sepulchrally. "Boys, there's a whopping arrest about to be made. For God's sake don't spill it yet. But when we get back there'll be a story that'll blast every rocking chair in New Orleans. There'll be plenty of time—it's only half-past two now—and you'll have the year's biggest Sunday circulation. Don't stop me—wait for me!"

He left them staring after him as he scrambled into the car beside Murphy and sat there chuckling. Murphy gave an order to the chauffeur and they started their chase.

It was hot; the pavement glistened ahead of them and the chauffeur squinted crossly at the glare on the wind-shield. After they had gone three blocks Wade peeled off his coat and after seven blocks more he unfastened his collar, leaning forward wearily to mop the back of his neck, but the smile he turned on Murphy was the eager smile of one who is expecting Santa Claus. Wade was thrilled—he was almost content. As the police car purred up the shining pavement of St. Charles Avenue and out toward the Napoleon ferry it was as if a separate tingle ran through him with every revolution of the wheels—for every revolution was bringing them nearer to Isle Bonne, and, if they were lucky, Terry Sheldon.

They took the Napoleon ferry, and Wade screwed his eyes at the dazzling sunshine on the river. He chuckled aloud.

"And it's glad I'll be," said Murphy soberly, "to bring this mess to a finish."

"You?" Wade drew a long breath. "At least you tried to give him the works, Murphy. It took me to moo like a contented cow."

He glowered at the river. The boat chugged to the wharf on the other side and the green car started its drive toward the bayous. Wade lit a cigarette and lay back joyously.

They drove along the bayou road, long and curving and cool; palm-trees reached up on both sides and long festoons of gray moss dipped from the live oaks and brushed them as they passed. For the first time in their long struggle they relaxed in a soft lush coolness as the wet air from the bayous blew around them. Wade puffed contentedly at his cigarettes, and even Murphy stretched his big legs in front of him and sighed with a sense of peace. They drove past a sleepy little town or two, where lived clusters of the people known as Cajuns, whose ancestors had been exiled from the country of Evangeline and who ever since had lived in the woods along the river. The little towns were quiet and lazy, for the Cajuns had not much to do in the summer but smoke their pipes and bable their soft patois in the sunshine. At last the chauffeur turned in his seat.

"I think we need water. I'll stop here."

Murphy nodded and they drew up at a filling-station where a sleepy Cajun youth shuffled forward to them. "No gas," said the chauffeur. "Just water."

As he started to fill the radiator Wade stretched his arms above his head and beamed luxuriously upon Murphy. "Nearly there," he said triumphantly.

Murphy grinned. "You wait till I see that lad."

"Think I'd better put some air in this back tire," the chauffeur announced, dragging up the air hose.

"Do for heaven's sake hurry up," grunted Wade. He opened the door. "Let's get some pop, Murphy."

An ancient flivver chugged up to the store on the opposite corner, and as Wade and Murphy crossed in quest of cold drinks a trapper leaped out and began shouting to the loungers in front. The store-keeper sprang to his feet with alacrity amazing in a bayou-dweller, and the loafers around him dashed toward the gesticulating bringer of news. Wade gave a questioning squint in Murphy's direction.

"Guess they've been shooting again?"

Murphy shrugged. "They're always killing each other, these Cajuns. We'll find out." He tapped the nearest youth on the shoulder. "What's the row, boy?"

A wild torrent of Cajun French poured upon him. Murphy shook his head. "Don't any of you lads talk English? What's the racket?" He pulled back his coat to show his badge. "I'm a policeman, see? You speak English to me."

"Police, hein?" Excited eyes turned upon him. The gesturing trapper in the middle of the group poured out his unintelligible tale.

"One minute, m'sieu!" exclaimed the boy Murphy had grabbed first. "Achille! Dere has come a man from dose police!"

The trapper pushed his way forward. "Dose police? Mon Dieu, but I have joy—I was tole to you—it was bad, bad—you can't know 'ow bad it 'ave become—"

"Somebody get shot?" cut in Wade.

"Mais non, m'sieu, dere was no one shot—one crazy artist man on dat island dey 'ave name Isle Bonne—"

"What?" Wade gripped his arm. "What happened? Talk, you!"

"I cannot tole you what 'ave 'appen—I don't know—my frien' Emile and me, we 'ave come up in one pirogue from dose bayou and 'e was dere—sacre bon Dieu, it was bad, bad—"

"For God's sake what happened?"

"It was so bad till I don't know dat I can tole you—we make a pass from dose bayou—we find dees man all burn up from death in de front from de cabin—"

CHAPTER TWENTY

WIGGINS leaned closer to the bar, his nose just clearing the rim of the rickey glass that stood in front of him. His impish face glowed, but there was at the same time a flicker of concern in the look he gave Wade, who was hunched over the bar gazing in fuddled appreciation at the bottom of his own empty glass.

"What do you think you're gonta do now?" Wiggins inquired caustically.

Wade looked down upon him with vacuous pity. "Don't you know? Have another drink, that's what. Tony!"

Wiggins shrugged. "Just one more, then. I got a lotta pictures in the soup now that the sports department will be crying for in about ten minutes."

Wade waved his long arms unsteadily. Wiggins eased further off. "Who cares about sport pictures?" Wade demanded. "Knobby-kneed girls playing tennis. Big hunks of beefsteak socking each other. Sports—"

"Oh, shut up. Doncha think we have anything in this town but murders?"

"*No!*"

Tony the bartender jumped and blinked under Wade's sudden ferocity. But Wade had subsided, and was morosely swishing the remains of his drink. Wiggins finished his rickey.

"You'd better come on before you get pie-eyed. They'll be wanting a new lead from you for that second Sunday edition."

"You," said Wade, "can go to hell."

Wiggins veered uncertainly between the inviting figure of Tony across the bar and the path of duty outside. It must be dark by now, he reflected, and he really did have to get out the sports pictures; if Wade wanted to stay here all night and get plastered Wiggins couldn't see that he had any business interfering, still, he was a little bit disconcerted by the savage intentness with which Wade was attacking the business of getting drunk. Wade had come in from Isle Bonne that afternoon looking like a man chased by ghosts; he had dashed off a story and then, yelling to Koppel to send O'Malley down to headquarters because he himself was going out awhile, he had grabbed Wiggins by the scruff of the neck and ordered him to come along to Tony's.

Wiggins had no objection to coming along to Tony's—he regarded Tony's as one of the few havens of peace left in a world that was always howling for pictures and more pictures—but since arriving at Tony's he had been somewhat appalled by the unaccustomed spectacle of Mr. Wade of *The Creole* seriously and methodically proceeding to get himself as drunk as a hoot-owl. Wade's limit, as Wiggins well knew, was three drinks; since one famous occasion seven years ago when Wade had gone on a riotous party and sent himself to the hospital for a week he had sternly restricted himself to moderation; but tonight Wade was getting drunk with a grim earnestness that Wiggins found almost frightening. Wade was not even enjoying himself, Wiggins thought as he looked at him. He gazed questioningly at Tony and strove to make up his mind. Wiggins did want another drink, but there was that second edition about to go to press, and while he knew perfectly well that it was none of his business he had a funny feeling that he'd like to drag Wade out if he could.

"I'm not a lousy newspaper reporter any more," Wade was saying. "I'm a hybrid. You don't know what a hybrid is. You don't know anything."

Wiggins picked up the glass Tony set in front of him and scowled across it at Wade. "You're drunk, you big sap."

"I'm not drunk. I'm hybrid. Half drunk and half sober. But I'm going to be all drunk in a little while, ory-eyed drunk for the first time in seven years. Big sabbatical event. Don't miss it."

Wiggins jerked his thumb over his shoulder. "Come on, let's screw. Drink that and we'll come back later."

"Come back?" Wade shook his head and closed his hand lovingly around his glass. "I'm not coming back, because I'm not going."

"Say, wise guy. You're a crimeologist, ain't you? Well, maybe you are to the rest of the world but to me you're just a fireman that gets there too late every time. Come on, let's screw."

"Oh, keep quiet and stay put." Wade tasted his drink with approval.

Wiggins sighed. Tony made good rickeys. But somebody ought to stop Wade. Still, Wiggins didn't know what he could do about it.

Wade finished his drink and called Tony again. Tony nodded brightly and replaced Wade's empty glass.

They had the place almost to themselves, for it was too early for most of Tony's patrons. Prohibition had made very little difference to Tony, except that he had moved his mahogany outfittings to the attic. The looks of the place had changed but little from the old days: battalions of shining glass were banked against the mirrors and the rail and the brass beer-taps were polished till they glinted in the light. Save for a nondescript lounger who sat at the end of a table reading the first edition of the Sunday *Creole*, Wade and Wiggins were the only customers. Wade lifted his glass and scowled as his unsteady hand let a splash fall on the counter. There was a paper propped up on the table behind him, and in the mirror he could see the front page screaming the reason why he was drunk.

"THIRD BIBLE MURDER"

yelled the front page of the sober-faced *Creole*. The letters were backwards in the mirror. For a moment they swayed and jumbled like a tumbling pile of building blocks, then he stood up and shook himself angrily.

Wiggins glared. "You make me sick," he snorted. "I never saw such a fool in my life. Seven years you've kept on the wagon, and now this egg gets burned up and you think you've gotta make up for all the drinks you've missed."

Wade smiled crookedly at his own reflection. "Stop the sermon and play your tambourine for awhile."

"You lay off me. You'll be looking for free coffee and doughnuts soon if you don't get back to the office." Wiggins surveyed him disgustedly. "What a sissy you turned out to be. This guy Sheldon ain't no skin off your nose. What the hell you so cut up about him for? Pack it in. Forget it. Put in a bid for that bathing beauty assignment in Galveston. Do you good. Forget your troubles. Say, you ain't no cop. You're supposed to write stories, not to go out and make 'em. Tell Koppel you ain't no cop."

Wade stared drearily into his glass. "Say, Wiggins. You're a good guy, and I wouldn't admit this to anybody else in the world. But I'm sick. I'm scared. I'm all to pieces." He gulped down the drink and the glass clattered on the counter.

"Well," snapped Wiggins, "why don't you let the mayor or some-body go to work? Nobody elected you to office. Some guy wants to burn up a lot of people—you should worry. Ain't anybody putting matches to you, are they? Come on back to the office. You've had enough."

Wade shook himself again. "Tony! The same. I'm going to stand right up here, Wiggins, and drink, and when I get through drinking I'm going to be out like a light." His syllables were getting troublesome; he gave another lop-sided grin at himself in the mirror. "Wiggins, I've got a hundred and ten dollars in my pocket and I'm gonna spend it all. Get me? Spend it all right at this bargain counter and buy me a nice big piece of black velvet oblivion."

The door of the speakeasy swung open, and Murphy, unseen by Wade or Wiggins, came in and looked questioningly around. Tony started; Murphy smiled. "Nobody but me," he said reassuringly, leaning on the end of the bar. His eyes were on Wade, who was continuing his speech.

"—black velvet oblivion, Wiggins, and as far as murders go they can set the town on fire and I'll leave the job of putting it out to guys like—"

"Me," said Captain Murphy.

Wade looked up. He grinned stupidly, took a step and grabbed the bar for support. "Hello, Murphy."

"How're you, cap'n?" said Wiggins. He sidled over and jerked his head toward Wade significantly.

Murphy nodded and beckoned to Tony.

"I'm all right. Gimme a bit of vichy and some lemon juice, Tony. You through for the day, you gentlemen?"

"I'm through," Wiggins announced. "I got work to do, but this monkey Wade won't lemme get away to do it."

"They've been calling the press-room for you," Murphy told him. "Say the sports men are on their heads. Better get back."

"He ain't getting back," objected Wade. "Ain't going back at all. He's on an assignment with me and he ain't going back till I send him back, see?"

Murphy nodded understandingly. "Sure, to hell with 'em. I wouldn't be bothered with 'em either. Keep him out and we'll all go on a party."

"'S a great idea," Wade approved. "Great big idea. We'll all have a party. You and you and me."

"Sure," chimed in Murphy. "Sure. If he goes back now they'll be chasin' him out to get that picture I just told the other boys about. But I guess it'll wait."

Wiggins snapped to attention. "What picture?"

"Why, there's an old fellow down here that's got some photo-static copies of a Gutenberg Bible leaf, and I thought it might be a nice thing to run along with the story. Picture was made from the Bible in the Morgan Collection, but it'll show 'em how a Gutenberg Bible looks on the inside."

"Gee—fair picture." Wiggins grabbed his coat. "I'll get out—who's got it?"

"I gave O'Malley the address just a minute ago. He's at headquarters phoning everywhere for you."

Wiggins was at the door. "So long, you drunken bum. I should get scooped because you're a high-breed? Ix-nay!" He bounced out.

Wade huddled over the bar, gazing bleary-eyed into the mirror. Murphy waved to Tony. "Tony, bring this gentleman another drink, now. You can't be laying down on the job like that. We're here to get drunk and we don't want anybody neglecting us." He took Wade's arm. "Let's go into the back room where we can be quiet, you and me. There's going to be lots of people in here before long and we can't have 'em in our way. Wish I could join you, but it's death to me right after dinner."

Wade grinned foolishly and allowed himself to be led toward the back door. "That's all right. Bring it in here, Tony."

"Bring some of that Bushmill's whiskey," Murphy ordered. "Me and Mr. Wade are going in the back room. And bring me a bottle of vichy and some lemons and some powdered sugar." He piloted Wade into the vacant back room and placed him at a table. "Excuse me a minute while I ask the bar-boy how his wife is. Auto broke her leg."

Wade agreed without interest. His eyes were on the bottle of Bushmill's and the glasses that Tony was bringing in. Murphy slipped outside and dropped a nickel into the telephone slot by the door.

"Police headquarters," he chirped brightly.

His nickel clinked back to him. "Headquarters? This is Murphy. Gimme Farrell's secretary. Miss Blake? Murphy speaking. If anybody wants me I'm at Raymond 5379. That's it." He hung up the receiver and buttonholed Tony, who was reappearing from the back room.

"Say, Tony, how long's that guy Wade been here?"

"Two hours, maybe."

"Mhm," said Murphy expressively. "I've looked all over town for him. I guess he's got a right to be upset, though. I am myself, just a little bit. Say, Tony, keep everybody out of that back room till we're gone, will you?"

"Sure." Tony bobbed in vast admiration. Captain Murphy was the only cop Tony knew who paid for what he drank. "These murders, now—"

"Shhh!" ordered Murphy sternly, and walked resolutely into the back room, shutting the door behind him. Wade was slumped over the table, his head on his out-crossed arms. For an instant Murphy stood quite still by the door, looking at him. There was an odd mingling of pity and exasperation on his face.

He sauntered over and sat down. Wade looked up, pushing his hand vaguely over his foggy eyes.

"Pretty tired, ain't you?" Murphy suggested.

"Damn tired." He fingered the bottle of Bushmill's.

"Sick, too, maybe," Murphy went on.

"Oh, I'm sick. Sick of everything." Wade dropped his forehead on his hands. "Murphy, you're an old policeman and maybe this thing doesn't get you the way it does me—but every time I think about that Sheldon kid I want to go off some place and cry."

Murphy smiled a slow smile. "I know how it is, boy."

Wade poured out a drink of whiskey and threw it savagely down his throat. "They've licked us. I guess we're only half smart, Murphy."

"They've done well, whoever they are." Murphy was soberly drinking his vichy and lemon juice. He paid no attention as Wade took another drink. "I thought we had the whole thing in a bag," he continued, "with that Dancy story. And now Sheldon—poor boy, being dead instead of the murderer we thought he was. The coroner tells me there ain't a chance it was suicide or accident. And not a devil's chance of telling who did it."

The details slowly made themselves clear in Wade's misty understanding. He rested his elbows on the table and ran his hand through his hair as though to rouse his brain to action. "What about the others?" he asked.

Murphy answered casually, but he was watching Wade with a keenness which Wade was too befuddled to observe.

"Everybody's got a cast-iron alibi furnished by members of the police department."

"Everybody?" Wade sat up; in spite of himself he was dragging back to sobriety.

"Sure. Not a chance. Dancy's in jail and there were two detectives at Gonzales' and two more at the library. We got to look for somebody else."

"Oh, I don't care what you do." Wade dropped his head again and his long fingers twisted in his hair. "Don't you understand? I'm sick of this thing. I'm nuts, Murphy. Can't you see I'm played out?"

"I know, I know, that's why I wanted to talk to you about it." Murphy spoke with shrewd sympathy. "Me and Farrell, we been talking it over this afternoon. You need a rest. We've appreciated what you've been doing—we know you've been at it about twenty hours a day and that you're about busted. We figured it would be a shame to let you go on in the state you're in."

Wade was staring, his red-rimmed eyes squinted in a frown of incomprehension. Murphy went on.

"So we thought we'd fix it for you to go down to the Gulf Coast for awhile. Say there's something over there you gotta look into. Get down to Biloxi or somewhere—just sort of ease you out of the Bible Murders."

"Thank you," said Wade with bitter sarcasm. "Very kind of you."

Murphy smiled. "It's all right. You ain't used to this sort of thing."

"You want me to go to Biloxi? Think I'd better quit?" Wade leaned over. He was drunk, but somewhere in his muggy understanding he was grabbing at words. "You listen to me, you big flat-footed ox. My name's Wade, see? Wade of *The Creole*. Ten years I've worked for *The Creole*. Worked there when I was a fair-haired cherub trying to make literature out of the vital statistics. Work there now when they count on me to bring in the biggest story in town. I've climbed flagpoles and I've battled strike-breakers, see? And my job is to do what I'm told to do. If I'm sent to chaperon a marbleshooting champion or to help a district attorney I go, and I stay with the damn job till it's finished. Get me? Sometimes I get lucky and scoop the town, sometimes I get a licking, but the guys that pay me know I'll be there all the time. I'm drunk now and I haven't been drunk in years. But you can get this straight and put it in your hat. I'm doing this job not because I like it but because I was told to do it. You babies can run this murderer from hell to Harlem but until you hang him, I'm in. I'm in whether you want me or not. And I stay in. Got that, you ape?"

He lurched to his feet. For a moment he stood leaning against the table. His cloudy eyes shifted. Then something glowing and nebulous slowly came into his face; his eyebrows drew together and his sagging mouth set itself in a line. His shaky hands clenched, his spine straightened, and as he drew himself up he faced Murphy with the steadiness that is the focus of a great idea.

"Murphy," said Wade, "damn you, I can solve these murders. I know how. You go back and tell Farrell that tomorrow I'm going to make Terry Sheldon give up his secret, and by tomorrow night I'm going to be brought back in cinders or else I'll come back knowing who the murderer is. I know how to do it and there's not one of you over at headquarters that can stop me."

Murphy half stood up. "You mean you want to go to Isle Bonne?"

"I mean I'm going to Isle Bonne. I'm going to follow every step Terry took this morning. Somewhere in that trip today Terry met the murderer and let out that he was on his track. That's what I'm going to do. I'm going down to Terry's cabin and I'm going to read that fool Euripides till I find out what he was talking about. You think I'm drunk. Well, I am, but I'll sleep it off before tomorrow, because tomorrow I'm going to be busy."

Murphy rocked back on the legs of his chair. "If you're going out on any such suicide scheme," he said stolidly, "I'm going with you."

Wade shook his head with a slow smile. "No you're not. Tell them to have some deputies around the island in case I need any help—but nobody's going to be with me. I've got a date with a dead man, Murphy, and three's a crowd."

He took a step, staggered unsteadily and straightened up with a jerk. "I can't talk any more now. It's too close to the next edition for me to see Farrell and don't you be holding me up here. You give Farrell my compliments and my message. I've got to work." He jerked to the door and banged it behind him.

Murphy leaned back chuckling. He picked up the bottle of Bushmill's and wandered happily into the front room, where he leaned over the bar and beckoned to Tony.

"Mr. Wade get out, Tony?"

"Sure, going hell-bent for somewhere, captain."

"Yeah." Murphy set down the bottle. "Tony, that's a peculiar drink."

"What you say? It cost me six dollars a pint. That's the best there is—straight off the boat—"

"Sure, I know." Murphy nodded in vast comprehension. "It's real Irish liquor, Tony, nearest thing to potheen you can get in this cock-eyed country. It makes well men sick and sick men well."

He grinned broadly and patted Tony's shoulder as he turned again to the phone and rang police headquarters. "This is Murphy. Gimme Farrell. Farrell? Murphy speaking. Just call your conference for about eleven o'clock tonight. Sure, I found Wade. He's all right. A long way from licked. He'll be there."

PART V
SUNDAY

CHAPTER TWENTY-ONE

MARIE came to the front door where Wade was waiting. "Here's a Euripides," she said. "It's an old copy with bad print, but Terry wanted Euripides yesterday and I gave him Alfredo's other copy."

Wade took the book and thanked her, but stopped as she spoke again.

"Wade, must you go to Isle Bonne alone?"

He nodded. "I've got to, Marie."

For a moment she did not answer, and Wade looked down at her, trying uselessly to check his sympathy till he had found what he was going to look for on the island. Marie seemed exhausted. Her gay yellow dress and her flashing makeup added emphasis to the desperate weariness of her face. At last she said, huskily, "I wish you wouldn't go. It—it frightens me."

"I've got to, Marie," he repeated. Then, in spite of himself, he added what he had been trying not to say. "Marie, I'm afraid for you. Be careful while I'm gone. And remember how sure I am that you aren't concerned in this affair."

She smiled gallantly. "You've been mighty good to me, Wade. But you be careful too."

He went toward the steps and turned to wave.

"Good luck!" Marie called from the doorway, "and good hunting!"

He went out to his car, relieved to think that at least she was with Alfredo today and not alone in her garret on Royal Street. The car purred and started forward, and Wade was on his way. Hard as it had been to follow Terry's movements this morning, hard as his interviews had been, he felt an anticipatory thrill as he drove.

Gonzales, punctiliously courteous as ever, had offered to go to the island with Wade if he could be of any service. Prentiss had seemed frightened when Wade had gone by the library to say he was going to Isle Bonne. Prentiss was more than uneasy, Wade had thought; the angry citizen who had thundered at the inadequacy of the law two days before had changed since Terry's death into a man in whom no quietening adjustment to reality could ever erase the knowledge of desperation. Marie—Wade stared through the windshield and thought of Marie. She was afraid, but she had insisted that it was not for herself—that she was sure the murderer's purpose did not include her. Wade was fairly certain that today the murderer's purpose was directed against himself; at his suggestion Dancy had been released from jail on bond, and the detectives had been removed from Gonzales' house and the library, so that every member of the circle that seemed most concerned in the Bible Murders was free to move at will. Wade crossed the river and turned into the road that led down to the island.

On a less terrible errand he might have thought that human problems could seem insignificant in the brooding silence of the Louisiana flatlands. But behind him, Wade knew, was a city stricken with fright; nursemaids in the Quarter were threatening their charges with the dreadful "homme de feu" when they were not good, boys and girls were building fires in which to burn paper dolls, editorial writers had called upon Farrell for results. Papers opposed to the city administration were making capital of the fact that the killer was still loose, and detectives in all departments were using every source of police information in an effort to unearth a single clue to the perpetrator of the Bible Murders.

It was very quiet on the road that led to the bayous. Though it was nearly noon, the marshes were hidden in a green darkness, and the road on which Wade was traveling curved between the two walls of forest in a strange bright strip. Here and there the woods broke and a little town swirled past his car; an occasional negro loomed up on a loping mule, and once or twice another car came out of the horizon and hurtled by with an explosion of dust; but as he neared Isle Bonne the traffic thickened. It was Sunday, and people were free to hustle out in an effort to see what the scene of the murder looked like, but not far from the bridge that led over the bayou he saw a deputy sheriff diverting cars from the direction of the island. Wade pulled up alongside of the deputy and showed his week-old badge.

"Keeping you busy?" he asked.

"Mon Dieu, Mr. Wade, tout le monde vient ici—everybody and de family from de whole parish—I tell heem no, not even my own cousin, go over from de bridge—nobody but Mr. Wade. It is orders." He gesticulated dramatically toward the approaching cars.

"Fine," nodded Wade. "You tell the other deputies I'm here and tell them to keep away from the cabin unless they hear shots or see smoke."

"C'est bien." The deputy grinned and nodded proudly. Wade threw his car into gear, crossed the bridge and took the side road that led to the cabin.

Isle Bonne is small and thickly wooded. Its only residents are a few trappers, and the cabins that dot the bayou shores are principally studios of New Orleans artists. Terry's cabin was set off at one end of the island, behind a screen of oaks and undergrowth. The trees grew thickly on three sides, and in front was a small grassy clearing. Wade shuddered as he stopped his car and walked to the entrance, for the grass was black, and the green stems of the surrounding bushes were charred and splintered. This was where Terry had come yesterday, to think with his hands.

He glanced at his watch. It was fifteen minutes past noon and the sun was high and hot, but the cabin, shaded by the interlacing oak trees, offered a cool workshop. Beyond the trees on the east side murmured the lazy waters of the bayou. Wade unlocked the door and stepped over the threshold.

He entered a gay rustic studio, lighted on three sides by vast windows and hung with brilliant modernistic pictures; the stands were cluttered with brushes and tubes of paint, and in the corners stood clay models in various stages of incompleteness. On a broad low table was Terry's modeling-clay, and at one side, under a window, stood a littered desk piled with books and papers. Wade set down his suitcase and crossed to the desk.

At one side of the desk stood a clay model, about eighteen inches high, covered with a cloth. Wade took off the cloth and studied it.

Here was Terry's preliminary study for his classical statue. The model stood on a flat base, and though it seemed at first sight nearly shapeless, after a moment's scrutiny its vague outlines seemed to become more definite—the folds of Grecian drapery, a sandaled foot, a bent leg, all done with a strange force that at once struck Wade with a curious sense of horror. The peculiar rigidity of the knee and foot, the straining at the instep and the toes curled as if frantically gripping at the ground—the harsh muscles of the leg, distended as though to the last limit of endurance—here was the whisper, mysterious, wordless, meaningless as yet, but the whisper of what Terry knew.

He stood looking at the half-made statue. The upper part of the clay had been roughly molded to give the lines of a human figure, a woman's figure, with a touch of classic grace but with more than a touch of distortion. The spine was strangely bent and the head thrown back, the line of the throat strained as though in a desperate clutch at breath. For the rest, Wade could tell nothing. He took off his coat and prepared for his vigil.

As he opened the windows, the rustling wind of the bayou blew upon him. Beyond the large room that Terry had used as a studio was a smaller bedroom, and beyond this was an impromptu kitchen. Wade felt for his pistols, sticking one into his hip pocket and the other into his belt, as he stood in the middle of the studio and looked around.

Tacked up over the desk was a sketch of a Greek theater, hurriedly but carefully done. On the desk lay a dozen smaller sketches, some of them incomplete, all of Greek women in various attitudes of agonized distortion. Beside them stood Terry's model. Wade finished munching one of the sandwiches he had brought and took out of his bag another stage-property—a photostatic copy of a leaf of the Gutenberg Bible in the Morgan collection, borrowed from its owner by Captain Murphy last night. He laid it on the desk and sat down, his chin in his hands.

Slowly he reconstructed Terry's last visit. The books Terry had borrowed from Prentiss and Gonzales lay on the desk. Fortunately, Terry had not been working on the model when he was killed, but had been sketching, probably another of those Greek women. Wade looked again at his watch. Twelve-thirty. By three o'clock yesterday Terry had been dead. A twig snapped outside; he started, and swore softly at his own nerves.

He looked at the books. There was a beautiful copy of the tragedies of Euripides, bound in scarlet morocco, with Alfredo Gonzales' name on the flyleaf, and a commentary also bearing Gonzales' signature. The others had the bookplate of the Sheldon library. Wade looked at them. There were several works on Greek tragedy, and a worn brown-covered book that he did not recognize. Its title, once stamped in gold on the cover, had been almost obliterated by time; Wade opened it, and saw that the inner cover had been carefully restored—probably, he reflected with a grimace, some of the work done by Quentin Ulman at that gruesome bindery by the river. He looked at the title-page.

"The Philosophy of Magic, Prodigies and Apparent Miracles, by Eusebe Salverte. With notes Illustrative, Explanatory and Critical by

Anthony Todd Thomson, M.D., F.L.S., etc." The date at the bottom was 1847, followed by a note, "First French Edition published 1829."

This, he noticed, was the second volume of the book. Terry had apparently not borrowed the first. Wade read the title again and frowned.

"Now what," he asked himself aloud, "was Terry doing with this?"

But Terry was past answering, and Wade did not know. He put the book down and studied the objects on the desk: a pile of books, a lump of clay just taking form, a photograph of a Gutenberg Bible leaf.

Would these, he wondered, be enough to enable him to follow the trail that Terry had started? He looked first at the model. That was what had given Terry the idea that had pointed to his solution. He pushed the books back and drew the model closer; it stood in front of him, alongside of the Bible leaf. What was it Terry had said—? A statue representing the epitome of human agony—a subject that would rival the Laocoon. Terry had said that at the time of Quentin Ulman's murder he had been in this studio working on some clay bases. But that was the day on which Dancy had given him the stolen Bible leaf. Had Terry really come to Isle Bonne to hide the Bible leaf, and then by a trick of imaginative analogy said he had been working on clay bases? Wade noticed that the base of the model was only a trifle larger than the copy of the Bible leaf that lay by it; the base would just cover the leaf if laid over it, with an inch or so on all sides to spare. Terry had had the Bible leaf that day—he had said he was working on clay bases. Perhaps this base? Then by a trick of like and like—

Wade picked up the model and laid it on the photo-static copy of the Morgan Gutenberg leaf. The leaf was hidden. Wade started and whistled softly. Picking up a scalpel, he turned the model over and struck the bottom. A hollow plunk answered. With careful briskness, he knocked the base on the edge of the table; the clay cracked, and the pieces fell on the floor.

Wade felt his hand quiver. He looked at the broken base. His eyes were wide with amazement and his breath came fast. From the hollow in the base he drew forth an oilskin packet.

With shaking hands he unwrapped the oilskin. Inside was something carefully covered with tissue paper. He tore off the paper, and in front of him lay one of the lost leaves of Dr. Prentiss' Gutenberg Bible.

He drew a long breath and wiped little drops of sweat from his forehead.

"I'm banking on you, Terry," he whispered.

He got up and looked out of the windows toward the trees and the bayou winding negligently in the distance. The Bible Murders. One leaf was where Terry had hidden it; the other eight?—He shrugged. And there was Terry's model, standing uncertainly on its broken base, holding in its vague outlines the secret of what Terry knew.

Wade walked back to the table and looked down, wondering at the strange travesty that had made Johann Gutenberg's masterpiece the cornerstone of a triangle of murder. He looked at the model. Terry had said, "Did you ever read Euripides?"

He sat down again and lit a cigarette. The cool green silence of the island wrapped the cabin with an atmosphere of impenetrable isolation. Here Terry had sat, thinking; here he had planned to read Euripides.

"Read Euripides," said Wade aloud. "He might as well have said 'read the daily paper.'"

He ransacked his mind for memories of Euripides, realizing hopelessly that the dramatist had drawn on nearly all the emotions of mankind for his themes. He stared hard at the clay model. That horrible struggling leg, that foot pressed into the ground as if in frantic search of support, that agonized distortion of the back—he looked thoughtfully at the foot. Terry had done his work well. Never, Wade thought, had he seen a more dreadful suggestion of struggle than in the lines of that distorted instep. He picked up the Euripides and turned to the index.

Alcestis. No, not there. The story of a woman whose love for her husband was so great that she offered her life for his—that had no place in this story of murder. *The Trojan Women*. The epitome of human despair, but hopeless despair—it offered him no solution. *Orestes*—a man pursued by furies—perhaps—heaven knew there had been furies loose in New Orleans—but he shook his head. *Electra*—a sister's devotion—no suggestion there of hate so horrible as this. *Medea—Medea*—there was hate, certainly, black hate and horror. Wade leaned back and reflected. Here was murder, perhaps the most horrid story of hate in all human literature. Medea, the woman scorned by her husband, the woman who in a paroxysm of fury killed her children on the day her husband cast her aside for a new bride. Medea, the most terrible woman in all the tragic legends of antiquity—but had she an answer here? He stiffened and looked at Terry's statue. Terry had shown a woman, not a child. A woman in her death-agony—Medea—Medea—

Something splintered in his brain. He sprang up, overturning his chair behind him. An exclamation of horrified dismay broke the dreamy silence of the bayou and startled the birds who basked in the sun outside.

"Good God! *Creusa!*"

Wade stood rigid, his hands clenched at his sides, staring down at the clay statue and at the book that lay face down on the floor where it had fallen. It was as if a bomb had exploded in his brain and the smoke were slowly clearing away as he remembered the dreadful tragedy of Creusa, princess of Corinth, who died in a flaming robe fashioned by the magic-working hands of Medea the discarded wife. Slowly, the details clicking in his recollection, he put together the story—Medea, cast aside by Jason for the sake of Creusa, had sent Creusa a bridal gown, an enchanted dress that burst into flames when Creusa put it on. And Medea, when word was brought to her of her rival's death, had laughed.

A cold shudder ran through Wade's body. He felt the sweat start from his forehead as he mechanically straightened his chair and sat down. Waves of unspeakable horror swept over him as he sat there, staring at Terry's model.

Creusa's robe, bewitched with fire—Ulman, Winifred, Terry. He pushed his hand over his forehead as though to clear away a fog. But it was incredible, impossible, insane—that today, in a twentieth-century city, a city of skyscrapers and taxicabs, there could be a murderer who could kill with impunity because he knew Medea's secrets!

But if it were true—

Wade pressed his hands against his throbbing temples. Medea had sent to Creusa an enchanted robe, a wedding gift; Creusa had put it on, and as she stood gazing into her mirror the dress had burst into searing magic flames. It was a myth, a dreadful legend turned into poetry for an Athenian festival, one of the thousand stories that dealt with the magic of the gods. *But if it were true!*

He stared wildly at Terry's unfinished model that had been meant to show the death-struggle of Creusa. So this was what Terry had known. What was it Terry had said? "I think with my hand. And Wade, my hands were thinking—and suddenly, as I worked, they thought of something so hideous, something so unutterably and incredibly evil—I can't say it now. It can't be said unless I know."

If Terry had guessed right—no wonder they had all had impregnable alibis for Terry's death! Wade began to pace the floor of the studio, his brain working in leaps. If it was possible that such a murder could be done today, a murder based on the enchantment of Medea, of course there could be alibis! He clenched his hands together behind him and walked faster. All that would be necessary was sometime to have access to some article of wearing apparel belonging to the intended victim—and who had had that? Marie—Prentiss—Dancy—Gonzales. Ulman and Winifred and Terry. The names danced furiously in his brain. Quentin Ulman had left the Sheldon Library on the day of his death, dressed as usual, presumably in the same clothes he had put on that morning before leaving home. How could the murderer have been sure the fatal poison would not take effect till Ulman was safely out of sight at the bindery? But wait—they had found Ulman's coat and trousers hanging on a rack in the bindery that afternoon. He had changed them for an overall; they had said Ulman kept an overall in the bindery, and wore it to protect his clothing from the chemicals used there. His overall had been in the bindery, perhaps for days before; and if it were true that the murderer possessed the knowledge of Medea, and that the lethal charge in the garment had no effect until it was put on by the person for whom it was intended, that death-jacket might have been waiting for Quentin Ulman for heaven knew how long, prepared and left there until chance should send him to the bindery to work. And every one of Wade's group of suspects could have gone to the bindery many times without exciting suspicion.

Wade stopped and gazed at the half-made statue of Creusa, as if trying to drag from it the awful knowledge of the ancient enchantress. He thought of Winifred as he had last seen her, exquisite in her brocaded Chinese suit, borrowed from the collection of Dr. Prentiss. But wait—he fought desperately for recollection—any one of them might have prepared that Chinese suit—Terry had borrowed it—Marie had been sent to Terry's apartment to fetch it, Dancy had delivered it to Winifred, and it had lain in her house half the day. But—he checked himself. It could not have been the mandarin suit, for she had worn it for hours. She had driven in her car to the Vincennes Club and she had taken part in the pageant. Was there something else? Yes—he remembered. She had said something about a mandarin coat. She said she had left it in her car. If her coat had been left in the car during all the time she was inside, anyone who wanted could have prepared it for its dreadful work.

He felt himself quivering with horror as he thought. The leaves rustled merrily outside the cabin, and the sun sloped over the trees as Wade paced up and down the floor of the studio, his hands knotted behind him, his head bent, his face distorted with the fearful thing that had come upon him.

Terry. Terry who had guessed the appalling truth, and who had died because he guessed too much; Terry who had gone carelessly from house to house, telling them all that he was coming to Isle Bonne; Terry who had openly borrowed Euripides, thus revealing what it was he had been seeking; Terry—Wade stopped short as if dazed by a blow—Terry who had left Luke Dancy alone in his bedroom during his conversation with Wade, and who had left his suitcase open within easy access to all the other three!

Poor reckless Terry, so stunned that he had not thought to guard himself against the fierce cunning that had directed the other two crimes!

But who was it that Terry had suspected?

Terry had said it was someone he had liked, someone who had been his friend. He had cowered in unbelieving dismay before his suspicion.

Wearily, Wade dropped back into his chair before the desk and began to read the *Medea* of Euripides.

Shadows starting from the edge of the cabin traveled slowly to the clearing and over the fringe of trees; the bayou to the east darkened. Isle Bonne was very quiet. Still Wade did not lift his head. He was back in the amphitheater at Athens, shuddering at the enchantment of Medea, and trying to link her crime to another crime thousands of years away.

Medea, a woman scorned in love, winding a fire of hate and death around her rival. Medea, who knew necromancy and the science of her day but who drew suspicion away from her plot with the wiles of her sex. Medea, who loved hard and lost bitterly. Medea—Marie.

Wade looked through the west window and the faint glitter of light outside, watching Medea. Medea, a symbol of power assailed, of a career in jeopardy, a calm, aloof worker of evil, a personage in her cult, a guardian of secrets; Medea, cast from her high estate and wreaking death because of it. Medea—Prentiss.

And yet, Medea was a mate, a sharer of a home, who lost to a younger and more fascinating rival. Medea was a member of a proud caste, descendant of a line of kings, a mate faced with ridicule, with desertion; faced with loss of luxury, with stigma, with abasement in the eyes of those before whom she had been her proudest. Medea, unwanted. Medea—Gonzales.

Wade wondered if the Grecian boy who played Medea in Athens had understood the envy, the hatred, the terrible ambition of his rôle. Medea was ambitious. She was politic. She had been scorned. Medea plotted in secret against those who had deprived her of her rights. Medea—Dancy.

He moved his chair closer to the desk and dropped his face into his hands. He saw Creusa. Creusa, falling in the quick death of the flames. Creusa the rival, Creusa the stumbling-block, Creusa the home-wrecker, Creusa the pawn.

He leaned back in his chair, and as he did so his eyes fell on the package of sandwiches he had laid on the desk when he came in, thick, homely sandwiches wrapped in oiled paper, and with a jerk that was almost physical he plunged back into reality. "What a lively sight you'd be, Mr. Wade," he told himself aloud, "chattering this kind of tripe to a jury!"

He laughed bitterly, imagining himself trying to convince the typical twelve good men and true that a murderer in New Orleans had used the magic of a Greek fairy-tale to gain his purpose. Stretching his cramped legs, he got up, unwrapped a sandwich and went into the kitchen for a glass of water. As he stood munching his honest bread and cheese he regarded the books Terry had brought to Isle Bonne with him, and wondered if Terry's theory had eliminated those four who seemed to him the most likely perpetrators of the crimes. He finished his sandwich and departed morosely for the kitchen to wash his hands. Back in front of the desk he stared at the books again.

There was that curious volume, Salverte's "Philosophy of Magic," wondering if in an obscure French book of a hundred years ago a man had explained how Medea had wrought her miracles. If he had, this still brought him no nearer to his main question, for the books at the Sheldon Library were open to anyone who chose to ask for them.

Wade reached scowling for the book. He was very tired. Pushing back his tumbled hair he glanced at the opening pages. With an exclamation of amazement he dropped the book as if it had suddenly gone hot in his fingers.

For M. Salverte, a hundred years ago, wrote a book based on the theory that the magic of the ancients was no magic at all, that the miracles of antiquity really happened, and only looked like miracles because science in those days was known to only a few initiates into the secrets of the temples. One by one M. Salverte took the so-called miracles of mythology and explained that they really happened.

Wade's fingers turned the leaves like a runner taking hurdles, half reading in his race to find what he sought. Suddenly he stopped, his eyes glued to a page halfway through the book. His face turned white, then grew greenish with understanding horror.

He closed the book and walked to the door.

"Terry, old chap," he said aloud, "why in God's name didn't you tell me?"

He took his revolver from his belt and fired two shots into the air.

CHAPTER TWENTY-TWO

CRISSCROSS lines of questioning and amusement appeared around Farrell's eyes as he read the letter brought to him by the Cajun deputy from Isle Bonne.

"Did Mr. Wade say anything when he gave you this letter?" he inquired at length.

The deputy gave an expressive shrug. "Sure. He say to me, 'Drive like one shot out from hell and tell Farrell if he don't mind what I say in de letter he turn out to be a lousy bum.'"

"Hm." Farrell stroked his chin and stared at Wade's closely-written pages.

"What happened down at Isle Bonne, Hercule?"

Hercule spread out his hands in a swift gesture. "She is very small, what happen. She is very quiet. We think, maybe Mr. Wade is dead, when all upon a sudden, in front from de cabin, we hear two queek shots, we run. We think maybe we find heem stretch out entirely dead, and Mon Dieu, when we get to heem, dere sit Mr. Wade, grinning like it was just Christmas, and he say, 'Come in, messieurs, have one sandwich.'"

"I see. Then what happened?"

"He is laughing, he say, 'It is one joke on my friend Farrell.' Den he give us a sandwich, and he write, and he give me de letter and he tell me to drive here like hell. So I did."

"He didn't let you read the letter?"

Hercule stood up, one hand on the doorknob. "I was going to de schoolhouse to learn dat reading, then a man he sell me what you call de read-io, and now at night I turn one button and a man he read me all what is from de papers."

"Good system. That's all, then, and thanks. Don't say anything about it."

"I am one oyster, Mr. Farrell."

Hercule went out, and Farrell, with a mighty sigh, picked up his telephone.

"Captain Murphy, please. Murphy? Farrell speaking. Come to my office as soon as possible. Yes, I know it's dark but you get busy and come on. Get a detail of eight men for special duty until six o'clock tomorrow morning. Step on it. I'll tell you more when you get here."

He hung up and called again. "Headquarters? Farrell on. Send a man out to buy two shoemakers' awls from somewhere and have him bring them to me at my office. Right away, yes. And send up a clerk for some dictation."

He groaned aloud, took another look at Wade's letter and made another call.

"May I speak to Mr. Gonzales? This is the district attorney. Mr. Gonzales, I have just had word of something I think you should know immediately. Will you be good enough to come down to my office as soon as you can? Bring Miss Castillo with you, and all the servants. We feel that everyone who has been connected with the victims of these crimes has been in a way under suspicion, and so has a right to be acquainted with our conclusions. I'll send two men up to guard your property while you are away. Thank you."

He called the Sheldon Library and gave the same summons, and then rang Dancy's apartment. As he turned from the phone after making his last call Murphy appeared with a group of policemen.

Murphy was belligerent. "Say, Mr. Farrell, I take orders and like the damn things, but what's the idea?"

Farrell grinned with relish. "Since you wouldn't believe me if I told you I didn't know, suppose we get to business. Leave the men outside for a minute."

Murphy waved his followers out with a lordly gesture, and approached the desk. "Say, what the hell?"

"Search me, Murphy. I got a letter from Wade. Come in!"

A clerk entered. In his hand he carried a couple of awls, which he was regarding with deep puzzlement. "They told me to bring these to you, Mr. Farrell."

"Quite right. Take some dictation. 'After an exhaustive and careful investigation by the office of the district attorney of the Parish of Orleans and by the district attorney of the Parish of Jefferson, where Isle Bonne is located, regarding the deaths of Quentin Ulman, Winifred Gonzales and Terry Sheldon, the district attorneys of both parishes are convinced that Quentin Ulman and Winifred Gonzales met their deaths at the hands of Terry Sheldon, who later took his own life at Isle Bonne in remorse for his crimes. The evidence supporting this theory is both satisfactory and conclusive, and will be presented to the coroner's jury of Jefferson Parish when it convenes next Tuesday. It is hoped that on the presentation of this evidence the verdict of suicide will be given in Sheldon's case and the other cases will be declared closed. Daniel E. Farrell, district attorney of the Parish of Orleans.' Please type that out and bring it back."

Murphy restrained himself till the clerk was out of the room, then he exploded.

"Farrell, it ain't the place of a cop to call the district attorney names, but you are one stiff-necked gaboon."

Farrell laughed. "Maybe. We're taking a chance, Murphy, and I don't know what it is. Wade sent me a cryptic letter with instruction to act upon it and I'm acting. If he's right New Orleans will owe him a medal; if he's wrong, I guess I'll get licked in the next election. Now I want you to get your men in and tell them to guard the houses of our various friends, who'll be away from home tonight. Put two men at each place, including Marie's flat."

Murphy stood up, shaking his head. "It sounds nutty to me. But I guess I don't get paid for my opinions. Boys! Come in here. Listen. Now, boys, I want two of you on each station that you are put at tonight and I want you to stay there till five-thirty in the morning. At five-thirty duty ends, and you'll report at First Precinct headquarters at six o'clock. I don't want you to do anything, no matter what happens, except to stand guard over these people's property while they are here, and for the rest of the night. Two at the Sheldon Library, two at Mr. Alfredo Gonzales' house, two at Mr. Luke Dancy's place and two at Miss Marie Castillo's apartment. Sergeant Mason will be in charge of this detail and he'll make the rounds of inspection, and any man that's missing from his post during the night will be on the carpet bright and early in the morning. Got that?"

He paused suggestively and lit a cigar. "'Nother thing now. Don't admit anybody into those houses while the occupants are out except myself or on written orders from me or Mr. Farrell. You got that? I want a man at the front of each house and a man at the back. I don't want any gatherings together to be smoking cigarettes or to be talking about the horse-races or any-think like that. I want the man at the front of the house to keep inconspicuous. Keep out of sight as much as possible. Got that? I want you to pay strict attention to business tonight and stay where you're put till you're relieved. In case you get any feeling of being lonesome spend your time thinking how tough it would be to be back driving a truck which is what you'll be doing if you don't obey orders. Make your report to me, sergeant. Take the detail."

He looked them over commandingly as they filed out, then slumped back into his chair. "Now, Farrell, what am I supposed to be doing?"

Farrell reached for the letter. "He's found something down at Isle Bonne. Read it."

Murphy read, slowly and laboriously, for like most people accustomed to use a typewriter Wade wrote shakily in longhand.

Dear Farrell:

I think we are coming to the end of the story.

Here is a plan that I want you to follow exactly. Sometime this evening on direct summonses get Prentiss, Gonzales, Marie and Dancy in your office. Have them accompanied by every member of their households. The point is—leave the houses empty.

Get them to your office by nine o'clock tonight and keep them there till after midnight. Justify this by saying you want no leak of your next step, and the city editions of the morning papers go to press by twelve-thirty this time of year. When you get everybody in, review the case in your own inimitable style. Be garrulous, voluble, loquacious and long-winded. Kill time. Then at about eleven-thirty tell them that after a conference with the coroner and district attorney of Jefferson Parish you have decided to issue a statement tomorrow morning saying that Terry Sheldon killed Ulman and Winifred and then committed suicide. Say that you do not want to announce this till morning because I am on Isle Bonne making an investigation and you think it might be embarrassing for me if you made the announcement before my return.

While they are all out of their houses, put a couple of officers in charge of each house. You can explain this by saying that you want to safeguard their property while their homes are empty, but have the officers stay on till daylight tomorrow. I suggest that you adopt throughout the gracious manner that you affect for juries.

At about a quarter of twelve you will get a phone call from me. Make it plain that this call comes from Isle Bonne. It won't, but that is none of their business. I will tell you that the solution of the murders will be complete by tomorrow morning when I get in, and that I will arrive sometime before noon. We'll talk quite a lot and I want you to put on a good act. I'll tell you that I am positive Terry did not do the murders but that he like the others was murdered and I can prove it and by whom. At first you are to be incredulous—tell me you have decided on a verdict of murder and suicide against Terry; but then take it seriously. Be impressed.

After you hang up, don't go too strong, but say that you are going to reserve your decision on the Terry verdict until I get in. Tell them that among Terry's effects I have found a clue as to who did the murders. Tell them that I refused to reveal this clue over the phone, but that you are going to hold up your conclusion till you can talk to me tomorrow.

Now this is important: tell the members of your little party that the brilliant Mr. Wade says Terry left indication of who did the murders but that Mr. Wade has not yet been able to determine the method employed. Be sure to get this in your little one-act play.

Have Murphy meet me at the Napoleon ferry at nine o'clock. Have him bring a shoemaker's awl and also a pint of whiskey. Doesn't this intrigue you? Well, forgive me, I must have my moment. All you have to do is a Belasco, while I'm staking my reputation on the difficult part of being the perfect Sherlock, and must be a little bit mysterious. All these details are devilishly important, Farrell. Have everybody out of the houses but the policemen. You have probably guessed by this time that whether he likes it or not the good Captain Murphy is going to make a lot of calls tonight, sponsored by your humble servant

WADE.

"Suffering mackerel," emitted Captain Murphy.
"I've called in the people," Farrell told him.

Murphy stood up. "Well, it ain't my business to think. But I must say he didn't tell us much."

"Only," amended Farrell, "that you're going to make a little inspection tour tonight."

"I guess I better take along some trick keys and other accessories for second-story work. I can get the whiskey in a few minutes."

There was a knock and a doorman put his head in. "Here's a paper the clerk brought up. Say's it's a statement you gave him. The people from the Gonzales house are outside."

"Just a minute," warned Murphy, "while I slip out the side door and get going. You got the stage all set, and Lord have mercy on your soul."

Farrell settled his tie and grinned.

Murphy made a bow. "So long, Mister Belasco. I'll see you in the last act."

Farrell waved. "Good night, Mister Barrymore," he said brightly.

Murphy bowed again. "Don't forget, next week we play East Lynne."

PART VI
MONDAY

CHAPTER TWENTY-THREE

AT HALF-past four Monday afternoon Murphy walked into Farrell's office and planted himself uninvited in front of the district attorney.

"This place," he volunteered, "is getting to be as bad as a repertory theater. Every night a different show."

"Have a cigar," suggested Farrell. He shoved his chair back and affably watched the captain exhale a cloud of smoke. "It's not the stage management that bothers me," he remarked, "it's keeping the customers satisfied."

"You mean the newspapers?" Murphy gave a grunt that summarily disposed of all such nuisances. "That boy Wade really seems to have something bright planned for tonight, but he ain't spilling it. How did it go last night?"

"Fine. I kept them here till twelve-thirty, and they all seemed peaceful enough. I didn't notice a peculiar reaction on anybody's part, though they all seemed pretty surprised when I read the statement relative to Sheldon's suicide. Prentiss put in a mild protest."

"How about that simp Dancy?"

"He just sat there and listened, and when I finished he came up and asked me if he could go. He left before any of the others."

Murphy gave a ruminative pull on his cigar. "What do you think Wade's got on his mind?"

"I don't know. What happened last night?"

"He didn't tell me anything. Last night we made the rounds of all the houses, but he left me downstairs while he poked around. I drove him up to my place after we got finished and gave him a good stiff drink and sent him to bed. He got up about eight-thirty this morning and I drove him over the river—he said he was going to pick up his car on the other side and drive back in case somebody was watching the ferry, so they'd think he's just come in from Isle Bonne. The only thing he'd tell me was that any of the four could have done it, but that he had a screaming suspicion of which one it was."

"What did he do all morning?"

"Don't ask me. He just waited long enough for my old lady to give him some coffee, and off he went."

The door burst open and in pranced Mr. Wiggins. "Hi, fellows. It gets more like Hollywood every day. Where do we put on this act?"

Before he could answer Wade came in, carefully shutting the door behind him. He came to the desk, his face fairly quivering with excitement. "Farrell," he breathed, "it worked!"

Farrell and Murphy stared at him in amiable bewilderment. "*What* worked?" Murphy demanded.

"Wait and I'll tell you." Wade swung himself to the desk. Wiggins crept closer to listen. "The big jolt came just as I figured it would. Remember I told you to tell everybody I was coming in this morning and going straight to my place to get some sleep? Well, after I brought my car back from the ferry I walked into my rooms just as I would have done if I hadn't slept over at Murphy's. I walked out to the balcony and drew the blinds. Then I came back into the room and looked around. It all looked normal and I was disappointed. Then, Farrell—catch your breath—then I remembered that what I was doing was catching some daytime sleep. So I went over to the bed and turned down the covers—and there, right in front of me, was the promise of fiery death. Excuse me if I can't help being a little bit dramatic about it, but if I hadn't known what to look for I wouldn't be here now."

"Lord!" exclaimed Murphy.

"But he didn't get killed," Wiggins inserted. "He's all right. Who did it, Wade?"

"I'll show you. Wait a minute—I've got some more company outside." He slipped off the desk and went to the door. "Larkin!" he called. A tall, spare young man entered and Wade led him up to Farrell.

"Farrell, this is Mr. Larkin from my office. And this is Captain Murphy, Larkin. Larkin works on our copy desk—he's an ex-captain of marines—and whenever there's any prospect of real excitement he manages to get there."

Farrell shook hands; Murphy grinned and asked, "Expecting another war, Wade?"

"I don't quite know what to expect, but I think there ought to be an unofficial witness."

Wiggins pulled at his elbow. "Say, Wade, where do you want us to set up the stuff? Pinning medals on guys don't win any kind of fight. When I was in the navy—"

"You won the war, we know. Now stand by for a minute, Wiggins. I want the room you use for the morning lineup, Farrell—the one where the plainclothesmen look at the new prisoners every morning. It's built enough like a projection-room in a movie studio to suit us. We'll use the screen. Wiggins is supposed to have stereoptican slides made of all the pictures he has on these murders. We have a projector all rigged up. I've told Prentiss, Gonzales, Marie and Dancy to arrive at five-thirty."

Farrell bit the end of a pencil. "You're sure it's one of them?"

"Pretty sure. You'll be convinced when the show goes on. Now when they come in, bring them down to the line-up room. All the lights will be on when they come in. Larkin will be sitting back toward the door. Don't introduce him. We want the murderer to be a little bit perplexed by the presence of a stranger, and we also want Larkin to be there on deck in case the murderer gets violent. We'll go down now and get ready."

He grabbed Larkin and Wiggins and made for the door. Murphy came after them.

"Say, Wade, is this all we're going to know?"

"Don't spoil my climax, officer. So long."

It was twenty minutes past five when Murphy came into the lineup room with Dancy, who seemed not at all at ease in the company he was keeping. Marie and Gonzales came in together, and as the doorman closed the door after them they stood still an instant, and slowly advanced toward the chairs Murphy indicated. Marie glanced at Wade, who stood at one side with Farrell, going over a sheet of notes. He did not look up.

Dr. Prentiss came in alone. Murphy showed them all to chairs at a long mahogany table, and took his place just behind them. Wade began to speak.

"The reason you are here this afternoon," he said, "is that I cannot agree with the district attorney's statement damning the memory of Terry Sheldon. It is my belief that Mr. Sheldon was murdered, just as were Mr. Ulman and Mrs. Gonzales."

For ten minutes he reviewed the case, while Wiggins, up in the projection-room, was throwing a light on the screen. Though the room was bright with other lights, the shifting white spot on the screen had a sort of ghastly threat about it. "And now," Wade went on, "we come to the investigation of these three murders at once and the hunt for a single criminal."

Dancy shifted in his chair. Marie was watching Wade with a strange expressionless face, her hands tightly laced in her lap. Dr. Prentiss was leaning forward, attentive to every word. Gonzales nodded gravely from time to time, as though to agree with the speaker. Murphy was laboriously adjusting his tie. Farrell sat very still at one end of the table, and Larkin, without attracting attention to himself, moved slowly to the back of the group. Wade went on.

"I am not going to review the terrible details of the murders, but I feel safe in telling you the method employed. But first, I would like to show you what I found in Terry Sheldon's cabin."

From under a pile of papers on the desk in front of him he brought forth the leaf of the missing Bible fragment. Prentiss was on his feet.

"Have you found the fragment? Let me have it, please! Where are the other leaves?"

His whole body was shaking with excitement. Gonzales was standing also, his eyes riveted on the leaf. Dancy had not moved. Marie was staring at Wade, wide-eyed with fear.

"I'll tell you what I believe to be true about the rest of the Bible in a few minutes. Dr. Prentiss, you will have an opportunity to inspect this just as soon as we are through here. I don't mind telling you now that this leaf was stolen with the purpose of unseating you at the library. The reason for the theft was to give Mr. Gonzales a chance to make a leisurely inspection of this part of the fragment, and at the time of your report to bring a court action that would relieve you of your trust."

"That," said Gonzales icily, "is a lie."

Both he and Prentiss were looking straight at Wade, their hands gripping the table's edge, as if conscious that it would be useless to attempt to take the leaf yet.

"No, professor, it is the truth, and no matter how complete the scheme of murder seemed to be, this fact of our case has a positive witness."

Dr. Prentiss wheeled upon the district attorney.

"Mr. Farrell, will you charge Professor Gonzales with the theft of the Gutenberg Bible, as well as the theft of the books that were found in his wife's room?"

"Just a minute," drawled Wade. "You were summoned here to witness my charge, and that will be not of theft, but of murder."

Gonzales pushed back his chair. "Mr. Wade, I refuse to be present at this farce any longer. I demand that you permit me to consult my attorney at once."

"You will all please consider yourselves detained as material witnesses," Wade cut in. "I'm going to finish." Dancy was jerking at his collar. Marie, who had sat white and stiff until now, suddenly covered her face with her hands. Her whole body quivered. Wade rushed to his conclusion.

"I want to tell you the rest about the Bible Murders. I want you to understand the havoc that can be wrought by a hatred that is hidden till it becomes a secret mania. I want you to know how someone in this room planned death for two persons and then was driven to commit another murder and attempt a fourth because the horrid secret must be kept. I will show you that these murders were done by devilish ingenuity, by inspired fiendishness—and now I will show you how!"

It was Wiggins' cue.

The room plunged into blackness. There was a scream from Marie. Something had appeared in the dark. Slow, smoky, but unmistakable, the climax had presented itself. For on the table, held in Larkin's grip, were two glowing hands.

CHAPTER TWENTY-FOUR

"PRENTISS did the murders. He's just admitted it."

Wade had walked into the room where Marie, Gonzales and Dancy were waiting for him. He shut the door and went on.

"When the lights were turned on down in the projection room and Larkin had Prentiss by the wrists, I knew we had the perpetrator of the Bible Murders. You see, the weapon he used was phosphorus."

"Phosphorus!" Marie exclaimed. She choked a little cry in her throat. "Of course. Horrible—!" She shuddered, and Gonzales slipped his arm around her and led her to a chair by the window. She glanced at Dancy, who stood uneasily on the other side of the room, looking as if it was all just a bit beyond his understanding, and then looked steadily back at Wade.

Wade met her eyes, and nerving himself for the rest of the story he had to tell, he turned to Gonzales.

"Professor, you were the real victim of Prentiss' hate. In a spasm of fury he told Murphy before I left the room that he had devised this whole ghastly plan for you."

Gonzales nodded silently. "Go on!" begged Marie.

"You see, Mr. Gonzales, you had him at last—the Bible leaves were faked."

Still Gonzales did not speak. He sat tensely, waiting to hear the rest.

"The whole story will be on the street inside of an hour," Wade went on, "for all the papers are rushing extras, but I think you three who have suffered through this should not be made to wait. Here's what happened."

Marie lit a cigarette and stared a moment at the match before throwing it down. He was glad to see that her hands did not shake.

"Prentiss bought the Bible leaves believing that they had really come from the press of Gutenberg. Then, after he had brought them here, heralded by newspapers all over the world, he discovered that he had been tricked. He knew that when you received his report at the end of this month you would demand an investigation by experts and that his cherished reputation as an unquestionable authority would be broken. He hated you. He has hated you for twenty years. You were the only person who threatened the maintaining of his single ambition—to be known as the ideal collector. For twenty years you had been watching hawk-eyed for him to make a mistake. You had continually questioned his judgment. Living alone, nursing a single passion, he let his hatred of you develop into a mania. The thought of seeing you triumphant, possibly being influential enough to unseat him and perhaps being given his post yourself, was more than he could endure. He plotted your ruin when he plotted the murders of your wife and Quentin Ulman. Those murders were simply the means to the end.

"He chose as his victims two persons whom you had a natural right to hate. He killed them in a way that might logically have been attributed to a husband made desperate by jealousy.

"His purpose was not to kill you, but to make you endure the bitterest conceivable humiliation and at last to make the state of Louisiana hang you for murder."

As Wade paused Dancy started with a sudden idea.

"Did Prentiss take the rest of the Bible?"

"Yes. He has already admitted that, and enough besides to hang him. He took the Bible leaves—that is, all but the one Terry had—and dropped them into the river. His first mistake was in not examining the leaves before he destroyed them. The leaf I found in Terry's studio will be a powerful exhibit against him."

"But why did he kill Terry?" Marie asked.

"Terry's murder was not part of the original plan. After Mrs. Gonzales' death I think Prentiss dreaded the possibility of having to commit any other murders to save himself, hence his tirade against the police department the next day. He was simply begging us to arrest you, Mr. Gonzales, before anybody suspected him. But Terry let Prentiss know that he had a clue.

"For Terry was the only one of us who had even a remote idea of how the murders had been committed. He told me that he got his clue from Euripides. Medea, in Euripides' play, killed her victim with a magic dress. Every one of Prentiss' victims put on a garment of some kind just before the end—Ulman the overall, Winifred the mandarin coat, and Terry the smock he had borrowed from the library.

"From what Terry said to me the last time I saw him, Mr. Gonzales, I think he suspected you."

"Terry—suspected me?" Gonzales sat upright, more astonished by this than by the revelation of Prentiss' hatred. "Terry? And I thought—poor boy!"

"I am sure he did," Wade answered, "and because of this he was not careful enough with Prentiss. He let Prentiss know that the mystery was about to be solved, and Prentiss killed him before he could solve it.

"I didn't know what it was Terry had discovered. All I knew was that I had let him go away alone to his death, and my job was to find out what had killed him. I followed him to Isle Bonne, and Prentiss tried to protect himself by planning a fourth murder with me as his victim."

Marie sprang up. "He tried to kill you? When?"

"This morning. But that was a trap—I'd planned that he should. That's how he got the phosphorus on his hands."

"But I don't quite understand," she said. "What did he do with the phosphorus? Did he use a sleeper?"

"Yes. Prentiss used phosphorus as his weapon. He painted the inside of the death-garments with the devilish stuff. In making his solution he used what you chemists call a sleeper. The sleeper," he explained to Dancy and Gonzales, "is anything that will check the volatile qualities of an ingredient in a formula. Pure phosphorus would ignite on being exposed to the air. Prentiss slowed it down. Then he used a detonator to offset the sleeper. That's something in the nature of a time-charge. I talked to the city chemist, and he suggested metallic sodium. You know that metallic sodium explodes with a fiery burst when it comes in contact with moisture. Prentiss put tiny pellets of the sodium in a shell of something easily soluble. These he put in the armpits of the garments.

"You can picture the steps in his killings. The victim puts on a garment that is painted with the phosphorus. In the armpits are two tiny lumps covered with a thin film. The perspiration that is always present in the armpits in this weather melts the film. The sodium is contacted, there is an explosion and the phosphorus is fired. The phosphorus burns with a fiendishly quick fire that eats in, and there's no chance for the victim to fight it. It's just like touching a hot electric wire to a match in a box. One big puff, and destruction for all the matches in the box. That was Prentiss' method of murder."

"It isn't a slow death, Alfredo!" Marie cried suddenly. "It works terribly fast. We can remember that anyway." She slipped her hand into his and turned to look at Wade again. "Wade, how did you find out all this?"

"I didn't," he answered. "Terry found it out. Terry solved the mystery of the Bible Murders, for he left me the only direct clue I ever received. You see, Terry had told me he had gotten his clue from Euripides, and he had borrowed some books that referred to the Greek drama, but among them I found a curious old volume written a hundred years ago by a French philosopher. As soon as he asked Prentiss for that book, Prentiss knew that Terry was on the track of the method of murder, for the old Frenchman suggested that Medea used phosphorus to make the death-dress she sent to Jason's second wife in the Greek play. He was pretty vague in his chemistry, but it sounded plausible. I began to think. Suddenly I remembered that every one of the murderer's victims had put on some garment just before the end. Ulman had changed his suit for the overall he wore in the bindery, Winifred had slipped on the mandarin coat that she wore as a wrap the night of the ball, and Terry had borrowed a couple of smocks. It was legitimate to assume that he had put one of them on when he went to work.

"Ulman must have started to the filling-station to get gasoline for the burner just after changing into his overall—that's why he died on the road. He and Terry couldn't see the phosphorus shine because they put on their death-garments in daylight, and Winifred couldn't see it because it was on the inside of that brocaded coat, under the lining. Prentiss must have put in the phosphorus before he sent the coat to her, and then brought two grains of metallic sodium, covered with a solution to keep out the air, and sewed them into the armholes when she left the coat in the car. We didn't notice the phosphorus smell partly because he used such a little bit of phosphorus and partly because the odor of burning flesh, and in Winifred's case, the odor of the burning gasoline, disguised it. The solution must have been in the smock Terry borrowed from the library. It looks as if Prentiss had prepared that thing in advance in case you, being a chemist, should give evidence that you were suspecting him."

Marie abruptly came over to him and gripped his wrists. "Come outside," she begged. "Please—I've got to ask you something."

He followed her, and when the door had shut behind them waited to hear what she had to say. For a moment she stood still, twisting her fingers nervously, then she lifted her head and asked in a voice just above a whisper,

"Wade—did—did you think it was Alfredo?"

"Well—yes," he confessed in a low voice. "You see, Prentiss had planned every detail to throw suspicion on Gonzales. I thought of Gonzales a long time down on Isle Bonne. I thought of Dancy too, and—forgive me, but I couldn't help it—I thought about you."

"Don't apologize," said Marie smiling. "I know you had to think about me. I suppose I'm a better chemist than Prentiss, and I could have worked out that formula with a lot less trouble than he took doing it. But how did you make up your mind that Prentiss was the murderer?"

"I never did, quite. I wasn't sure whose hands were going to shine when I turned off the light. But if it hadn't been Prentiss I should have been surprised. I'd thought about it pretty thoroughly, and I eliminated you and Dancy. I couldn't entirely eliminate Gonzales, but at the same time I couldn't convince myself that he had really done it, because on the only occasion I'd seen him and Winifred together his attitude had suggested that he didn't care enough about her to kill her.

"So I began to wonder if it would be possible that someone else had committed the murders with the intention of throwing suspicion on Gonzales. Prentiss was the only person who hated him, but that was just a theory and at first it seemed impossible to prove.

"Then I got my idea. The old Frenchman had mentioned phosphorus. I'm no chemist, and like most people all I know about phosphorus is that it shines in the dark.

"So I got an awl and made a nocturnal call on everybody's house while you people were listening to Farrell's fairy tales last night, and searched for rubber gloves. You all had them, Marie, and not a single pair had phosphorus on the outside."

"I suppose," she suggested, "that Prentiss threw away his gloves after using them, and kept new ones. Gloves that had evidently been used to handle phosphorus would be pretty damning evidence."

"That's a logical suggestion. Of course you had rubber gloves for your hospital work, and Prentiss and Dancy had them for work in the bindery."

"And Alfredo has them," she added, "for those funny medieval chemistry experiments he likes to try—I think I told you he dabbled in chemistry."

"Yes, I remember. Anyway, I punched every pair full of tiny holes, too little to be noticeable. You'd better not wear yours again, or you'll be catching diseases up at the hospital."

"All right. And I'll warn Alfredo."

"You remember that I got Farrell to tell all of you that I knew who did the dirty work but didn't know how?"

"Yes. Why was that?"

"Well, I figured that whoever was responsible would come to my house the next morning and fix up something lethal for me, using phosphorus, and handling it with those punctured gloves. I'd had Farrell keep the cops at the houses till daylight so the murderer wouldn't have a chance to get out till morning and so wouldn't see his own hands in the dark. When I came home, along about noon,

I looked things over. I darked my apartment and examined all my clothes. They were as innocent as new-laid eggs. I remembered that I'd said I was coming in from Isle Bonne that morning and was going to catch some daytime sleep, so I gave the bed the once-over. At first it looked all right too, but when I turned down the lower sheet I saw my mattress had been touched with phosphorus—my mattress, mind you, so that the lower sheet covered it and I wouldn't have noticed a thing if I'd darkened the room and gone to sleep. And believe me, Marie, if I'd slept in that bed, in this weather, there'd have been plenty of perspiration to fire the little grain that would ignite the phosphorus.

"You see, Prentiss made his error when he believed my story about not understanding the method of the murder. He figured that having been up all night at Isle Bonne I'd tumble into bed to make up some sleep before I did anything else.

"But as soon as I saw that mattress I knew my trap had worked and that somebody had a touch of phosphorus on his hands and didn't know it. So I got all of you down here, timing it so you'd come in daylight. I got you into the dark room and turned off the light. You know the rest of it."

"Yes, I know," she whispered. "But you did think, didn't you— that Alfredo had done it?"

He nodded.

"So did I," she went on desperately. "I've got to confess to some-body what a brutal fool I've been—Wade, Alfredo has been so good to me all these years, and I thought Alfredo killed them. I treated him horribly, Wade—I was cruel—"

He gripped both her hands in his so tightly that she winced. "Marie, you thought Alfredo was a murderer, and yet you went home with him the day after Winifred died?"

She tried to take her hands away, but he still held them. "What made you so reckless?" he insisted. "If you had been right didn't you understand that you would have been his next victim if he had suspected that you knew?"

For a moment she did not answer. "But I had to," she said at last. "I had to, Wade. I thought he had killed Quentin and Winifred, and you were working so determinedly that somehow you would find proof of it, and if he had suspected you were coming too close to the truth he would have tried to kill you too. Neither of his alibis was perfect. He could have left his office at the university and come back again the day Quentin was killed. He could have slipped out of the ballroom and back the night Winifred died without being noticed. I thought that if I was there, with him, I could see what he was doing and stop it, or warn you in time. You had been so incredibly decent to me. Then when Terry died I was nearly insane. Alfredo had gone to his room that afternoon—he said he was going to get some sleep—and he could have gone out by the balcony outside his window without the detective's seeing him. The day you went to Isle Bonne I didn't let him get out of my sight. I pretended to be frightened and begged him to stay with me. When he went to his room to dress that afternoon I stood outside in the hall and heard him moving around. Last night—he doesn't know it and I'd rather die than have him know—I slipped upstairs before he went to bed and locked the balcony window and hung the key around my neck, and after he was asleep I locked his bedroom door. I got up early this morning and unlocked it and waited in the hall till he came out. I love Alfredo—he has been like a big brother to me, and but for him I don't know how I could have stood it after father died, and I wouldn't have told even if I'd actually seen him commit the other murders—God knows he's had reason enough to want to kill that woman—but I knew I couldn't stand around and let it happen if he was going to kill you."

She had not looked at him as she spoke, but had stood with her eyes on his hands that were holding hers so tightly that it hurt, so that until it happened she did not know that he was going to kiss her.

There was an explosion of flashlight powder and as they started and looked around in the smoke Mr. Wiggins bobbed brightly into view.

"Just thought I'd let you know I was here," he announced cheerfully. "Say, Wade, you better come in. I got something to tell you."

"What's that?" Wade had stepped back with a legitimate scowl. Wiggins spread out his arms.

"I got good news for everybody. But I guess you better let me tell him first, Miss Marie. Come on, Wade—you gotta phone the paper."

He had grabbed Wade and shoved him inside the office before Marie had caught her breath in the acrid clouds with which Wiggins had announced his presence. She followed them inside, where she saw Wade hurriedly dialling a number at the telephone. In the middle of the room was Wiggins, looking considerably like a pin-wheel as he bubbled an exciting announcement to Dancy and Gonzales. Marie went slowly over to where Wade stood by the phone.

"Calling Koppel," he told her. The smile he gave her was somber.

She put both hands anxiously on his arm. "What happened, Wade?"

"Prentiss is dead," he said. "Suicide, yes. He had a couple of poison tablets on him—I suppose he got frightened when his scheme to kill me didn't come off this morning and brought the poison in case anything happened. Marie—don't look like that! It's easier this way."

She had suddenly pressed her knuckles against her mouth as if to smother a cry of horror. "Yes," she said faintly, "I—I suppose it is."

"City desk," said Wade into the phone. "Wait for me a minute, Marie," he added, turning quickly to her. "This won't take long."

She turned away from him toward the window and stood looking at the blinking lights outside. "Say, honey!" said somebody at her ear.

It was Wiggins. "Don't you be upset," he urged soothingly. "Ain't you glad it's all over?"

Marie gave him a crooked little smile. "I don't know," she owned. "I guess I am."

"Then what makes you all cut up about it?" he demanded. "Don't you get worried. It's easier like this."

"I know it is, Wiggins," she answered after a pause. "But he was always good to me. He paid me more than I earned at the library, because he knew I needed it so."

"Oh, that ain't no wreath," Wiggins cut in. "Anybody'd be good to you. It just comes natural. Let's go over and see what Wade's barking about."

He grabbed her hand and piloted her back to the phone. Wade smiled at her and motioned her to stay till he was done.

"Does this make the extra, Koppel? Fine. I have the detailed report from the city chemist, and I'll send it in for the first regular edition.

"Larkin got everything else, didn't he? I guess they'll open the codicil to old Mike Sheldon's will in the morning. The afternoon papers will have first crack at that. Too bad, but don't blame me—

the big denouement came in time for us. That's all, I guess. Sure, that's all. No, I don't want my picture in the paper. No, honest. Oh, Koppel, for the love of Mike have a heart—"

The receiver was suddenly grabbed from Wade's hand and Mr. Wiggins ducked under his elbows to plant himself at the telephone.

"Hey, Koppel! That ain't all. Say, that ain't more than half. I gotta picture for you—bringing it in right now—sure, Wade's picture, only he don't know I got it—get away, Wade! Koppel! Tell him to get his knee out of my ribs! Wait a minute, Koppel, this is a scoop—run a box alongside of the Bible story and say that Mister Wade is going to be engaged to Miss Marie Castillo of Bible Murders fame or if he ain't he's a lousy bum and I can prove it because I got a flashlight picture of him kissing her—quit that, Wade! Koppel! He won't let me talk! Let go of my ear, you simp! Koppel! Listen! He's trying to crack my backbone! Call her an heiress, Koppel, yeah—she's coming into the Sheldon money that Prentiss has been having because that's the way the will is and Terry didn't leave any .children leastways I hope he didn't him not being married—stop it, Wade! Koppel! This big ape is beating me up right here in police headquarters!—So long."

CODICIL TO THE WILL OF MICHAEL SHELDON

I, Michael Sheldon, have this day signed my will, the instrument by which I hope to punish Julian Prentiss and Alfredo Gonzales for the suffering they have brought upon me.

I am a rich man, and because my daughter Muriel was my only heir I wished to make sure that she would not be married only for her wealth. Therefore, when she wished to marry Julian Prentiss I told him that I intended providing her with only a modest competence, leaving the bulk of my property to charity. While this was not my intention, I wished him to believe that it was, and on being told that Muriel would never possess a large fortune Prentiss found it convenient to dissolve the engagement.

Muriel was very young, and she had been carefully shielded from unpleasant knowledge. While I was glad that she had discovered the duplicity of Prentiss before it was too late, for her the experience was bitterly cruel. I was glad when she seemed to forget it in her affection for Alfredo Gonzales. To all appearances Gonzales loved Muriel, but warned by her earlier disappointment I told Gonzales also that Muriel would never be a rich woman. In a short time he contrived a lover's quarrel and told her their engagement was at an end.

Muriel's first experience had nearly broken her heart; the second wrecked her confidence in life. She was too young to be glad she had been saved from marriage with either of these men; she found herself believing that they were typical. She took her own life, and her mother's life was shortened by grief.

By the terms of my will I have set these two men in opposition to each other, giving one of them a large private income and the opportunity to handle the income of the rest of my property, and to the other the power of censoring these expenditures. To one of them I have denied marriage; with my knowledge of both their characters I am convinced that the other will contrive to marry a rich woman and will be unhappy in such a union. Also, knowing both of them as I do, I believe that the circumstances that must follow such an arrangement as I have provided for will, before many years have passed, result in tragedy for them both.

This codicil is to be opened when the custodian of the Sheldon Library has either died or has been declared incompetent for his post. If I know these men as well as I think, the suffering caused to the other will by this time have been so great as to satisfy even my desire for his punishment. I therefore direct my executors, upon reading this document, to pay the head trustee of the library two hundred thousand dollars from the general library fund. I trust that by this time he has learned that there are things in life that money does not buy, and knowing this, will be better able to enjoy those things that money can pay for.

MICHAEL SHELDON.

THE END

Milton Keynes UK
Ingram Content Group UK Ltd.
UKHW021641010924
1453UKWH00041B/211